TURBULENT INTRIGUE

TURBULENT INTRIGUE

A Billionaire Aviator Novel

Melody Anne

Montlake
Romance

Published by Montlake Romance, Seattle

www.apub.com

Amazon, the Amazon logo, and Montlake Romance are trademarks of Amazon.com, Inc., or its affiliates.

ISBN-13: 9781542046206
ISBN-10: 1542046203

Cover design by Eileen Carey

Cover photography by Regina Wamba of MaeIDesign.com

Printed in the United States of America

I want to dedicate this book to Emmy McCormack. You have changed my life in all the best ways. You make me realize the person inside me has always been there, wanting to come out. I'm stronger, happier, and ready to say, "I can" instead of "I failed." I love you!

NOTE FROM THE AUTHOR

This book was so fun for me to write. I truly enjoyed both Ace and Dakota. I've never made a heroine quite like her, and she mimics very strong women I have so much respect for. Something that will be fun for readers is to look for all the places she gets common sayings wrong. I made sure to change them just enough to make it fun in both her internal thoughts and when she's talking to people. The more flustered she gets, the more she will slay a common saying. Send me messages and let me know when you find them.

PROLOGUE

The house was in utter disarray, with the doors hanging on their hinges, the floors scattered with blood and soot, the walls torn to pieces, priceless paintings broken, vases shattered.

Nestor walked through the rubbish, his face blank, the men around him uneasily looking around as they carried weapons in their tense fingers. Slowly, the group advanced, walking through the hallways, practically hearing the cries for help.

It was over. The fight was over, but the blood splatter told the story of a vicious battle. War had been waged, and someone would pay the price. They moved to the kitchen, where the walls had been blown apart, where it was impossible to tell the blood from the ash.

Nestor stopped. His men were silent. Maybe it was seconds, and maybe time didn't matter. But finally he looked up, his eyes filled with hatred, his body trembling.

"Find out who is responsible for this," he said, his voice cold. "They will pay."

Those were the last words spoken in this broken house. Revenge would come swift and with purpose. People would die.

CHAPTER ONE

ONE DAY EARLIER

His adrenaline pumping, Ace Armstrong watched as the final pieces went into place in the huge house he was using as a front to draw in the heavy players in this drug cartel. There was one person he was after in particular—Anton Pavlov. He was the worst of the worst in this twisted family, having killed hundreds of people with his own hands and thousands of others through his command.

But he couldn't just go after Anton. He had to take down the entire gang. If he didn't, there would be loose ends—there would be too many people seeking revenge. When this was over, Ace wanted it to be *absolutely* over. He wanted to be able to go home without putting his family in danger.

When he had walked away from those he loved so many years before, at the reading of his father's will, when the old man had listed the provisions to earning their inheritances, he'd been angry. Over time, that anger had faded, but then he'd stumbled into a man who had recruited him for the CIA. He'd thought he'd found the right path in life. It had been the right thing for him for many years.

Now he was so hard from the outside in that he wasn't sure his family would want him back. But the recent tragedies that had plagued his brothers had sent a yearning through him that made it impossible for him to stay away any longer. The sooner this case closed, the quicker he would be able to go home and make sure his loved ones were still okay.

"We've finished setting up, Mr. Smithers," the caterer said, breaking Ace out of his reverie. He'd gone by the name Steve Smithers since this operation began. He didn't hesitate at all when the man spoke to him.

"Very good, Emanuel. Thank you for the hard work," Ace told him.

The man turned and walked away. Ace moved through the house. Everything was in perfect order. The lights, decorations, and food were good enough to host the president of the United States. That's what it had taken to lead Anton, and his colleague Nixon, to Ace.

Hidden cameras covered every inch of the place, and Ace had three concealed weapons on him. The waitstaff were all undercover CIA agents who had orders to protect the operation at all costs. They wanted this documented, and they wanted to make sure no stone went unturned.

It was almost showtime. He was more than ready. One more quick walk-through, and then he went and changed. In the blink of an eye, people began moving through the large mansion.

The party was going off without a hitch, and Ace felt like a monkey in a suit in the custom-made tux that fit him to perfection. He had to dress the part of a successful member of the drug cartel. A lot of money passed between people in this business, and anyone who got in the way of that money trading hands would be eliminated. It was simply that cut-and-dried.

"He's moving toward you."

The slight nod of Ace's head wouldn't be noticed by any of the goons wandering this ridiculously spacious mansion. The heads-up was delivered to him through a nearly invisible earpiece by one of the men watching the cameras. The man prepped Ace so he was ready when Anton stepped up to him a couple of seconds later.

"You outdid yourself for this party," Anton told him.

"Only the best for you. You told me this deal was big, so we want to make our guests comfortable," Ace easily replied.

"You are my most trusted asset in this organization," Anton told him. "Not an easy task in only four years."

"I appreciate your trust in me," Ace said, though the words practically choked him.

"Your body language is expressing rage. Better be careful," the man in his headpiece said.

Ace forced himself to relax. It was almost time for this to go down. He certainly didn't want to give himself away at the last minute. At least he didn't have to try to smile. His reputation for being a coldhearted bastard was a useful tool.

"I want to thank you, Steve. You've been invaluable to me and have helped us make a lot of money," Anton told him.

Though that was exactly what Ace had been trying to do—trying to ensure the trust of Anton. It still made him sick, how easily he'd been able to infiltrate the gang. He played the bad guy too well. Maybe that was truly who he was.

People who met him learned quickly not to cross him in any way. It had taken him time to cultivate the image of a stone-cold asshole. He took pride in passing that test—even if it was for the sake of the bad guys and to ensure his position to take them down. He feared, though, that it had changed him into the villain he'd been trying so hard to portray.

For eight years, Ace had worked for the CIA as an undercover agent with limited contact with the outside world. For the past four years, he'd been on one case, had been working on closing that case, ensnaring a world-renowned drug cartel who knew very well how to cover their tracks, how to keep in the shadows. He'd been their chief pilot, his past flying lessons coming in quite handy.

It had taken years for him to earn the trust of the top family members, but that was exactly what he'd done. And now it was almost over.

He'd managed to make his entire family hate him—to keep them safe. But he wanted to go home, wanted to see if there was any way he could let go of this fake life he'd created and possibly have a different future than the one he'd lived since walking away from his family home.

There was a commotion by the door, and both Anton and Ace turned to see three large men walking into the room behind a small, older man wearing an original Westmancott suit that Ace knew was valued at over seventy thousand dollars. Money wasn't something Ace had ever needed to worry about, growing up the way he had, but still, the thought of wearing something that ridiculous made him scoff at the drug dealer.

This was definitely a world where prestige and envy meant everything. No true emotion could ever be felt in a world of deceit and greed. Ace might have grown up with money, but he'd also had incredible parents. He could even admit he'd long ago forgiven his father for his meddling ways at the end of his life. While Ace might not have agreed with his father's intrusive wishes, he could now let that go and move on, remembering his father for the many good years he'd given Ace and his brothers.

"Let's make sure our party guest is pleased," Anton told Ace.

"Of course," Ace said.

The crowd parted for the two of them as they met Nixon Westworth in the middle of the room.

"I apologize for being late," Nixon said. "My team was concerned by safety issues."

"Safety is of the utmost importance," Anton told the man.

"Yes. Still, I don't think I want to stay longer than need be," Nixon said with such arrogance, Ace found himself grinding his teeth together as he, Nixon, Anton, and the man's goons walked out of the room into a quieter place where they could speak.

The sound of the partygoers was drowned out the moment they closed the door behind them. Then they immediately got down to business. Ace stood by as second in command as Nixon and Anton came up with reasonable terms, then they all shook hands. It was almost civilized—that was, if a person didn't know what they were trading.

But the bottom line was that the operation had been a success. They had done it. Ace felt like smiling, knowing they had placed the final nail in the coffin of the Pavlov family. They also would get Nixon, which was an added bonus.

"We got them," the voice in his ear said, unease still in the man's voice. Just because they had them didn't mean the coming battle was going to be easy. The lives of good men could very easily be lost in the fray.

"I'll be taking my leave now," Nixon said. "I look forward to future business arrangements."

"Me as well," Anton told him. Ace simply nodded at the man, who smirked. Anton might trust him, but Nixon was an even more cynical man, if that could be believed.

"He's not leaving the house" was the warning in Ace's ear, making him tense. It was about to get a bit more hairy in only a few seconds. Nixon wasn't getting away—none of them were.

They all walked out into the ballroom, and as Nixon began heading for the front door, it was kicked in, SWAT team members piling into the house. Anton and Nixon both stopped a few steps in front of Ace.

"If everyone cooperates, there's no need for people to get hurt," one of the SWAT guys yelled.

Of course, they were dealing with drug lords who would much rather go down shooting than surrender. Ace watched Anton pull out a weapon and take aim at a SWAT member. Ace couldn't blow his cover, and he hoped like hell he wasn't about to get shot down, but he wasn't letting these criminals escape. No way.

"Drop it," SWAT commanded.

Anton's eyes narrowed as cold fury flooded his expression. He didn't like being in this position.

"You damn well better have my back," Anton told Ace.

"Always," Ace said, knowing he sounded convincing.

A bullet whizzed past them, and both Ace and Anton jumped for cover in opposite directions. When Ace lifted his head, Anton was nowhere in sight. *Damn it!*

"Where is he?" Ace shouted.

"He's not on camera," the man in his earpiece replied.

"The bastard isn't getting away," Ace said.

He jumped to his feet and fought his way through the chaos of the mansion, trying to avoid being shot as he hunted for Anton. There was no way after all of this that he was going to give that man freedom. And Ace knew if Anton got away, he would hide, making it virtually impossible for them to find him again.

"Got him, Ace. He's in the back of the house. Agents are closing in. Don't blow your cover."

"Thanks."

Ace might not want to blow his cover, but he wanted to see the takedown, that was for sure. He took off in the right direction, being able to travel through the place with blinders on if he needed to. He'd familiarized himself with his surroundings, knowing this fight was going down.

Another bullet flew past him as he turned a corner, this one ripping the fabric of his tux. Shouts of pain and anger could be heard behind him. More police and agents were swarming the house as the fight continued.

"We're getting control of the situation, Ace. Stay out of the fight," the agent in his ear commanded. The man knew him well, and knew it wasn't easy for him to back down.

Ace didn't need to reply. Finding Anton was all he was focused on at the moment. He made a left and then halted. Anton was standing against the west wall in the kitchen, firearm in hand, his eyes wild as he looked around him, agents surrounding him. Ace edged closer, still staying out of sight even though it nearly killed him.

"Do you really think you can get away with this?" Anton snapped.

"We already have, Anton. You can leave this place in cuffs," an agent said with a smile tilting his lips, making him look quite feral, "or you can leave in a body bag. The choice is yours."

"You'd like to see that, wouldn't you?" Anton snarled.

"I'm not going to lie to you. I think this world would be a much better place without you in it," the agent told him. "But I also want you on trial, where the families of the victims you've terrified for decades can see you get what you deserve."

"That won't ever happen," Anton said with a leer. "A man like me isn't so easily captured."

"Give it up, Anton. It's over," another agent yelled. Ace's feet were twitching with the need to jump into the scene and take this man down.

"I will kill everyone who has ever crossed your path," Anton promised as he glanced at the men moving in even closer.

"You will do nothing more than rot in prison," a man told him.

"Go to hell," Anton shouted.

"You first," the agent replied, a mocking smile pulling up the corner of his lip.

Ace watched Anton's finger twitch on the trigger of his gun before a shot rang out, barely missing the agent in front of him. The agent no longer hesitated as he fired on Anton, dropping the man to the ground.

The agents rushed forward, instantly kicking away Anton's gun and covering the wound to the man's chest. They all wanted to see him face a jury. But they had known his death in this battle was a definite possibility.

Anton screamed curse words at the agents as blood spat from his mouth. The wound could be fatal, which wasn't what Ace needed or wanted. He wanted him in court, facing his crimes.

"Don't let him die," Ace snapped into his earpiece, still staying out of sight. Let Anton think he'd been shot. "This bastard will face his accusers in court." Ace's leg hurt, but he didn't have time to analyze if he'd been shot or not. He was too focused on the man on the ground—so close, yet so far away.

"He's not going to make it," one agent said.

"Get him out to the ambulance. He doesn't get an easy out," Ace told the agents, who nodded while they spoke into their mics. The danger still wasn't over, but Ace lowered his gun. The guy he'd been chasing for four years had been shot. Ace could soon go home. But now wasn't the time to relax.

Even so, he was tired. Ace was far too young to be this exhausted. But this sting operation was indeed over. It was time to figure out what he was going to do next. He stepped up to the back door when someone behind him shouted. Ace turned in time to see Anton with his finger on a black remote that he must have slid down from the sleeve of his jacket. Why hadn't the agents frisked the man?

"Good-bye," Anton said before an evil chuckle escaped his throat.

"Stop him," Ace shouted, forgetting about staying out of sight as he took a step toward Anton. But it was too late. Everything blurred as Anton's laughter was amplified in the small space.

An explosion erupted, sweeping Ace off his feet. Hot fire burned around him; his skin felt like it was boiling before he slammed back down to the floor, his head cracking on the hard marble as his body flopped like a rag doll and the lights went out.

CHAPTER TWO

Dakota Forbes wasn't a meek woman—not by any means. And when she wanted something, she had no problem going for it. Yes, sometimes she was impulsive, and yes, that could certainly get her into trouble—once in a while. But without a little danger, life was too dang boring.

She smiled as she sat back at the small airport—in the cool zone, the place only those with a special badge got to be. She didn't know why that made her feel haughty, but maybe it was because she was somewhere the average person couldn't access. She watched small aircraft lift off into the sky and then land again. It was utterly mesmerizing.

Yes, this might be another impulsive decision, but the joy in her heart, and the itchiness in her body, told her it was the right one. She stood up and moved inside the hangar, where Sherman was speaking to a young teenage boy with hair too long and eyes filled with excitement. She probably wore the exact same expression he did.

"Okay, you go out and chop some of that hair off before we get started. A pilot needs to be able to see," Sherman told the boy, who eagerly nodded.

"Will do, sir," he said before he turned around and spotted Dakota.

The boy smiled at her before he began walking, and she had to fight to keep her laughter in when the teenager added a bit more swagger to his awkward gait. She was used to teenage infatuation. She *was* a cheerleader for the Seattle Seahawks, after all—at least for one more season.

Though it filled her heart with sadness, knowing her time with the Seahawks was almost up, it was a day she'd known was coming for a while. She was almost twenty-seven, and playtime was over. Now, she needed a career she could do for the rest of her working years.

Looking in front of her at the slick red plane with smooth curves, long wings, and crystal-clear windows showcasing leather upholstery, she couldn't help but sigh in enchantment. She had made the decision to become a pilot.

Her brothers all flew, and she'd shown a little interest when she was younger, but not enough to take the lessons she'd been offered. At that time in her life, cheering was her passion. Now she was finding a love for something else.

Maybe it was simply that she needed to do a job that caused her adrenaline to pump, and something that couldn't pigeonhole her. People often thought of pilots as men, but she was there to prove she was just as capable as any man, if not more so. She would work harder, put in more hours, and kick some ass at becoming a pilot. Soon, she'd be flying the biggest and baddest planes out there.

Okay, when she wasn't in dreamland, she could admit that it might take a little while for her to work up to the big planes, but that wasn't going to stop her from getting there someday. She wanted to step onboard a huge plane with four stars on her shoulders. She would double dare someone to call her a flight attendant. A smile of anticipation curved her lips at *even* the thought of it.

"You look like I did the first time I laid eyes on a plane," Sherman said as he sneaked up to stand next to her. "Of course, way back then, in the olden days, my plane sure wasn't as pretty as this one," he added with a laugh.

"You really like to milk this wise-old-man thing, don't you?" Dakota said with a laugh. She actually didn't know Sherman's age, but if she were to guess by his eyes alone, she would put him at twenty-one. They had a youthful sparkle in them that automatically made her smile and want to draw closer to him.

Dakota was from a great family, but that didn't mean her heart didn't have room to draw more people into her circle, and men like Sherman were one in a million. She was so glad her best friend had married Sherman's nephew, ensuring Dakota would have him in her life forever.

"An old man has to do whatever he can," Sherman said, but he couldn't keep the smile off his lips. "So, you want to become a pilot?"

"Yes!" she said, excitement screaming from her. "I should have done this years ago, but then again, I don't think I would have given it the proper attention back then. I'm now ready to be the best pilot in Seattle, maybe even the world."

"I have no doubt you will achieve whatever you set your mind to," he told her.

"You know me well. I don't quit," she assured him.

Sherman laughed. "No, I've learned that for sure," Sherman said. "And I love your determination. You will do well with this endeavor, and lucky for you, I've found you the perfect trainer."

"Great!" Dakota told him. "When can we start?" She was ready to do it right this minute.

Sherman laughed again. "Slow down there, Turbo," he told her. "I'm going to send you home with materials, and I'll let you know when you get to do your first lesson."

"I knew I wouldn't be flying today, but . . ." She trailed off, unable to take her eyes from the beautiful plane in front of her.

"Don't you worry. It won't be long," he assured her. "And you know what?" He trailed off, making her want to jump up and down.

"What?" she said when he didn't continue quickly enough.

"I don't think you're the kind of girl to be in a slow plane. I think you can handle an upgraded model." They both stared at the plane in front of them.

"Oh, yes, please," she said. "I will study every aspect of it, and I'll be safe," she assured him.

"I have no doubt about that," he told her with a pat on her back.

"Can I stay awhile longer and watch the planes coming and going?" she asked.

"Of course. I have a few more things to do," Sherman told her.

He moved over to where he had a desk and cabinets and pulled out several items. He handed them to her, and then he walked back over and sat down. She took the handful of material and moved outside, sitting down in a nice grassy place in the sun as she began devouring it all—that was, when planes weren't taking off or landing.

They were in a small airport in Washington away from Seattle, which Sherman assured her was a much better place to train than SeaTac, where it was way too busy. After a long lapse of time, she moved back inside the huge hangar and went over to a wall where a bunch of photographs were proudly hung.

She got caught up with one picture. She knew it was the missing brother—Ace Armstrong. It was taken when he was young, and a boyish smile filled his face as he stood before a plane, wearing a ripped shirt, holding up a piece of the worn cotton with the date on it to commemorate the event. His first solo flight.

There was so much happiness in his eyes. She knew from what she'd been told that he'd been away for a really long time, and the family didn't know why. She suddenly wondered what his story was and what would make him want to leave the loving embrace of his family. She couldn't seem to take her eyes off him.

After too much time, she shook her head, forcing herself to look away. Dakota had a thing for people in need. She didn't understand why, but she'd been that way since she was a young child and had found a small boy at the playground who'd fallen off the monkey bars.

She'd immediately gone up to him and assured him all people fell off once in a while. When he'd gazed at her with those crushed eyes, looking as if he didn't believe her, she'd climbed the monkey bars and purposely fallen, spraining her ankle, which she hadn't intended on doing. Graceful falling wasn't in her DNA.

But when he'd smiled at her, she'd known it was totally worth it. Sometimes a little bit of pain was needed to heal someone else. She'd never looked back from that moment on, constantly driven by the need to make others happy.

She had no problem making herself happy as well. And deciding to become a pilot was making her incredibly joyful. It was a new day, and she was more than ready for it to begin.

CHAPTER THREE

Pulling from what could only be described as a deep sleep, the first thought Ace had was how he'd never thought about how loud silence could be. Tuning in, he heard the ticking of machines and the quiet breathing of people around him, and he knew for sure that silence was louder than screams.

He wasn't alone, which automatically made him tense as he tried to remember where he'd last been. He chose not to open his eyes, giving him time to assess the situation. He had to figure out exactly where he was and who was with him. His head was throbbing—his body aching in unbearable ways—but he couldn't focus on that right now. First, he had to understand his surroundings. He had to figure out if he was safe or in danger. There always had to be an escape plan in motion.

"Is he waking?"

Ace tensed. He tried not to, but he knew that voice—knew it well. It was his uncle Sherman. Oddly, he felt a strange stinging sensation in his eyes. Irritation flooded him. Ace Armstrong didn't cry—not ever! He refused to let such a weak emotion fill him. But knowing his family was with him made his fight-or-flight response instantly dim.

The stinging stopped, and he made sure he didn't move, not so much as his pinkie finger. He concentrated instead on his other senses. He smelled strong antiseptic and heard monitors pinging. He listened beyond the silence, and he could hear voices in the distance, outside the room he was in.

It was a hospital.

He wasn't in danger. Good. That gave him more time to figure things out. His uncle Sherman was there, and Ace was sure he wasn't alone. The last thing Ace could remember was an explosion. It had pulled him from his feet and then sent him straight back down to the ground—hard. He tried to assess the damage to his body. It was difficult to do when he was trying so hard not to move.

Wiggling his toes the slightest bit, he wanted to weep in relief that he wasn't paralyzed. He twitched his fingers and found that his body had many areas of aches and pains, and he might have a cracked rib or two, but other than that, nothing seemed to be broken. Good. That meant he'd be back on his feet again very soon.

But then what? Ace had no idea. The job was done—the job he'd been working on for years. He suddenly had no purpose—and no desire to keep working for the CIA. The only thing the job had given him was isolation. He wasn't sure where he stood in life, or with his family, but he was tired of being a different man from who he truly was. Not that he knew exactly who he was.

It was time to open his eyes. It was odd how difficult it was for him to do something so simple. But he was afraid to face his uncle, afraid his brothers were going to be there as well. He'd been such a dick to them to keep them safe, and now he wasn't sure he could turn that switch off.

Ace had long ago learned not to be afraid, though, so he pushed back the feeling of anxiety and slowly opened his eyes to look around the large hospital room. Sherman; his mother, Evelyn; and his three brothers—Coop, Mav, and Nick—were all gazing at him. There was a mixture of emotions inside him at the sight. On one hand, he'd been avoiding them for so long that it was ingrained in him to run—to keep them safe. On the other, he missed them—was glad they were there.

"Good to see you awake," Sherman said, drawing Ace's eyes to his favorite uncle.

"How long have I been out?" he asked, surprised by the croaking in his voice. Ace cleared his throat and focused his attention on his brother Cooper. For some reason, he was having a difficult time looking any of them in the eyes. He blamed it on whatever the hospital was pumping into his system. He assured himself he would be back to normal very soon.

"We got a call late last night. You've been out about twelve hours," Sherman told him. He then frowned as he stared intensely at Ace.

"What?" Ace asked, grateful some strength was coming back to his voice.

"Don't you think you should have told us you are in the CIA? We've been worried about you," Sherman said. The man had a way of making Ace feel like he was a thirteen-year-old boy again, getting caught behind the family home making out with the caretaker's daughter.

"My position was classified," Ace told him.

"We're family. That trumps everything," he said.

"We thought you were in some serious trouble," Nick said, making Ace look in his brother's direction. "You could have come to us."

"No, I couldn't. The case I was working on was dangerous. It could have gotten you all killed," Ace told him.

"You could have had a safe haven to come home to," Cooper pointed out. Ace turned but was afraid to see the judgment in his older brother's eyes. That's not what he saw. It was almost worse, because Cooper was looking at him with acceptance.

He'd been such an ass for so long, and his brothers were still there for him. Ace didn't know what to think. He again blamed the damn medication the hospital was giving him.

Pushing the button on his bed, he raised it so he wasn't in such a vulnerable position. When he was sitting up, he felt the aches and pains in his body, but he was strong enough not to need the crap filtering through his veins. He reached over and ripped the IV out, making Maverick jump from his seat.

"What in the hell are you doing?" Maverick snapped as he grabbed the sheet and held it over Ace's now dripping arm.

An alarm went off, and a nurse ran into the room, approaching the bed and reaching for him.

"Don't touch me," he told her. She froze where she stood and looked around the room. It was filled with large men who must seem pretty dang intimidating. She took a step back.

"What happened?" she asked, moving to his monitors and pushing a few buttons.

"I don't want this damn IV in my arm. I'm going home," he yelled.

She seemed flustered, but Ace didn't care. He wanted out of the hospital. He shifted on his bed, hating how weak his body felt. He was winded from this little bit of movement.

"The doctor hasn't signed you out," she told him, seeming to get some of her nerve back. "Did you rip your IV out?"

"I don't like being drugged," he told her.

"You can't just rip it out," she said, moving toward him again.

"If you try to put it in me again, *I'm* going to play doctor on *you*," Ace warned her, his voice lowering to lethal levels.

She was smart enough to back off. "I'm getting the doctor," she said before her eyes moved around the room again, and then she made a quick retreat.

"That was a bit uncalled for," Sherman told him.

"Yeah, I'm an asshole. I get it," Ace said with a sigh.

He shifted his legs off the bed and touched his feet to the cold ground. His body was breaking out in a sweat, and he was growing more frustrated by the minute. Weakness was for the pathetic. He refused to allow any kind of injury to hold him back.

"You're going to fall on your ass if you try to get up," Nick warned.

"I'm stronger than I look right now," Ace assured his brother.

"I got ripped apart in a helicopter crash a year back, and I thought I was tough too. I just made life a hell of a lot harder on myself and everyone else by fighting every step of the way," Nick told him.

"You look like you're doing well now," Ace said. He wanted to tell his brother he'd been there when he'd been in that terrible crash, that he had been worried for his family. He didn't say that, though. His siblings couldn't know he'd kept an eye on them through the years. He didn't know why they couldn't know, but he just knew the shell he'd placed around himself was the only thing keeping him intact. At least for right now.

"I am, because I pulled my head out of my ass and let my soon-to-be wife help me," Nick said.

"You're getting married?" Ace asked.

He'd kept up on his brothers over the past several years, but this was news to him. He felt a pang and didn't know what to think about the situation. It wasn't as if he'd made it possible for his brothers to get ahold of him, but he still couldn't help feeling hurt about not knowing.

"Yes, I am. In two weeks," Nick said, his face transforming with a radiant smile that even shot light from his eyes. His future wife must be one hell of a woman to put that look on Ace's brother's face.

"Congrats," Ace told him. He actually meant it. But when he realized he was allowing too much softness in his voice, he immediately firmed his lips. Going soft wasn't acceptable.

"Thanks," Nick said, his stupid grin growing even brighter. "Let's get you on your feet so you can be my best man."

The words processed in Ace's head, and he felt that damn stinging in his eyes again. Good thing he'd ripped out the IV, 'cause he was obviously a mess due to the ridiculous drugs they'd forced in him.

"I haven't been around. Don't you think Coop or Mav would make a better best man?" Ace said with a laugh that had no merriment in it.

Nick moved to his side and placed his hand on Ace's shoulder, refusing to allow Ace to look away. His smile dimmed, but there was sincerity in his expression as he reconnected with his brother.

"I love all of you equally," Nick told him. "But from the moment I asked Chloe to marry me, I knew I had to find you, knew you had to stand beside me."

Silence was once again booming in his ears as Ace tried to keep himself together. Ace loved all his brothers, but he and Nick had been paired off for a lot of their lives. They simply had a truly special bond. But even though Ace didn't deserve Nick's loyalty, it meant the world to him that he still had it.

"Well, I can't stand anywhere as long as I'm locked up in this room," Ace said, clearing his throat as he looked away from his brother.

"That wasn't exactly an enthusiastic yes, but I'll take it," Nick said with a laugh. He squeezed Ace's shoulder, and then Maverick stepped up on his other side.

"If you insist on getting up, then we'll help you. I'm sure you could use the bathroom," Mav told him. Mav wasn't being as open as his other brothers, and Ace could see that not all was forgiven between the two of them. Hell, he'd expected Maverick's chilliness from all of them, but if he were being honest with himself, he'd have to admit it hurt.

"I don't need help," Ace grumbled.

"Okay, then humor us," Nick insisted.

Ace quit arguing with them. It wouldn't do him any good, anyway. Then he was glad they were there when he managed to rise from the bed. His legs shook as he stood there for a moment, one brother on either side of him. His first step made him feel like an infant trying to walk for the first time, but after he made it a few more steps, he felt a little more sure of himself.

They made it to the bathroom door, and Mav backed away, but Nick stayed at his side as he stepped through.

"I've got it. I don't need you to hold anything for me," Ace told him.

"That's good," Nick said with a laugh. "I think that's going above and beyond for brotherly love."

Ace showed his first real smile in a long time. He stepped forward on his own and let out a sigh of relief when Nick shut the door, leaving him alone in the bathroom. It took a lot of effort to make it to the wall and grab ahold of the bar before he sat down and looked longingly at the shower.

He might hate weakness, but he knew he was in no shape to step in there yet. Instead, he sat on the toilet and laid his head in his hands as he let the reality of his situation settle in on him.

He was back home again. His family was on the other side of the wooden door, and he didn't have to hide from them anymore. He was taking too long and Nick knocked on the door, but Ace assured him he was still fine. He just needed a few moments to compose himself. Ace was truly home—where he had belonged all along.

What scared the hell out of him was he could hear his uncle and brothers whispering—which they obviously didn't do too well—while he sat there fighting a breakdown.

"What do you think he will do now?" Maverick asked, that note of suspicion clear in his voice.

Sherman was the first to speak to that question. "Don't any of you worry. I have the situation all taken care of for Ace." The grin Ace was sure his uncle was wearing couldn't be masked by a closed bathroom door. Ace was almost sure his life was going to get a hell of a lot harder than it had been in the CIA.

His throat seemed to close as he tried to swallow. What new fire had he just been pushed into? And how quickly could he escape?

CHAPTER FOUR

Ace adjusted the ridiculous bow tie that was trying to strangle him as he looked around the crowded ballroom. Only for his brother would he be willing to slip into a monkey suit and dance for the masses.

He'd been in the field for so long pretending to be someone else that he wasn't quite sure who he was anymore. It wasn't a feeling he liked at all. On top of all that, to be thrust into a regular life with the force of a hurricane wasn't helping.

He was on leave from the CIA, had managed to find a tiny apartment in the city of Seattle, and was finding it more difficult to reintegrate into normal society than to dodge a bullet. Why was it so much easier to live a lie than real life? He wasn't sure.

He leaned against the wall, desperately wanting to sneak out of the room and smoke a fine cigar. But he'd promised Nick he'd stay for the entire wedding and at least part of the reception. He wasn't sure how long he'd actually last, though.

"Ace, time to take a walk down the aisle," Mav said, stepping up to him and slapping him hard on the back. Ace had a feeling Mav really enjoyed getting a slap in, even if it was under the ruse of brotherly camaraderie. The two of them were eventually going to have to talk about things.

Even with that thought, Mav's words sent a shiver of fear straight down Ace's spine. He felt a shudder rip through him. Walking down any aisle might just be worse than a death sentence.

"I'm not the one taking the walk. I'm only here for moral support," Ace said through clenched teeth.

"Don't worry, brother. When you see who you get to walk next to, you'll be more than willing to take that plunge," Maverick told him with a wicked laugh.

"I don't think so," Ace grumbled.

But he followed Mav through the crowd, letting out a sigh of relief when the doors closed and they were in the back hallway of the massive hotel where the wedding was taking place.

Mav cracked a few more wedded-bliss jokes as the two of them took a left and then went through another set of doors to where the rest of the wedding party waited—minus Nick, who must be at the head of the aisle. Standing there in a fitted suit surrounded by his family while they analyzed him must be punishment for what Mav would deem as Ace abandoning his family. Of course, he *had* left them. In all honesty, he probably deserved the discomfort he felt.

"They just sent everyone in to take their seats," Cooper said. It had been a long time since Ace had seen his brothers so dressed up. He wouldn't go so far as to say they looked good, but Nick certainly had gone all out with his wedding. Okay, maybe they did look pretty damn good. Ace wasn't exactly known for being humble.

"I'm so glad you're here, Ace. Nick has been very worried about you," Chloe said as she moved through the throng of people and came right up to Ace, throwing her arms around him and squeezing.

"Don't mess up your dress," Ace told her, but he surprised himself when he hugged her back and actually felt a slight tug to his heart.

"You skipped out on dinner last night, so I have to hug you when I can," Chloe insisted, squeezing a little harder before she let him go. She stepped back with tears in her eyes. "I'm just so happy you're here." A tear slipped from her eye, and he reached for her cheek to help before stopping himself.

"We better get you down the aisle before my brother comes out here and kicks my ass for holding you up," Ace said, having to clear his throat.

"Okay, I'll quit trying to make you feel uncomfortable, but get used to me, 'cause I'm a sorta in-your-face kind of girl," she warned.

Ace was grateful when she turned her attention to her bridesmaids. He looked over at the smirk on Maverick's face and sent a glare his brother's way as he adjusted his tie for the millionth time.

"Looks like you're partnering up with me," a woman said. Ace turned to give her the mandatory smile that was expected, and then his jaw just about hit the floor. "I'm Chloe's best friend, Dakota Forbes."

Ace stood there like a stupid man while he tried to find his voice. She had bright green eyes with a Disney-type sparkle to them and high cheekbones that didn't need even the barest touch of makeup. Her lips were full, the kind that were most definitely made for kissing, and they were painted bright red, making his mind instantly go to the gutter.

The maid of honor dress she wore was red, matching her lips, and hugged her delicious curves in all the right places. His thoughts definitely sank farther down into the gutter, and he was grateful his brother hadn't decided to get married at a church or he feared he might be struck down by lightning for the immoral thoughts rushing through him like crashing ocean waves.

"Hey, big boy, my eyes are up here," Dakota said with a laugh, snapping Ace's gaze from her terrific breasts to her laughing eyes. She licked her lips, and his pants became unbearably tight. He had instant thoughts about where he wanted those painted lips of hers to be on and around his body.

Ace was never a man without words, but he couldn't seem to find a single syllable in his vocabulary as he gazed at this woman. Had he known his brother's wife-to-be had such a delicious best friend, then maybe he would have made it to the dinner the night before. Damn, he'd missed out on staring at her during what normally would be a very tedious meal—and possibly talking her into coming back to his tiny apartment with him. Well, weddings were all about the hook-ups, weren't they? The mood he'd been in all day had just improved a hundredfold.

"Did you say Forbes, like in *the* Forbes?" he asked when his brain was working somewhat normally again.

She laughed out loud. "I know you think that's a unique line, but you would be absolutely amazed how much I get asked that. And before you expect an answer," she said before pausing, "some things are better left to mystery."

Ace was growing hotter by the minute next to this damn woman. He might even be falling into instant love—well, that was if he was capable of such an emotion. If he was, this woman would be holding his heart already. He could say with certainty that he was, however, in lust.

"Ready to walk down the aisle?" he asked, his lips turning up in a confident smile.

"Hmm. Are you?" she said, giving him such sass his pants felt as if they were on fire and his heart was surely going to beat out of his chest.

"Oh, I'm certainly ready for anything," he told her. Yes, he was going to bed this woman!

"Be careful, Ace. You might get caught if you aren't careful," she warned him.

Ace decided to ignore the cold sweat breaking out on the back of his neck. This woman was sugar and spice and everything nice. She was confident, beautiful, and capable of making him ache in so many ways, he couldn't remember ever feeling such hunger. It had been too long since he'd taken an interest in the opposite sex, and she was waking him up in such pleasant ways.

"She's your new sister-in-law's best friend. Not someone to bed and run from," Cooper whispered in his ear, instantly irritating Ace. He didn't respond but shot Cooper a look that clearly told him to mind his own business.

Dakota looked between the two of them, but she didn't seem at all concerned that Cooper was whispering to him. She seemed to be floating as she stood before them. He wondered what it was that made her so damn happy.

The music started, and Ace found himself standing at the back of the line as his brothers and their wives walked side by side down the aisle. Too quickly, it was his turn to do the same.

Dakota slipped her arm in his and gave him one more blinding smile before she began moving. The sweat on the back of his neck dripped down his back as he stared straight ahead, trying not to scope out the crowd for signs of danger.

The gorgeous woman next to him helped ease that response in some ways, but in others, she made it worse, because he felt the instinctual need to make sure nothing happened to her. The intimate setting—rose petals on the ground, ribbons festooned down the aisle—made this so much worse.

There was no way in hell Ace had ever thought he would follow his brothers down the matrimonial aisle. But standing beside a beautiful woman as they made their way to the front of the decorated room put frightening things in his head. He was almost glad when she pulled away from him to go stand next to the other bridesmaids. Then the wedding march music began and Chloe walked down the aisle, her eyes shining and focused solely on Nick.

Ace looked down as he stood beside his brother. Maverick was beside him and patted Ace on the back as if he could hear the turbulent thoughts rushing through his brain. This time the pat didn't seem like a punishment, but Mav pulled back quickly, making Ace think, for just a moment, his brother might have forgotten he was supposed to be angry with Ace.

Ace didn't hear a word spoken in the ceremony, didn't pay attention as his brother spoke words of love to his new wife. All Ace seemed able to do was glance across to the other side of the stage, where Dakota looked so delectable. Her eyes clashed with his several times during the ceremony, and the little wench didn't seem at all shaken up like he was. At one point, she even winked at him.

That was most certainly a good thing, Ace determined. It meant she was just as interested in him as he was in her. But even though he told himself he didn't give a damn what anyone thought, his brother's words kept repeating themselves in his mind—she wasn't just any woman, and she couldn't be messed with. The marriage made Chloe Nick's bride—and that meant Dakota was now part of their family. *Crap!*

Looking up for only a moment before his eyes once again zeroed in on the ground, Ace made sure he turned his lips up as Nick kissed Chloe. He clapped when he heard the rest of the room come together in applause. And then he moved behind his brother and Chloe and accepted Dakota's arm in his as they made their way back down the aisle.

He didn't dare breathe in her scent the entire walk, but as soon as they exited the door, he pulled away from her. She patted his arm as she smiled at him, and he cursed his traitorous body and how much he wanted this woman.

"That was so beautiful. Chloe deserves a man as wonderful as Nick. I almost had to kick your brother's ass for hurting my best friend, but he wised up and now I adore him," Dakota said.

"Wait. What?" he asked as her words processed in his head. She stared at him, waiting for him to continue. "You almost kicked Nick's ass?" That was something he would have loved to have seen.

"Yeah, I grew up with four brothers, and I don't take crap from anyone," she said with a laugh. "Nick was having a crisis of conscience or something, so I came to beat some sense into him. But he realized he was in love with Chloe, my beautiful and amazing friend. Albeit he thought he was having a heart attack, but still, he got the point rather quickly after realizing what the chest pains were all about," she continued.

Ace couldn't help it. A burst of laughter started low in his belly and then exploded from him. He could just imagine the scene—his brother gripping his chest as he tried to understand what in the hell was going on with him. Once he started to laugh, it seemed there was nothing on earth that was going to stop the sound.

Dakota's lips turned up, and soon she was laughing with him. She had no idea what was going on inside his brain, but she didn't seem to care. She just continued laughing as she reached out to him again and held on as she bent over.

"What in the heck is so funny?" Sherman asked as he looked back and forth between the two of them with an eyebrow raised.

Ace felt tears in his eyes, he was laughing so hard, and even still, he couldn't stop. Soon Cooper and Maverick were standing beside them, looking at the two of them with concern, which only made Ace laugh harder. It had been so long since he'd last laughed, he couldn't even remember when it had been. The sound was so strange that it amplified his laughter even more.

It took several moments for him to get control over himself. Finally, he stood up straight and sent a beaming smile toward Nick, who was greeting people but still looking over at Ace with an obvious question in his eyes.

"Sorry, Dakota just told me how she had planned on kicking Nick's ass, and it struck my funny bone," Ace said, a few more chuckles escaping.

All sets of eyes turned to Dakota, who shrugged.

"When did this happen?" Cooper asked, new admiration showing in his eyes.

"You haven't heard the story?" Ace asked. He was oddly pleased he had been the first to hear it. It made him feel a little less out of the family loop.

"No, but I'm eagerly waiting," Maverick said, getting a little closer.

Dakota told her story again, which had Ace chuckling just as hard, but this time Maverick, Cooper, and Sherman joined in. When they all looked over at Nick, their brother was obviously aware the joke was on him, and it was obvious he wanted to step out of the greeting line and join in on the fun. His new wife gave him a reassuring squeeze, and he turned away from his laughing family to continue greeting guests.

"Dakota, you are truly a member of the family now," Uncle Sherman said.

Ace wanted to groan with frustration. That meant the woman was completely off-limits. It looked like this reception was going to be boring and torturous as well. If he were to hook up with Dakota, the family would expect a commitment from him, which he couldn't offer. This side trip home was only until he was healed, and then he'd be off on the next mission lickety-split. He couldn't make up his mind if he was staying with the CIA or leaving. Damn his luck and his indecisiveness!

"It's time for a toast, or at least it's time to start drinking," Ace said.

He pulled away from the group, but he felt them hot on his heels as he made his way into the ballroom. Even without looking at Dakota, he could still feel her presence. Now that he knew she was there, he couldn't seem to focus on anything other than her.

He went straight for the bar and ordered a double scotch. He had a feeling it wasn't going to help him. When Dakota shot him a look from across the room that was full of fire and humor, he downed his drink and ordered another. The long night had just become what would feel like an eternity, no end in sight.

He'd rather be back in enemy territory than try to resist these urges that he hadn't felt in such a long time. But even thinking this, his eyes were drawn back to the woman again—and he knew the night had only just begun.

CHAPTER FIVE

Dakota couldn't help but smile as she watched the incredible view of Ace Armstrong walking away from her. She'd heard a lot of stories about the rebel brother of the family, and she had to say they hadn't done the man justice. His old photos hadn't done him justice, either. He'd most certainly grown from a boy to one hell of a hot man.

Her heart was thundering, and she actually felt her skin tingling from nothing more than simply being in his presence. He was a dangerous man—and Dakota had a serious problem with hazardous males. He was something she didn't want a cure for. She also had a thing with wanting to meddle in people's lives—she could see the restlessness in the man's otherwise confident eyes and wanted to ease his pain.

He'd been away from his family for a long time, and he looked like a lost and frightened animal who'd been dragged home. That brought every meddlesome instinct alive for Dakota. If there was one thing she knew how to do, it was delve inside the areas of a person's mind where they wanted to keep you out. The harder someone tried to hide from her, the more she wanted to know his or her story. Sure, Ace had flirted and given her as much sass as she was doling out, but she had a feeling it was automatic on his part, as if he was desperately trying to hide something behind his witty banter.

Now she wanted to jump right in with both feet and get to know him—and it had nothing to do with the size of the man's shoulders, which rivaled those of the Seattle Seahawk football players she cheered for. And it certainly had nothing to do with his emerald-green eyes or square jaw or far-too-kissable lips. Nope, she assured herself. It was all about the discomfort she saw in Ace's eyes and how desperately he was trying to mask it by flirting and showing a grin that didn't quite reach the windows to his soul.

Okay, if she were being completely honest with herself, she might admit his body didn't hurt, she thought with a smile as the man turned around and their gazes locked. But he was now her best friend's brother-in-law, and knowing how rebellious he was, he probably wasn't sticking around. She might be a little terrified of relationships, but she also gave her heart to people, and she feared one day she would give it away and never get it back. She'd seen the devastating results of that happening. And Ace would leave when he was better. She knew that for sure. She was now a little lost—a feeling Dakota didn't relish in the least.

Insecurity wasn't a feeling Dakota was familiar with. Sure, she'd had moments of weakness, just like every other person on the damn planet, but she didn't allow those emotions to define her—didn't easily accept defeat, and didn't crawl into a hole feeling sorry for herself.

Life was simply too short to be angry, sad, or insecure. She preferred to smile through the pain and turn that frown . . . another way. She scowled as she tried to remember how that saying went. Chloe teased her relentlessly that she couldn't get popular idioms right. Dakota disagreed. She figured it was just that the sayings were wrong. Dakota liked to think only of the positive in life.

Ace started moving back toward her, and Dakota's spidey senses began tingling. Hot damn, there was an air of danger about the man that was sending signals to all the right places on her needy body. It had been too long since she'd been in a relationship. Though she might be the world's biggest flirt, and she sure as heck loved a hot make-out session, that didn't mean she gave it up to all the great-looking men who sent a signal her way. Ah, the damn morals her mom had taught her. She wished she didn't have them, and she really wished she didn't have such an open heart.

But her mother had never told her it was wrong to drool over a sexy man. She let her imagination run as wild as it wanted. And she had one hell of an imagination. Right now, she was picturing sweaty bodies entwined with not a stitch of clothes between them.

Just because she wasn't ready to jump into the flames didn't mean she wasn't going to look—and possibly even drool—a heck of a lot while around Ace. After all, she'd already decided she was going to find out every little thing about him, so her reward would be an active imagination.

"Hold this, Ace."

The moment his uncle Sherman gave Ace the tray of wineglasses he'd been moving for some odd reason, Dakota knew it was a mistake. It felt almost as if she were in a thriller movie and about to watch the ditzy girl open the basement door because she heard a sound down there.

Ace took the tray, and it teetered precariously in his hand. The fool didn't even lift the other arm to try to stabilize it. She made her feet move forward, but before she'd taken two steps, she knew she wasn't going to make it.

"Ace . . ." she called out to him. He looked up, and the tray turned sideways just as she reached his side—just in time for a whole lot of champagne to spill down the front of him, some of it splashing onto her, surely ruining her incredibly beautiful *and* expensive heels.

The horrified expression Ace wore was too much for her to take. The noise of the metal tray hitting the ground and glass shattering had every person in the room going silent, looking their way.

"I . . . I don't know why he handed this to me," Ace grumbled.

"Me either," Dakota said, trying desperately to hold in her laughter.

"What in the hell was he doing with it?" he said, looking less embarrassed and more irritated.

"Mr. Armstrong, I'm so sorry. I don't know how this happened," a man said as he pulled out a towel and handed it to Ace.

"It's no problem," Ace mumbled. The man continued apologizing, leaving them to believe he must be the manager of the hotel or the head caterer. He was probably worried he was going to get into trouble.

"It's not a problem, Jean," Sherman said as he patted the man's back. "I spilled a glass of bourbon on one of your waitstaff and insisted on taking the tray from her while she went and changed. I didn't give her a choice. Then Nick was calling me over for a picture, so I handed the tray off to Ace. My nephew obviously wasn't coordinated enough to handle it."

Ace sent a scowl his uncle's way before he looked at Jean. "It's really okay. I'm fine, we're all fine. The floors, on the other hand, have gotten slightly abused."

"I already have janitorial on their way to clean up the mess," Jean assured them.

"See, no harm done," Sherman said, wrapping an arm around Jean's shoulder and dragging him away as he continued mumbling apologies.

When they were a safe distance away, Dakota wasn't able to hold it back any longer. She smiled first, her throat hurting with her attempts at keeping the laughter locked up inside, but when Ace sent her a knowing glance, she lost it.

Laughter spilled from her, and the glare he sent her way only made it that much worse. He had a choice to make in the next few seconds, and it would tell her a lot about his character. He could either join in with her and appreciate the humor of the situation, or he could stomp off to places unknown feeling sorry for himself. It would tell her if she would be able to make the slightest difference in this broken man's life or not.

The cleaning crew arrived, and the two of them scooted over to allow them to clean up the mess. Dakota was laughing too hard to offer to help. Besides, she didn't think she'd be able to bend in the tight dress she was wearing.

"Looks like you've decided to make another impression at this wedding too," Maverick said as he patted Ace on the shoulder.

"Does he make a habit of dropping trays?" Dakota asked.

"Nope. At Coop's wedding, he came in and . . . um, did some things, then decided to deck Nick. Seeing as this is Nick's wedding, hopefully he'll just stick with dropping trays," Mav said, chuckling at his own humor, not looking the least bit concerned that one of his brothers had been punching his other brother who knew how long ago.

"Well, maybe we should try to find you a new shirt," she began, looking down his lean body, "and possibly some pants."

Suddenly, he smiled as he sent her a wink that had her cheeks heating. Damn, he had too much of an impact on her. She might have to be a little bit careful in the man's presence.

"You can dress me if you want, darling," he told her.

"Here's my key. I have clothes in my room," Mav said with a snicker before he disappeared. There was no way Dakota thought it was a good idea to go to a hotel room with Ace.

"I've got the key. I'll take you up on that offer," Ace told her.

She hesitated before speaking. "I think you can find the room on your own," she said, wishing she hadn't offered her help.

"You took part in doing this to me. I think you need to help fix it," he assured her, grabbing her arm and moving her through the throng of people. The crowd had lost interest in the situation and had gone back to celebrating Nick and Chloe's wedded bliss.

Dakota was, for once, oddly quiet as the two of them reached the elevators and Ace pushed the button for the top floor. Of course, the room had to be on the top of the thirty-story hotel. That would put her in the small box with Ace for that much longer. Normally, she wasn't so nervous about such silly things.

But as the doors closed the two of them inside, she was hoping it would stop along the way so that someone would join them. She certainly wasn't going to be able to delve into Ace's brain and possibly bring out his love of living if she couldn't even manage to have a neutral conversation with him. She scolded herself before flashing him a bright smile.

"Are you glad to be home?" she asked.

His body stiffened as if he wanted to reject her question, but she was impressed when she noticed how he forced himself to relax and smile back at her.

"So far it's been incredibly . . . eventful," he said.

"Life is boring when we aren't stimulated," she assured him.

At the flash in his eyes, she wondered if maybe she should be a little more cautious about which words she chose to use around this virile man. He'd been gone for a long time, and she wondered when he'd last had a relationship. Of course, a person didn't have to be in a committed partnership in order to relieve some sexual tension. She didn't want to think about Ace bumping parts or whatever.

"I'll tell you this much, Dakota," he said as he moved toward her, unbelievably making her fall a step back. She hated retreating, no matter how far she was pushed into a corner. "Life has most definitely become more exciting with you in the picture."

Dakota had a choice to make. She could either put him in his place, or she could go full throttle ahead. She chose the latter. She grinned as she lifted a hand and placed it against his chest.

Dang, she wanted to squeeze those hard muscles, but she somehow managed to keep her fingers flat as she held the man off. He looked eager—as excited as she felt. But she would be the one who kept a cool head during this.

"I've decided you need my kind of therapy, Ace," she said. He tensed beneath her hand, his heart skipping a beat. "So you can give me all the come-on lines you want, but you won't scare me away, and it takes a hell of a lot more than some pretty words to get me into your bed."

Dakota enjoyed the shock in his eyes. Then she didn't know what to think about the sparkle that took the place of that surprise. It was true that this man had some issues going on inside him, but he also had confidence in spades.

"Bring it on, Doc. We can see who wins," he told her.

Dakota's heart thundered as the elevator doors opened. She wasn't sure if she should step out with him or push him out the door and retreat. He made the choice for her when he moved forward and then turned to give her a look that obviously called her a coward.

Dakota moved forward. She didn't back down—not ever.

CHAPTER SIX

Ace wasn't a man to sweat a difficult situation, but he felt nerves skittering through him as he and the incredibly sexy Dakota Forbes stepped up to his brother's hotel room door. He wouldn't admit it, but his fingers shook slightly as he swept the key down the lock and saw the green light telling him it was okay to push the door open.

"I think you have it from here," Dakota told him.

"Are you afraid I'm going to bite you?" he asked, sending her a challenging look. Her shoulders stiffened, and she stepped forward.

He hadn't known this woman long, but already he was learning what made her tick. She didn't like to be considered weak, and all it took was a challenge and he had her doing exactly what he wanted. There was power in that knowledge. He liked it.

The sound of the door closing behind them was louder than a gunshot at close range. Damn, Ace wanted to push this woman up against a wall and make her scream. But he had to tell himself that anticipation was part of the fun. He also had his brother's annoying voice in his head telling him he couldn't just mess around with this woman. And since he would certainly be leaving again, all the two of them could have was a quick fool-around session . . . or two.

Ace's clothes were soaked, and his first order of business was getting out of them. He shrugged out of the tuxedo jacket and let it drop to the floor. Turning, he felt immense pride at the awe in Dakota's eyes as she gazed at his white shirt, which was plastered against his chest.

Ace would never allow his body to go to hell. He worked out hard and had no problem standing seminaked, or fully nude, in front of another person. Body issues were for those who didn't have confidence. It didn't matter what showed on the outside. In reality, all that mattered was how a person felt on the inside. And Ace felt perfectly fine with how he looked.

He began undoing the buttons on his shirt, his eyes never leaving Dakota's. She did her best to act as if she weren't affected, but Ace knew when a woman desired him, and it wouldn't take much for him to have Dakota screaming beneath him.

If only his damn brain wasn't messing with him, wasn't telling him this woman was off-limits. He never had been one to have a moral crisis, but at the moment, it seemed that's exactly what he was going through. It would almost be better to be back in the constraining CIA world, where he'd run on pure instinct. Not only that, but he would be leaving as quickly as he'd arrived. People around him tended to get . . . hurt in one form or another. Would he be willing to risk this vibrant woman, be willing to see that beautiful light in her eyes dim? No. He realized that with absolute clarity.

"I should give you privacy," Dakota said, her breath coming out a bit too fast for her to pull off her nonchalant attitude.

"I'm fine. I have nothing to hide," he told her.

The last button on his shirt came undone, and he reached for the cuff links and quickly undid them, then pulled the wet material from his chest. It didn't come off easily, and he still felt sticky when the shirt was gone.

"I might need a sponge bath. Want to help me with that?" he asked her with a wicked grin.

He figured she'd finally go running for the hills—the smart move on her part. But Ace felt himself thicken painfully when she gave him a sassy look and stepped closer. To hell with his brother and his own morals—if this woman wasn't going to resist him, who was he to turn her down? He pushed down the logical brain, far more willing to listen to his southern hemisphere.

She ran a finger down his sticky chest, and Ace nearly came in his pants—something he hadn't done since he was a teenager. He didn't care. It would at least give him sweet, sweet relief.

"I think you're a big boy and can wash yourself," she said. Then she lifted her finger to her luscious red lips and sucked. "*Mmm*, good wine. Too bad it went to waste."

Ace pulsed painfully as he looked at the woman in shock. She was every wet dream he'd ever had come to life, and her confidence was enough to make him want her all the more.

"It hasn't gone to waste. You can lick it off me," he said, his voice husky.

She leaned forward, and he thought for a moment she was going to do just that. His heart thudded in anticipation of her sweet tongue on his entirely too hot skin. Who needed sponge baths when a hot woman was there with fingers and a capable tongue?

"Tempting, but I think I'd rather get it fresh from the bottle," she said. She ran a finger down his chest again, circling it around his stomach before she stepped back, moving over to the suitcase resting on a bench near the window.

"You are a hell of a tease," he told her. He should be angry, but he was more amused and impressed than anything else.

She turned and looked at him, her scorching gaze taking in his entire body, from his sweating forehead all the way down to his toes and back up. He noticed how her eyes took a few extra seconds on his very hard package. It pulsed beneath her glance. He felt as if she'd just caressed him.

"I don't tease," she finally said as she licked her lips, making him sweat even more. "However, I also don't give in to arrogant men who think it's their right to have whatever they want. I've already told you I want to know you." She paused, and he held his breath as he waited for her to go on.

"With the right attitude, something might happen between us," she told him in her forthright manner. His body responded as if she'd just produced a damn condom. "*But* if you act surly and egotistical, you'll find yourself on your own. Go take a shower while I find you something suitable to wear."

She turned away from him, not worried in the least about him having a comeback to her words. Ace stood there for a moment, wondering if she was right—wondering if he should tuck tail and do her bidding. He sort of liked the thought of that.

But instead, he moved toward her. Ace wasn't the type of man who ran from a challenge, and Dakota was throwing one after another at him. It was time he showed her he wasn't the typical pushover she dealt with.

Dakota turned just in time for him to reach around her and haul her up against him. She didn't seem as composed anymore as he looked into her eyes for a beautiful moment. He grinned at her and then crushed his mouth against hers.

The kiss was even better than he'd imagined. Her soft lips instantly molded to his, and he swept his tongue inside her mouth, feeling as if he'd arrived home. One hand tugged against her hips as he pressed against her. He was leaving no doubt whatsoever in her mind about how much he wanted her.

Ace was losing his sense of reality as she reached up and tugged his hair, her hungry groan captured by his mouth. He gripped her tight ass and squeezed, his body throbbing painfully.

Pushing forward, he pressed her against the window and ravaged her mouth, his hands sliding up her hips, tickling the undersides of her luscious breasts. She was incredible, with curves in all the right places and tight muscles where he appreciated them the most.

Breaking away from her mouth, he ran his tongue down her jaw before he sucked the skin where her pulse was beating out of control. She groaned again, and the sound pulsed in time to the beat of his erection. He could practically taste sweet relief in the air.

"Let's take advantage of this room," he said, his voice vibrating against her skin. Yep, the little brain was most certainly winning his internal battle.

Dakota moved her hands to grip his face, and the desire sparking in her eyes gave him hope. She was a sexual woman and she wanted him, that much was incredibly clear.

"*Mmm*, Ace, you *are* a temptation that should most certainly come with a warning label," she said, her swollen lips turning up. "But you aren't getting into my pants—or I should say *into my dress* . . ." She paused, and his heart thudded. "At least not tonight."

Ace's breathing was out of control as he waited for whatever this dynamic woman was going to say next. He had never been as on edge as he was in this particular moment. He was most certainly her captive audience, and she knew it.

"We might get to enjoy each other, but you have to play nice first," she said. Then she pushed him away.

Ace knew he could challenge her, knew he could pull her close and have her be his willing puppet if he pushed the matter. But he found he had entirely too much respect for this woman to even attempt that.

He had to close his eyes and take a few calming breaths as he fought the urges of his body with the rationality of his mind. He also had a feeling that taking her once would never be enough. If he opened this door, he was going to be her willing slave. What frightened him was how much he didn't care about that.

"What do you define as playing nice?" he asked.

She moved farther away from him, going back to looking through clothes. She didn't say anything as she dug out a pair of slacks and a polo shirt. He hadn't shared clothes with his brothers in a long time, but he didn't have much of a choice at the moment. It was either that or a sticky tux.

"You might want to wash out your underwear and blow-dry them," she said as she tossed the clothes on the bed and then moved toward the door. He wanted to rush to her and grab her, tell her there was no way she was leaving him in this condition. His feet seemed planted to the floor, though.

"You haven't answered my question," he said, happy when she turned back around and looked at him. "And maybe I don't wear underwear."

At those words, she glanced down to the large bulge in his pants, and he pulsed. He hurt so damn much. Just a simple stroke of her fingers or those full lips and he'd explode in the most beautiful of ways.

"This is a day-by-day thing, Ace. You'll figure out the rules as we play the game," she said with a beaming smile. Ace couldn't help but grin back at her.

"I think this is a game I'm going to win," he assured her.

She opened the hotel room door, still grinning at him. "I hope so," she said. Then she stepped through the opening and walked away from him. He'd thought the sound of the door closing when they'd entered the room had been unusually loud, but the clicking of the door as she exited was like a bullet to his chest.

He stood there for a long time, looking at the shut door, his body on fire, his heart thundering, and his mind filled with a million questions. This woman was the best thing to enter his life in many years.

Stripping the rest of his clothes away, he found himself grinning from ear to ear as he took a quick shower. His body might be throbbing, and his blood felt like lava in his veins, but it was all worth it. Ace had no doubt whatsoever that he was going to get the girl.

With that knowledge, he did as she suggested and found himself hand drying his underwear before he hurried into his new clothes. He wanted to get back down to the party and chase the girl. This was one mission he wasn't allowing himself to lose. He just hoped she was ready for him. She didn't have any other choice.

CHAPTER SEVEN

Dakota was off balance as she walked back into the room filled with hundreds of people all laughing and drinking and having a great time. They had no idea what had just taken place on the highest floor of the hotel, but Dakota felt as if it was written all over her cheeks.

She was flushed and hot, and her body was feeling things she hadn't imagined ever being able to feel. She'd barely been able to keep it together as Ace's hands had roamed across her body, as his mouth had masterfully worked her lips. Never before had she been as turned on as she'd been with that man worshipping her body.

Dakota was used to men giving her attention. She was a flirt, was confident in herself, and felt as if she had nothing to prove. But being with Ace was like being on another planet. She had never felt such an immediate and intense attraction to another person.

It might be foolish of her to make the man her pet project. But she'd already made a decision, and she wasn't one to turn away from a choice she'd made. It would be weakness on her part if she tried to back down now, and there was no way she was going to allow that to happen.

"Where have you been, young lady?"

Dakota jumped guiltily as she looked at Sherman, who was grinning at her in such a knowing way that she was afraid he knew exactly what she'd been up to with his nephew. Why she felt as if she'd done something wrong, she wasn't sure.

"I was helping Ace," she said, her voice unusually subdued.

"Good, that boy needs some help. He's been gone from this family for a very long time. We're grateful he's back home," Sherman said.

"Yes, your entire family is back where they belong." Dakota turned to find a giant of a man standing on her other side, making her feel completely dwarfed.

"Dakota, meet my good friend Joseph Anderson," Sherman said.

Dakota looked back and forth between the two men, both of them larger than life. She smiled, feeling completely at home in their presence. They reminded her of her own family. She had a feeling they would fit right in with her rowdy group.

"It's a pleasure to meet you, Joseph," she said. He surprised her when he gave her a hug, taking her breath away.

"The same to you, darling," Joseph said. "So, you're taking care of our little Ace, are you?"

"I have a way with lost souls," she told Joseph before she looked at Sherman, not sharing that she wanted to pick Ace's brain. "And even though Ace has been gone for a while, I also think he's right where he wants to be."

"From the moment I met you, young lady, I knew you were going to be good for Ace," Sherman said. She was growing a little suspicious of the light in his youthful eyes.

"Don't be getting any ideas," she said as she scanned the room. "I'm not looking to walk down any aisles."

"Ah, the heart wants what it wants," Joseph told her. She again looked back and forth between the two men.

"And sometimes the soul just needs a pick-me-up," she said, hoping she was stopping these two men in their tracks. She didn't want someone trying to match-make her.

"Sometimes that is one and the same," Sherman said.

Dakota couldn't help but laugh. These men were certainly forces to be reckoned with. Dakota appreciated so much more what her best friend had gone through while working with this family. They were intimidating, and Chloe had been so lost for such a long time. Sometimes a girl needed her best friend, and sometimes she needed a family who held open their arms.

"I'm so happy Chloe has all of you now," she said, emotion clogging her throat.

"We are the ones happy she's a part of our lives," Sherman assured her.

"Did I marry the wrong man?" Chloe asked as she walked up to the group and hugged first Sherman and then Joseph.

"Of course not," Sherman said with a smile.

"Good. 'Cause you, my sweet new uncle, are my favorite family member," Chloe told Sherman.

"Ah, you are good for this old man's soul," Sherman told her.

Chloe laughed with true joy, something that made Dakota incredibly pleased to hear. Her friend had laughed far too little in her traumatized years with an abusive father and neglectful mother.

"And you are good for this once-broken soul," Chloe told him.

"Now don't you go and make me cry at this happy occasion," Sherman told her, a suspicious sparkle in his eyes.

"I wouldn't dream of it," Chloe told him. She wiped a tear from her own cheek before turning to gaze at Dakota. Her eyes widened, and then her grin grew.

"Where have you been?" she asked, and Dakota found herself squirming on her feet. She didn't like being the one under the lens of the . . . telescope. She'd much rather be the one looking through the magnifying lens.

"Not that it's a national secret or anything, but I was lending a hand to your new brother-in-law," she said. She found herself unable to keep looking into Chloe's eyes.

Her best friend laughed, which immediately drew Nick to her side. He wrapped an arm around her, and then Dakota had four sets of knowing eyes on her. She put her trademark smile on her lips and faced them all with her shoulders squared.

"I'm sure Ace was mighty pleased to have a helping . . . hand from you," Nick said with a pause and a laugh.

Dakota sent him a warning look. "I took you down once, Nick Armstrong. Don't think I won't do it again, *even* on your wedding day," Dakota threatened.

Nick held up his hands and laughed. "You are scary, woman. You win," he said. Chloe couldn't stop grinning.

"What would a wedding be without some family drama?" Chloe asked. "And I just have to point out how much I love saying the word *family*." She choked up at the end of her sentence, and Dakota admired how Nick pulled her closer to him and kissed her cheeks as his eyes sparkled.

"We are so blessed to have you with us," he assured his new wife. Then he turned to Dakota. "And you are just as much a part of us now."

Dakota moved forward and hugged Nick. "I love all of you," she told him.

"What's going on here?" The entire group turned as Ace approached. He had a cautious look in his eyes, which intensified when he found himself the target of their gazes.

"We're just having some sentimental moments," Sherman told his nephew. He stepped right up to him and slung an arm around Ace's wide shoulders. Ace seemed uncomfortable for a moment, but then he forced himself to relax. Dakota didn't miss a moment of it, and his reaction only stiffened her resolve to learn about this man.

"Sentimental moments are for fools or those who can't stand the reality they live in," Ace said.

Joseph looked at him as if he were insane. "Now that's just not the right kind of attitude to have, boy," Joseph told him.

Ace knew better than to argue, so he just shrugged his shoulders. Dakota didn't miss how he stepped closer to her. He was already leaning on her, whether he knew that or not. She'd have to be careful to be there for him without it leading to more than what it was. She wasn't sure how not to cross that line—not with this man.

"Did you know Dakota is going to be taking flying lessons as she embarks on her new career?" Sherman asked, changing the subject. The man obviously knew his nephew was uncomfortable, and he was trying to steer the conversation in a new direction.

"Yes, I can't wait," Dakota said with honesty. "All of my brothers fly, and they have a total god complex because of it, so I'm determined to not only become a pilot but to be better than all of them," she said.

Nick laughed. "You go, squirt," he said.

"Oh, Nick, don't you mock me *or* my dreams," she told him.

"I'm not mocking you," he assured her. "Flying just isn't as easy as you might think it is."

"The best things in life are the hardest to learn *and* require the most endurance to achieve. The harder it is to fly, the more I'm going to enjoy it," she told him.

"The problem is that the pilot I had all set up to train her broke his leg," Sherman said.

"You have a replacement, don't you?" Dakota asked. She had been excited about this for a while, and there was no way she was letting go of this dream of hers.

"Well, since you brought that up," Sherman said with a grin before he looked at Ace. Dakota caught on really quickly to what was happening, and she wasn't sure she liked the direction of his thoughts.

She definitely felt drawn to Ace, but that didn't mean she wanted him invading every aspect of her life. The flying thing was something just for her. But she couldn't say that with all eyes on her and Ace.

"What?" Ace asked, looking confused.

"You still have your instructor's license, don't you?" Sherman asked.

"I don't see what that has to do with anything," Ace said.

"Because you're not working right now, and I have a job I need filled," Sherman said slowly, as if his nephew wasn't too bright. Dakota had to agree with Sherman's approach. Ace wasn't catching on too quickly.

"What?" Ace said again, looking more confused.

"Dakota is starting flight lessons next week, and she needs an instructor. I'm volunteering you," Sherman said. "Is that clear enough?"

Ace gave his uncle a withering glare before his eyes focused on Dakota. She shrugged her shoulders. The ball was now in his court.

"I've got a lot going on," he said. Dakota tensed next to him. She was feeling a bit rejected, not something she was used to—and she didn't like it one little bit.

"What are you doing?" Sherman asked, his gaze narrowing.

Ace stumbled over words as he looked down at his feet. Wow! It seemed his uncle was shaming him. Dakota felt bad for him now. And she felt like the rope in a tug-of-war game she hadn't asked to be in.

He looked from her to his uncle and then back to her again, and she could see the shift in his eyes. His uncle was challenging him, and it appeared he didn't like to back down from a challenge any more than she did. That could be a bad combination for the two of them.

"You need a teacher, huh?" Ace suddenly asked, his attitude doing a one-eighty, the confusion and annoyance vanishing as his lips turned up. She had no doubt he was thinking of teaching her a lot more than flying. She flashed him an equally confident smile.

"Yep, it looks like it," she told him before she winked.

Lust flared in his eyes, and Dakota wondered if she was playing with far more fire than she could manage. Even if that was the case, she couldn't seem to stop herself.

"Then I guess I'm your man. When's the first lesson?"

The rest of the people around them might as well have faded away as they gazed at each other. The powerful connection between the two of them was so much more than she could handle, but that only made this whole thing that much more exciting for Dakota.

"Next week," she said.

"I have all the paperwork," Sherman said, breaking their intense connection. She was a little grateful to the man.

"Good. You can give it to me tomorrow," Ace told his uncle, though his gaze never left Dakota's.

"Then it's all settled," Dakota said, hating that her voice was a little breathy.

"This is far too much business on my wedding day," Chloe said before she looked at her husband. "Take me out on the dance floor and hold me close."

"I thought you'd never ask," Nick told her, immediately pulling her away from the group. Dakota was mesmerized by their love as she gazed after them.

"That sounds like a great idea. Let's dance," Ace said, taking Dakota's arm and pulling her away, not giving her a chance to refuse.

Dakota liked a man who knew what he wanted and didn't hesitate to get it. She followed him to the dance floor. When he pulled her into his arms, she let her mind go blank and allowed herself to do nothing more than feel.

It was the best decision she'd made in a long time. Being in Ace's arms felt like being home. It was right where she belonged, and she'd learned long ago to chase her dreams and not fight them or try to analyze them too much.

CHAPTER EIGHT

Slow music played, and Dakota fit in Ace's arms as if she'd been made just for him. Normally Ace avoided slow songs like they were the plague, but as Dakota melted against him, he knew it was the ultimate in healing after being analyzed like a bug on a slide since he'd returned. He could get lost in this woman—in the magic she seemed to bring with her very presence.

Yes, he knew he was potentially putting her in danger, and yes, he knew he was leaving again soon and shouldn't make these connections, but he couldn't seem to stop himself, and he was getting really tired of the internal battle. It was just a dance, he silently muttered.

He wished he could let go of the edge of danger he constantly felt, but too much had happened to him while he was away with the CIA. He understood his family wanting to know about it, wanting to understand why he'd been gone. They probably thought it had been easy on him. They were wrong. But Ace didn't articulate that too well, so they looked at him as if he would bolt again at any minute—which he actually might. Being with Dakota, though, he felt a moment of relief from the guilt he was constantly carrying.

And though he did want to mend the fences he'd built between himself and his family, right now all he wanted to do was get lost in

Dakota's embrace. He wanted to selfishly keep her all to himself and not allow anyone else into their little bubble.

"Your family obviously loves you," Dakota told him. He wondered if she was a mind reader along with all her other talents.

"I've been away for a very long time. It takes some getting used to, being around them again. My family certainly isn't the hold-back kind. They will say what's on their mind, and they will make sure you listen to their very emphatic opinions," he told her.

"Is that hard for you?" she asked.

The way her manicured nails trailed along the back of his neck as she spoke was mesmerizing. It made him want to open up to her about anything and everything. She was casting a spell over him, and he didn't even care . . . much.

"I knew it would be difficult coming home," he admitted. "I wasn't sure what my family thought about how I've behaved over the last several years."

"How did you behave?" she asked. She snuggled a little closer to him, and though he was pulsing with need, he also felt sweet comfort in her embrace. He wanted to harden himself against that but seemed unable to do so.

"I pushed them away. It's what had to be done."

"Why?"

He sighed as he pulled back so he could look into her lovely green eyes. There was such warmth in them, such understanding. He felt as if she was looking straight into his soul. He didn't like that feeling.

Leaning down, he brushed his lips against hers, not caring who was watching them. Her eyes closed as she kissed him back, and he slowly moved them to the easy rhythm of the song.

"I had to push them away to keep them safe," he finally answered.

"Is it easier for you to push people away?"

Ace actually thought about that for a moment. "Yes. It's what I'm supposed to do," he told her.

"You haven't pushed me anywhere," she pointed out.

He smiled down at her as his hand caressed her lower back.

"That's because you are a force of nature who has my complete attention," he said. He couldn't help himself from bending down again and running his lips across hers as he let his hand drift over the top of her butt.

Her eyes flared, and he knew he was getting himself way too worked up in such a crowded room. He was going to announce to everyone there exactly how he felt about this woman, and he didn't think his brother would appreciate that too much. Flashbacks of the last Armstrong wedding wove through his head, and he actually felt . . . shame. What the hell!

"I'm also stubborn and like to get my way," she warned.

"That has been more than obvious from the second I met you," he said with a laugh. It was strange to be laughing so easily when he hadn't done so in years. Being here with this woman, with his family surrounding him, had lifted a weight off his shoulders he hadn't even realized he'd been carrying. He wished *all* the weight would evaporate.

"This is moving mighty fast, Ace," she said. There was still a sparkle in her eyes, but he could see an edge of fear in there too. He knew how she felt. It was frightening when a person had such an impact on you. Besides that, Ace had learned long ago not to try to hold on to things too tightly, because it made it more painful when they were ripped away from you.

"I've been warned that you're off-limits," he told her. Secretly he added, by his family *and* himself. He knew the smart thing would be to make her stay as far from him as humanly possible. Maybe while he was home he could send her on an all-expenses-paid vacation. Nope. He couldn't even imagine doing that.

She smiled at him. "And that probably made you want to claim me that much more."

He loved that she wasn't afraid to say exactly what was on her mind. Why had he ever bothered chasing women who pretended they didn't want to be caught?

"Yes, I might have to admit that intensified the appeal," he said. "But even without the warning, you're a beautiful, confident woman. I'm sure you're very used to being chased."

"But if you aren't pursued for the right reasons, then it's no fun," she said.

"Are you giving me permission to chase you, Ms. Forbes?" he asked, letting his hands slide along her hips now. He wanted to reach between them and feel the sweet weight of her breasts, but their lack of privacy stopped him. Maybe he could dance the two of them out to a patio and have his wicked way with her. That was an appealing thought. Maybe he could give himself this one night . . .

"You can try to catch me, but it might not be as easy as you think," she warned him.

Ace smiled as a chuckle escaped, and he pulled her lower half tightly against him, making sure she felt the power of his attraction to her.

"Not only *can* I catch you, but I can assure you, you would never want me to ever let you go," he replied.

She smiled, her eyes sparkling, her hips pushing into his in a sweet swirl that had his head spinning.

"Are you telling me you want me forever, Ace Armstrong?" she asked with a teasing smile. "Has your brother's wedding given you ideas?"

He knew his eyes must have shown the terror those words held for him, because Dakota laughed. He lifted his hand, giving her a smack on her delectable butt cheek. That only made her grin more.

"If you think you can scare me away, you will learn I'm not like most guys," he told her after several moments.

She gave him an intense stare before leaning her head against his chest and swaying with him as the song merged into a new one. Luckily it was still a sweet, mellow beat, so he didn't have to release her just yet.

Ace slowly moved the two of them through the crowd, spinning them as easily as a dancer from the twenties, his footwork perfect, her steps matching his with ease. His body was hard and his heart was racing, and he still didn't want to let her go.

The air thickened between the two of them, and Ace couldn't stop touching her, couldn't find the will to end their dance and let her go. In a few hours' time, he'd fallen under this woman's spell, and the thought of their perfect night ending was enough to make a cold sweat break out on his neck.

Ace might not be looking for love, didn't even know if he would recognize it if he were to find it, but he wanted something more from this woman than just a single night. He might not want forever, but he wanted more than just a single moment. And that was dangerous territory for him *and* for her.

Ace felt worried about the intensity of his feelings for this woman. To ease some of his anxiety and let air into the cocoon the two of them had formed in the crowd of people, he grabbed her hand and spun her in a circle before pulling her back to him. Her laughter was his reward, and then the song changed, a fun beat filling the room.

More people around them began dancing, laughter and talking surrounding them. He thought about pulling her from the room and taking her somewhere they could be alone, thought about all the things he'd like to do with her, but he was afraid of how he was going to feel if he made this moment any more intimate than it already was.

"You are full of surprises, Ace, and you have made this wedding a lot more fun than any other I've been to," Dakota told him as they continued dancing.

"You are bringing out something in me I didn't even know was there," he told her. "Or it could be the whisky I've drunk all night."

She smacked his arm. "It's *all* me. Besides, I've been told that alcohol simply allows us to do what we aren't brave enough to do without it."

"I'm a superhero, baby. I'm not afraid of anything," he said.

"If you just add a little chest pounding to that statement, I might believe you," she said.

He pounded his chest, knowing he was willing to do just about anything to make this woman laugh. It was sweeter than the music playing and the wedding cake combined.

"You know what, Ace?" she asked with a mischievous smile. He was afraid to respond. He was quickly learning he didn't know what would come out of her mouth next.

"What?" he finally asked.

"You smell delicious. I could lean into you all night and simply smell you."

Ace's arousal pulsed at her words.

"You are trouble, Dakota," he told her. "Why couldn't you have said this stuff while we had a nice empty hotel room all to ourselves?"

"Because then I might have done something I would regret in the morning," she said with a wink.

His mind was once again filled with images of the two of them entwined together, sweaty and naked. This night was going to be the death of him if she had her way about it.

"Damn, woman, you are killing me," he told her. "And trust me, there is nothing we would do together that you'd have *any* regrets about."

"Good. I'm finding it's quite fun torturing you," she admitted.

"My family might kill me if I haul you away over my shoulder, but then again, it could certainly be worth it," he said. But his words also brought to mind all the villains he chased. They might literally kill her if they thought they could get to him because of it. That didn't sit well with him—not one tiny bit.

"There might be a closet nearby we could sneak into," she told him as she bit her bottom lip, driving him crazy.

"Ace is very familiar with closets," Nick said with a laugh, interrupting the two of them.

Unbelievably, Ace felt his cheeks heat as he refused to meet Dakota's eyes and vowed to punch his brother again. That might just have to become an Armstrong wedding tradition. Too bad it looked as if Nick would always be the one getting hit.

"I feel there's a story here," Dakota said with laughter that surprised him, though he didn't understand how he could still be surprised by anything that came from this woman's mouth.

"Well, you see—" Nick began, but Ace cut him off.

"Dakota doesn't need to hear stories of the past," Ace warned.

"Oh, she certainly does," Dakota professed.

"Don't you have a bride to entertain?" Ace asked.

"I'm pretty entertained right now," Chloe said as she danced with her husband.

"And I need another drink," Ace told all of them.

Though his arms felt empty as he pulled away from Dakota, the sound of her laughter made clear that Nick must be telling her of Ace's youthful indiscretions. He continued straight to the bar, where he downed another double.

The smartest thing Ace could probably do at this point was to run as fast and as far from Dakota as he possibly could. But as he turned around, his eyes seeking her out, he knew he wasn't going anywhere.

He wanted to get to know this woman, wanted to understand how she was able to make him feel so many emotions he'd kept buried for years. He knew pursuing her might not be the smartest decision he'd made in a long time, but then again, he always survived no matter what choices he made. But what he couldn't avoid was that even if he survived, what if *she* didn't? He wouldn't be able to live with himself if harm came to this vibrant woman because of him.

Even knowing all of this, it didn't take long before staying away from Dakota was impossible, so he found her at the table with the rest of his family and sat next to her. Heat poured from her body, and though he tried to focus on the conversation, he gave up after a while and simply focused on the sound of her beautiful voice.

If he was really careful and didn't go out in public with her, he could make this work—for a short time. He tried telling himself that was the smart and safe thing to do. But it was only an excuse, because he wanted her, had to have her. The two of them together would be absolutely epic.

CHAPTER NINE

Two days after the wedding, Ace still hadn't thought of anything other than the beautiful brunette who'd so easily slipped beneath his defenses and caught his attention. After leaving Nick and Chloe's wedding and saying a very disappointed good-bye to Dakota, he'd told himself his feelings had been caused by the atmosphere of the event and the amount of liquor he'd consumed.

If that were truly the case, then why was he still thinking about her? Why did he want to find out exactly where she lived so he could go stand before her house with a boom box in hand, vowing his loyalty to her?

Because he was an idiot, he decided.

Even while sitting in Cooper's house with his family, getting ready to go to a game, he still couldn't focus on what was going on around him. Dakota filled his thoughts during the day, and she certainly filled his dreams with erotic visions that woke him up hard and unsatisfied.

"Are you ready for some football!" Mav yelled, breaking Ace from his brooding. Mav was still holding back from him in a subtle way, but Ace couldn't seem to find it within himself to talk to his brother about it. Probably because he felt he deserved it.

Ace also couldn't help but laugh at Mav's excited voice as the man entered the living room. They were all wearing their Seahawks jerseys with plenty of warm clothes beneath. Seahawks games were as cold as hell, but there was nothing like a live game.

"It's been a long time since I've sat in the stands," Ace admitted. Now, the thought gave him some anxiety. He was all too aware of the danger of being in a crowd like that, and how difficult it was to get away if things went to hell.

"Just another reason it's good to be home," Nick said as he joined them.

"Right now, we should be pregaming, though," Ace told them as he grabbed a bottle of Corona and took a large guzzle.

"Couldn't have said it better," Maverick said, grabbing his own bottle. "Good thing Coop's the designated tonight."

"We could have had Sherman drive us," Cooper said as he looked at his brothers with a scowl.

"This is brother-bonding time," Nick said. "You've all been complaining the last few days because I haven't been around."

"Yeah, I'm surprised you're coming out now. Since you tied the knot, that noose around your neck is getting pretty tight," Ace said.

"Don't knock it till you try it," Maverick warned.

"I never thought I'd see the day you'd be spouting the virtues of matrimony," Ace told him.

"Me either," Mav said. "But damn, I can't live without my woman."

"I hear you there," Coop said.

"And you don't have to," Lindsey said as she stepped into the room wearing her own jersey. "Now, you boys can go and have a great time alone," she added with a smile as Chloe and Stormy entered the room, looking just as adorable as Lindsey, "or you can have *our* company along with you."

"Oh, please don't leave us on our own," Maverick said as he moved over to his wife and easily lifted her from the ground before giving her a big kiss.

"Agreed," Coop said, his mood improving exponentially.

"It's up to Ace," Chloe said as she smiled sweetly at him. "We can go in our own vehicle if you want to have brother bonding."

Even if Ace had wanted that, he was on the spot with everyone in the room looking at him. It wasn't a hard decision to make, though. He liked his brothers' wives.

"I think the view will be a lot better if we go together," Ace said. The women beamed at him, making him feel like he'd just won an Olympic medal.

"Ah, thanks, sweetie," Chloe said, coming up to him and giving him a kiss on the cheek.

Ace didn't know how to deal with all of this open affection. It wasn't what he was used to, and it would take him a while before he got the hang of it. Cooper laughed, and Ace looked over at him. He was sure Coop knew just how uncomfortable he was.

"Since the ladies get to join you, I'm insisting on coming," Sherman said as he stepped into the room. "And since I brought transportation, I don't think you'll say no."

They all turned to see Sherman standing in the doorway wearing a jersey. It was odd to see him in something other than one of his sweaters. Each of them gazed at him in a bit of shock. He sent them a glare.

"I can join the crowd and wear a jersey for my favorite team," he grumbled. But he plucked at the material as if it was foreign against his skin and he didn't like it one little bit.

"It wouldn't be the same without you, Uncle Sherman," Nick said with a laugh. "And that means *you* get to join in on the pregaming," he told Cooper, who immediately grabbed a beer.

"I'm in," Coop said with a laugh.

Ace looked around at the rowdy group and wondered how he'd managed to survive for so long without them. For years, he'd been an outsider, peeking in the windows as the rest of his family had thrived and grown.

He still wasn't sure he fit in with any of them. The urge to flee was so intense he felt like he should have his running shoes on standby. But he kept those thoughts to himself. He wasn't yet sure how long he had until his next mission, and he was determined to enjoy his downtime while it lasted.

They soon piled into the limo, and laughter surrounded Ace like a protective shell as they made their way to CenturyLink Field, where the Seahawks were playing the Raiders. It would be a good game.

"I used to go to the games only to watch the cheerleaders," Nick said with a grin as he punched Ace's arm.

"You would, perv," Ace replied.

"I bet that's *all* you'll be looking at tonight," Cooper said with a knowing smirk.

Ace was confused as he gazed at the grinning faces looking at him. He had no idea what in the world they were talking about. But he didn't trust the expressions on their faces, especially when the women laughed in a wicked way.

Not only was he nervous about being in such a large crowd with what he deemed insufficient security, but now there was something wicked going on with his family. This night didn't seem like it was going to be a hell of a lot of fun anymore.

"I'm not some horndog, only interested in looking at women in short skirts," Ace said with a scowl.

"I bet there's *one* woman you'll have eyes for . . . all . . . night . . . long," Coop said, dragging out the words.

The group laughed, and Ace was even more confused. He sipped on his beer and scowled at them. Maybe he'd been gone long enough for his family to have gone nuts. That was very feasible. Besides, the thought of staring at any woman other than Dakota was downright unappealing. He was in more trouble than he was going to admit even to himself.

"Let him be surprised. It's more fun that way," Maverick said with an evil glint. Yep, his brother wanted payback.

"Surprised about what?" Ace asked.

"Oh, it's nothing. We're just having fun at your expense," Nick told him.

Ace didn't trust or believe any one of them. They were showing far too much delight on their faces. But it wouldn't do him any good to try to extract from them whatever it was they were going on about, so he sat back and let out a relieved breath when they got to the crowded stadium. At least they'd somewhat taken his mind off the dangers of the crowded place.

They entered through a VIP entrance and then moved inside to special field seats. Though Ace hadn't ever watched a game with this great of a view, he'd been lucky enough to grow up with money and had sat in many of the best seats in the house. But even he was awed by this new experience. Even if he felt too exposed.

"How did you manage this?" he asked as they sat in cushioned chairs while they watched the stands fill up and the teams come out to do warm-ups. Ace tuned into the conversation between his family members, but he also continuously scanned the arena.

"I have connections," Sherman said with a grin.

Ace sat back and decided to enjoy the show as much as he was capable. A server came to them and presented fresh beers and snacks, and Ace tried to relax. If it weren't for the stress of being in such a large crowd, he'd actually be enjoying all of this. It certainly was much more fun than sitting in his cramped living room.

The women jumped up when the cheerleaders came running out of the tunnels, shouting and getting the fans on their feet. Ace glanced at them before focusing again on the football players. He was determined to prove his family wrong and not watch the damn cheerleaders—not for a single minute.

"You're missing out," Mav said with a nudge in the arm as the cheerleaders ran by in front of them.

"I'm here for the football," Ace grumbled.

"That's too bad, 'cause we dance a lot better than they do."

Ace's head whipped around as Dakota stopped in front of them, wearing a ridiculously short skirt and bra top that was showing far too much of her beautiful cleavage. Ace's jaw dropped, and he found he wanted to grab her and cover her up, but as quickly as she'd shown up, she was gone again.

Of course! She was a cheerleader! That explained it all. The perkiness, the confidence, the way she'd drawn him to her. She had to be brainless on top of it. Weren't all cheerleaders? But . . . Damn it! She hadn't seemed like that—not at all, not like the cheerleaders at his high school. His thoughts were so muddled, he was beginning to wonder if he had a concussion.

Ace heard his family chortling as he put their teasing remarks together in his mind. No wonder they'd been saying he was going to be staring at the cheerleaders. They were right, but he wasn't happy about it.

The group of women stood about twenty feet in front of them as they performed a routine, giving Ace an incredible view of Dakota's luscious body as she kicked her legs high and jumped in the air, her breasts nearly spilling from her ridiculous top. He wanted to jump over the fence, haul her over his shoulder, and take her away.

His brothers were laughing, and he wasn't sure if they were doing it at his expense or not, but all his focus was on one woman only. Guess he was going to watch the cheerleaders the entire game after all—or at least one of them.

Dakota met his eyes several times over the next couple of hours, and Ace felt his body tense as he watched her do an incredible job of entertaining the huge crowd as the Seahawks pulled out a nice lead over the Raiders. Ace didn't even give a damn about the score of the game.

His brothers tried engaging him in conversation, but he couldn't concentrate. Between his awareness of Dakota's proximity to him, and his eyes constantly scanning the crowd for danger, he was a bundle of nerves, ready to snap at a moment's notice.

It also didn't matter how cold it was outside—he was hot and bothered as his eyes swept across Dakota's curvaceous body. He hated that the entire sporting world was getting the same view he was. Her performance should be for him only. It shouldn't be in this arena where she could get ambushed, where others were taking advantage of her. His mind was a mess.

When the game finished, Ace let out a breath of relief that they'd survived the event with no one getting injured and without him jumping over the barrier to save a girl who had no need of saving. He stared after Dakota as she passed by them and winked. His brothers called out that she'd done great, and she blew them a kiss.

Another cheerleader caught Ace's eyes and smiled at him in a way that assured him she'd be more than happy to go home with him. He turned away, not at all interested. He wanted only one woman right now, and he didn't see that changing any time soon.

"Let's get out front. Dakota is going to dinner with us," Chloe said.

Ace was the first person on his feet. His mood improved greatly at knowing he was about to be with the woman who was consuming entirely too many of his thoughts. He didn't wait for the rest of his family, just marched through the crowd and out to where the limo was waiting for them. He let out an enormous sigh of relief the minute he stepped through the tunnel. Damn, his muscles hurt—they'd been so tense all night.

His family met up with him a few minutes later, and then he paced as the crowd filed from the stadium. He was waiting for one person only, and she was taking her sweet-ass time.

When Dakota finally came through the private entrance, Ace felt his heart thunder in his chest. She had looked delicious in her cheerleading uniform, but damn if she didn't look just as amazing in a pair of tight jeans and a sweater that hugged her in all the right places.

He had now seen a lot of her luscious body, and clothes did nothing to hide the visuals that were permanently tattooed on his brain. He needed to strip her down and see the final pieces of her body he hadn't yet been privileged to view.

Soon, he promised himself. Very soon he would have her naked and sweaty beneath him. He feared if he didn't, bad things might happen. Could a man go crazy with lust? Yeah, he decided. It was a real possibility. Maybe he should just voluntarily commit himself now.

"You did wonderfully, beautiful," Chloe said, the first to grab Dakota. "As usual."

"Thanks, darling. I had fun," Dakota said. She looked over Chloe's shoulder and met Ace's eyes. Hers widened a bit, and he realized his emotions might not be as masked as he'd been hoping.

"Ready for some food after that workout?" Nick asked.

"I'm starving. I think I could eat an entire cow," she said with a laugh.

"Hey, sugar! Want a ride?"

Ace froze as some dipshit guys in a raised Chevy pickup stopped in front of them, their eyes on Dakota, drool practically spilling from their mouths. He took a step toward them, ready to beat them into a bloody pulp.

"Get out of here, Gary, and go see your wife," Dakota said with a laugh.

"If you insist," the man said with a wicked smile before he pulled away.

Ace was shaking with the need to smash something. He turned back and looked at Dakota, who was smiling at him, clearly understanding the rage he was feeling. He didn't like her seeing his instant jealousy at another man coming on to her.

"That's just Gary. He's a dear friend," Dakota said. But he had a feeling she was thinking she had Ace right where she wanted him—hook, line, and sinker. Maybe she did.

"Let's get out of here," Cooper said, laughter in his voice.

Ace didn't say a word and didn't dare touch Dakota. Instead he moved to the limo and climbed inside. He had damn well better learn how to get himself under control. If not, he was going to be in for a world of hurt.

He looked down at his feet, but even without seeing her, he felt it the moment Dakota stepped inside the limo—the large space suddenly became suffocating. He wasn't going to survive this woman. He now knew that, as sure as he knew his own name. She was going to take him on a wild ride, and he wasn't ever going to get off.

And maybe that's exactly what he wanted to have happen. If the decision was taken out of his hands, then he would have nothing to feel guilty about.

CHAPTER TEN

Dakota had been cheering for the Seahawks for three years, and never had she had such an intense game as the one she'd just participated in. It was even worse than the first time she'd taken the field, hoping and praying she wouldn't fall on her ass in front of the tens of thousands of people in the stands, along with the millions of people viewing her from the comfort of their living rooms.

But with Ace's eyes on her the entire time—and she had felt his gaze burning into her—she'd had to concentrate even harder than normal on not messing up. The man was messing with her in far more ways than she felt she was messing with him. It wasn't something she was used to, and she was more determined now than ever to get the hell over it.

Stepping inside the limo, she didn't even give herself a choice of what to do. She swiftly moved through the large seating area and plopped herself down right next to Ace. She felt his body tense beside her, and that gave her a bit of her confidence back. She was certainly affecting him as much as he was her—that helped a lot.

"Did you enjoy the game?" she asked as sweetly as she possibly could.

The intense look he sent her way set her core to boiling levels as she squeezed her thighs together. The man looked as if he wanted to kick everyone out of the vehicle, which slowly began moving, and take her right there on the seat.

Dakota was thinking that wouldn't be such a bad idea. Her hormones were going crazy, and she could use the relief she was sure only he could give her. Of course, with all eyes on them, it might be best to behave—at least for now.

"Yes," he told her shortly. It took her a moment to even remember what she'd said to him. She pulled herself together quickly, though, and gave him a beaming smile.

"Good. I like happy fans."

His expression didn't change, but if possible, his eyes darkened even more as he leaned in closer to her. Dakota's breathing was coming out in short pants, but she was sure she was covering it up well.

"I aim to please," Ace told her.

"I appreciate that in a man," she said, making sure her hot breath whispered against his ear. She saw the shudder pass through him and felt herself on much more level ground again. If they were torturing each other equally, she could consider that a win.

"You know when you play with fire, you usually get burned," he said, this time his breath rushing across *her* ear and neck. She was the one shivering. Dakota decided to take it up about a dozen notches.

"I enjoy the fire, Ace. Haven't you figured that much out about me yet?" she asked as she let her hand trail across his thigh before settling it on her own lap.

She glanced at him out of the corner of her eye and was immensely pleased by the rigid set of his jaw and body. She knew she was going to pay for her torture of him, but she didn't care. Inflicting the pain was well worth it—at least for this moment.

"When I get you alone . . ." he began, and Dakota laughed, causing several people in the vehicle to turn their way.

"What's so funny?" Chloe asked.

"Oh, Ace was just telling me a terrific joke. Want to share it?" she asked as she turned to him with big eyes and patted his thigh, letting her fingers trail off close to where she was sure he was pulsing. It would look innocent to anyone watching, but she knew what she was doing to him.

Ace looked up at the group, and she had to choke on the power she felt in being a woman. Looking natural and naive wasn't as easy as it appeared. But she managed to keep her expression light as she waited to see what he would say.

"Knock, knock," Ace grumbled.

Cooper burst out laughing. "I think we've missed out on an inside joke," he said as he stared their way.

"Yeah, Dakota has quite the sense of humor," Ace told them. This time it was his turn to torture her.

He slung his arm around her shoulder, dipping it into her back, his fingers resting on the side of her breast. She sucked in air as she sat stiffly in his embrace. If she pulled away, he won. She decided to squirm just a little bit closer and rubbed her thigh against his.

"Yes, she does," Chloe said with a smile of affection.

Dakota could always count on her best friend. Whether Chloe knew exactly what was going on or not, she would always side with Dakota and help her make the man suffer. That's what besties did for each other.

They arrived at the restaurant, and Dakota let out a sigh of relief. As the group began piling out of the limo, Ace's fingers rubbed along the side of her breast, and her nipples beaded painfully as her core pulsed with heat.

"This night is only just beginning," Ace warned her as she stood up on shaking knees.

Ace quickly stood behind her and rubbed against her backside. She sucked in air at the feel of his powerful arousal pressing against her. Damn, she wanted to close the limo doors and stay inside with him. She had never wanted to jump into a fire as much as she wanted to right now.

This time it was Ace who positioned them once they were inside the restaurant. He sat in the back of a booth beside her, his leg pressed up against hers. When the group was relaxed, eating appetizers and chatting, he reached over and ran his hand from her knee to the top of her thigh, his pinkie finger nearly brushing against her panties.

She squeezed her legs together and barely managed to keep her moan of frustration and pleasure from escaping. Her forehead beaded with sweat, and she grabbed her water glass and downed the entire thing.

"Guess you get pretty hot doing all those routines," Maverick said, looking like his comment was innocent, but at this moment she didn't trust any of the Armstrong men. They surely all had to be as suave as Ace.

"Yes, it gets pretty hot and sweaty," she said with mock naivety before looking Ace straight in the eyes. "We really do get a workout, twisting and turning in all directions. I'm always famished after a game."

She blinked her eyes at him and smiled, loving the flare of fire in his eyes and how his jaw tensed even more. He squeezed her thigh in punishment, but she could imagine the sort of images rushing through his mind at her words.

"Don't worry, darling. I'm definitely going to show you new moves," he said against her ear.

"What was that, Ace? I didn't hear you?" Sherman asked loudly.

"Nothing, Uncle," Ace said as he looked down. Dakota snorted. She was both incredibly turned on and having a lot of fun at the same time. She could honestly say it was the best night she'd had in a while.

The rest of the evening continued with Dakota and Ace seeing who could torture whom the most. By the time it was over, Dakota wasn't exactly sure who the winner was. Normally she came out the victor, so she didn't know if she wanted to keep playing games with Ace or not.

Of course, she squashed that thought immediately. Dakota didn't go running for water just because the going got rough. Or something like that, she assured herself. When the limo pulled up to her place, she was having a hard time balancing as she rose.

"I'll walk you to the door," Chloe said.

"Not a chance," Ace interrupted. "I'll do it."

Not one person argued with the man, and she wanted to call all of them traitors. She refused to look any of the Armstrongs in the eyes. They might have an inkling of what had been happening the entire night, but it would only be suspicion and not fact. So she had to rest assured that she had kept it hidden.

The silence of the night was overwhelming after being in the boisterous limo, but Ace placed his hand on her lower back as she walked as quickly as her legs would carry her to the front door. She fumbled in her purse, looking for her keys, shocked when she found that her fingers were shaking.

"Are you nervous about something, Dakota?" Ace asked, oozing with smugness.

"Nope, just drank a bit too much wine with dinner," she replied.

"I don't think so," he said, boxing her in against her door just as she wrapped her fingers around her keys. "I think you had fun playing tonight, and now that we're alone you're nervous," he guessed accurately.

"Well, you don't know me very well if you think I get spooked so easily," she assured him.

"Hmm," he murmured as he leaned his body against hers. His touch was incredible, and she couldn't even begin to pretend she didn't like the sensation of craving him.

His lips fluttered across her neck, and her heart thundered as she anticipated the moment his lips would touch hers. She'd kissed him several times the night of the wedding, and each kiss had been better than the last. She didn't mind another taste of him one little bit.

71

"Are you going to pretend you don't want a good-night kiss?" he asked before his tongue swept down the curve of her neck, making her lean her head back to get more.

"No," she said. Why lie? It didn't do either of them any good.

He looked up, delight in his eyes. His arms wrapped around her as he dragged her tightly against him, then pulled her leg up so he could settle between her thighs. He let her feel his arousal pressing right where she wanted it.

"I like a woman who knows what she wants," he told her.

He quit talking as his mouth took her lips in a harsh kiss that sucked all the oxygen from her. Dakota's arms wrapped around his neck as she clung tightly to him and gave back just as much as he was giving.

She squirmed against his body, heat overwhelming her as she got lost in Ace's embrace. It would be so easy to let it all go and fall captive to him. She wanted to do just that, but she couldn't—not yet. She'd just become another notch on his bedpost.

With reluctance, she finally pulled back, sure that her eyes reflected the same desire she saw in his. Her fingers trailed across his jaw.

"You are an incredibly good-looking man," she said with a wobbly smile.

"Why don't I send the family home and take you inside for a nightcap," he said, his voice pleading.

She actually thought about it for a few seconds before she sighed with reluctance. She wanted so badly to say yes to him, but they both knew she wasn't going to do that.

"Good night, Ace," she said. Then she pushed him back. He stepped away willingly, though with reluctance.

"It might not happen tonight, but it *will* happen," Ace assured her. He then took the key from her hand and unlocked her door, pushing it open. "Go inside before I change my mind about being chivalrous and follow you."

Dakota didn't say another word as she stepped into her house and turned to look at him one final time before she shut the door in his face. She leaned against it as she listened to his steps moving down her walkway.

She heard the limo pull away and then walked slowly into her living room, where she sank down onto her couch and grabbed a magazine off her coffee table, fanning her flushed cheeks.

Dakota wasn't going to be getting a heck of a lot of sleep tonight. And she feared the entire week was going to be shot. Her flying lessons began tomorrow, with her and Ace in very tight quarters with no one else around.

She wasn't sure she was going to make it. She certainly knew she wasn't going to without falling into the man's bed. As much as she knew it would be wise not to do that, she couldn't help herself. She wanted him as much as he wanted her, and it might be better to just get it over with.

By the time Dakota climbed into bed, she was no closer to finding answers than when she'd first set eyes upon Ace. Maybe the problem was she needed to quit thinking and go with basic animal instinct. That made her smile as she finally fell asleep.

CHAPTER ELEVEN

Ace was leaning against the small four-seater Cessna 400 he'd chosen for Dakota's flying lesson. Yeah, he knew this wasn't a plane most students would fly for the first time, but Dakota wasn't just any student. She could handle the sexy plane and would appreciate its composite construction and lack of lumpy rivets. He also wanted to impress her. Besides that, Sherman had assured him she was ready for a powerful plane.

Ace had a clear view of the door, and he was highly anticipating the moment she walked into the room. In his life, Ace had done a lot of jobs, had been to many places. Never had he thought he'd so look forward to teaching someone how to fly.

But he was more amped up about this job than any other he had ever had. The thought of the two of them being side by side for hours high up in the sky was unbelievably appealing to him. He was closing in on making her his. And his conquest couldn't come soon enough.

He feared the consequences of making Dakota his own, but his need for her was outweighing his reservations. Besides, he reasoned, he had come up with a solution by keeping their relationship in the dark. Plus, Dakota was more than capable of giving back just as good as she got. She was certainly the right kind of woman for him.

When the door opened and Dakota finally stepped through, Ace didn't move from his position, but his entire body tensed as she drew closer to him. This was where he wanted to be and the woman he wanted to be with. Could he be losing his mind?

"Is this the plane?" Dakota asked. She made a wide circle around him as she looked at the clean lines of the beautiful plane.

"Yep. She's perfect for you," Ace told her.

"Why is it a she?" she asked, a hand on her hip and sassiness in her voice.

He laughed aloud as he followed her around the plane. She reached out and caressed the cool white metal like he imagined she would touch a lover. He was instantly hard and uncomfortable again.

"All planes are referred to as female," he informed her.

"I think you need to prove that. Maybe I want to call it . . . Bob," she said with a raised brow.

"Honey, with these curves and beauty, she couldn't have anything *but* a lady's name," he assured her.

She laughed, allowing him to win the argument. And Ace had no doubt whatsoever that she was indeed *allowing* him to win. He'd never actually investigated to find out why planes were referred to with female names. But flying had been the good old boys' club for so long, he was sure that's where the naming of planes had originated.

"She's a Cessna 400 with low wings, a carbon-fiber composite design, and, most importantly, a *very* comfortable interior," he said as he opened the door and let her look inside at the clean leather upholstery.

"There's not a lot of room in there," she said as she looked from the inside of the plane to Ace and then back again.

"Nope. We'll be squished in nice and tight," he said, his tone clearly telling her that was a perk to this job.

"Where do I pay for my lesson?" she asked.

Ace gazed at her at a loss. "Pay?" he questioned.

"Yes. This is a flight school. I'm supposed to pay," she told him.

"I'll talk to Sherman about it," he said, shifting on his feet. He wasn't going to talk to Sherman, because she wasn't paying. He wasn't taking money from the woman, especially when he would be more than willing to pay her to be up in the air with him.

"*I'll* talk to Sherman about it. I don't trust you," she said with a knowing smile.

Yeah, so would he. Ace absolutely wasn't taking money for this gig. He planned on some after-hours activities, so money was definitely off the table.

Dakota simply smiled at him, and he knew that she knew exactly what was going through his mind. It wouldn't ever be easy to pull the wool over this woman's eyes. She was too aware of herself and her surroundings.

Ace led her over to a desk, popped open a book, and leaned in behind her as she went over some basic techniques of flying. Her brows furrowed as she read the material, glancing up at him every once in a while.

Ace missed those days when he'd first learned to fly. Every single part of the reading materials had fascinated him. But nothing had compared to when he'd sat in the cockpit for the very first time. There had been a thrill then that he still felt when he took the controls of a plane. He could rise above the land and soar like the birds. There was utter freedom in the act of flying.

Then he'd flown for the drug cartel, he remembered with a frown. That had dampened his love of flying, because he knew what and whom he'd been transporting. He didn't want those thoughts invading his mind at this moment, but it was hard to pull himself out of that dark place. Dakota's presence made it a little bit easier.

"You ready?" he asked, shaking his head to clear it.

Dakota looked at him as if he had a screw loose. He wanted to tell her that since he'd met her, there wasn't anything bolted down securely in his head anymore, but he held that in. Those words wouldn't exactly inspire confidence in his student.

"Ready?" she said, her voice hesitant. He found he liked knocking her off-kilter. The woman was so damn confident. He was used to being around women who knew they were beautiful and knew how to use their bodies. But with Dakota, it was different. She had an aura about her that spoke of competence as well as confidence.

"You didn't learn how to walk by sitting on your ass. You can't learn how to fly by reading a book," he said, holding out his hand to help her up.

She accepted his fingers, though she seemed unsure as she stood up next to him.

"I didn't think we'd be getting into the plane so soon," she said. Ace smiled at her as the two of them drew closer to the plane.

"It takes many hours of hands-on experience to learn how to fly. It's no different than driving, really. The biggest difference is you're in the sky if something goes wrong. Like driving, though, you have to act quickly, be prepared, and use your training to keep your wits about you and deal with emergencies properly."

"You aren't exactly inspiring confidence," she said with a sassy glare.

Ace's smile grew even bigger.

"You have plenty of that on your own. I don't need to stroke your ego," he assured her.

They climbed inside the small cockpit, and Ace wasn't complaining at all with her pressed up beside him. He had to help her with the seat belt, and that just made him smile all the more. His pants were achingly tight, and her perfume was saturating the air.

Normally, he wouldn't mind that one little bit, but he had to be in trainer mode, and it wouldn't do either one of them any good for him to be distracted. He wasn't going to be able to ravage this woman if he got them both killed.

"Everything is new and exciting the first time you fly. But most pilots will say that feeling never really goes away. You are either born to fly, or you're one of the many who prefer to be shuttled around. I can see the lust in your eyes. You're going to make a hell of a pilot," he assured her.

"I'm scared, I admit that," she said with a chuckle. "But you also might be right. I think I was meant to do this."

Ace had known a lot of female pilots in his lifetime, but none as sexy as Dakota. He normally wasn't one to ever be the first officer, but he would make an exception with her. Flying in the sky, just the two of them, sounded as close to paradise as he could imagine.

"As long as you're open to new experiences and you take charge of your learning, this will be as smooth as butter," Ace assured her.

"Well, I'm as smooth as a porcupine, so I've got this," she said seriously as she gazed at the controls.

Ace waited for her to laugh, but she didn't. "You really don't get idioms, do you?" he said after a few moments. She looked at him with guileless eyes.

"What do you mean?"

"Smooth as a porcupine?" he asked, with raised brows. She still looked at him in confusion. He just laughed as he pulled out the preflight checklist. She narrowed her eyes at him.

"Douglas Adams said that flying is learning how to throw yourself at the ground and miss," Ace told her. "So let's make sure we miss."

"I can promise you, I want to do exactly that," she said.

During the next twenty minutes, he taught her how to go through the checklist, and then he showed her how to start the plane. She hung on every word he spoke, and Ace was glad he was the one teaching her how to fly.

The thought of her in this plane with some other guy sent feelings through him he didn't want to analyze. He was already beginning to think of this woman as his. It was a frightening thought, so he pushed it to the back of his mind and refused to focus on it.

They taxied out to the runway, and Ace spoke to her through her headphones. "Even when I'm the one holding the controls, make sure you follow along so you can feel how I'm maneuvering the aircraft. This will build positive muscle memory and lead to good habits from the beginning."

"Got it," she told him as the plane revved up. They got clearance for departure, and Ace pushed in the throttle and gazed straight ahead. He could feel Dakota next to him as she held her controls and looked through the front and side windows. She was loving every moment of her time in the plane.

They climbed easily into the clear blue sky. Ace was able to let go of his raging desire for a while as he instructed her on the basic motions of flying. She was a fast learner, and he knew she'd be doing her first solo flight by the time she had ten hours logged. He was almost bummed about that.

"You don't want to rely too heavily on your flight instruments. You are training to become a pilot under the Visual Flight Rules, or VFR, so that means the majority of time you're flying, you need to be looking outside the plane. A lot of students rely too heavily on the instruments, and if something goes wrong, they don't respond quickly enough," Ace told her.

"The view is better outside the windows anyway," she told him.

He decided not to take offense to that. He knew what it was like to fly—when first learning, a trainee can be so in love with every aspect of flying, it feels like no one else exists.

"Exactly. There's no need to look at the artificial horizon on your panel when you can glance out the window and see the real thing. Of course, your instruments are needed and incredibly helpful, but they are there to validate what you are already seeing. The FAA recommends that pilots' attention be outside the cockpit ninety percent of the time."

Ace could see that Dakota was getting too relaxed simply being a passenger. He couldn't allow that to happen. She was born to be a pilot, not a passenger.

"Take over," he told her, removing his hands from the yoke.

"What are you doing?" she asked, her fingers gripping the control wheel, her knuckles turning white.

"You have to learn by doing," he assured her. He didn't tell her he could take over at a moment's notice. He needed her to believe in herself. He leaned back, his hands going behind his head in a relaxed gesture.

Her eyes flashed to his before they quickly darted forward again. She held on to the stick tightly. She was keeping them perfectly level. He was impressed.

"I want you to bank left," he told her.

"I can't," she said, the plane not veering an inch from its forward trajectory.

"You can do it, Dakota," he said calmly.

He felt a shudder pass through her body as she tensed even more, but then she took in a deep cleansing breath, and the plane began turning left. Ace had a difficult time taking his eyes from her beaming face as she learned what it felt like to make a plane do exactly what she wanted it to do.

"I'm doing it!" Her excited voice through his headset was music to his ears.

"You're doing a hell of a job," he confirmed. "I want you to go in a 360-degree circle now."

This time she didn't argue with him. She made a much wider turn than needed, but as they made it around into a full circle, he knew she officially had the flying bug. She would never go back to feeling the same way about the ground again. Ace really liked that he had been instrumental in Dakota's first hands-on flight.

They stayed in the sky for about two hours, and still, Dakota pouted when it was time to come back down to the ground. He let her descend then laughed when they missed the runway—twice.

He finally had mercy on her and took over the controls, bringing them in for a smooth landing. When they got back to the hangar and Ace stopped the plane, he turned to her and said, "Good job."

The beaming smile she gave him took both his breath and his words away.

"You are so stunning," he said, utter awe filling him.

"Thank you," she said, though he knew she wasn't talking about the compliment he'd just given her, but about the experience they'd just shared together. She was on such a high, better than any drug. There was nothing that compared to your first time flying.

Dakota launched herself across the tiny space between them, her arms circling his neck as she clung tightly to him. She thanked him over and over again. Ace didn't hesitate as he put his arms around her and squeezed.

Her scent was enfolding him, and he wanted to be somewhere a hell of a lot more private than a public hangar. Dakota pulled back, and then her lips were only inches away from his. He wasn't going to resist the temptation of her sweet mouth. Not giving her a chance to protest, he gripped the back of her neck and pulled her to him, his mouth covering hers in sweet, sweet relief.

Dakota gasped into his mouth, her lips opening to his hungry tongue. Then, like she did with everything in life, she embraced him with hunger and excitement. Her fingers dived into his hair as she pressed more tightly against him and kissed him back with as much hunger as he felt.

By the time the two of them broke apart, Ace was ready to explode in his pants. This woman was twisting him apart, and he didn't even care.

"Let's go back to my place and celebrate your first flight," he said with an attempt at a smile.

Dakota looked at him as if she was trying to decide. Ace's heart pounded as he awaited her decision. If she said no, he might actually die. But if she said yes, he might burst with excitement.

She licked her lips in the most enticing of ways, and his thickness pulsed. Then she bit her bottom lip, and he thought about stripping them both down and just going for it right then and there. To hell with anyone who might walk in.

"Not yet."

It took a moment for Dakota's words to process in his befuddled mind. She was telling him no, but she wasn't telling him never. Hot damn!

"Any time, anywhere," he said huskily.

She smiled at him, her tongue darting out to wet her lips again.

"I'll keep that in mind," she said.

He was thinking seriously of pulling her back to him when she let him go and opened the door, quickly jumping from the plane. Ace leaned back in his seat and concentrated on his breathing techniques for several moments. His body was pulsing so painfully he was afraid of even moving.

"I've gotta run, Ace. Thanks again for a great day," Dakota called to him.

He turned in time to watch her tight ass sway as she exited the hangar. Then he leaned back and closed his eyes. With Dakota around, he would never be bored, that was for sure. He also didn't have time to be stressed. She was a ray of light in a dark world. And he was falling for her more and more by the second.

CHAPTER TWELVE

Dakota paced her house as she fanned her hot cheeks. She couldn't quit smiling. She'd had such an exciting first flying lesson, not to mention being pressed close against Ace's side all afternoon. It had been a thrill in so many ways.

This man was getting under her skin unlike any man before him, and she wasn't in the least bit afraid anymore. It had scared her a little bit at first, but she'd gone beyond that to now being excited for her next visit with him.

She could tell herself all day long that it only had to do with her wanting to help him, that her instincts had kicked in and she knew he needed the kind of therapy she was known for giving, but her connection to him went way beyond that.

She was attracted to Ace in the most basic of ways. Her instincts were to follow through on that attraction. When he'd invited her to spend some private time with him, she'd been more than willing to say yes in a big, bold, exclamation-mark kind of way.

But part of the fun was the anticipation. She'd waited so long to get to this point, and she was terrified of being let down if things didn't turn out as she expected. Still, Dakota wasn't sure how long she was going to be able to hold out. She wanted this man—and she knew she was going to have him.

Her energy on high alert, Dakota cleaned her place from top to bottom, working up a good sweat as she blasted music and danced her way through her house. Life without music would be a tragic thing. It didn't matter what the task was—if there was music playing, it was always better.

When her doorbell rang in the late evening, Dakota almost missed it. When it rang again, she sighed as she tried to decide if she was going to answer or not. She was on a roll and didn't feel like stopping. At the third ring, she decided the person wasn't going to leave.

She left her music on high as she floated through her place and swung the door open. It drove Chloe crazy that Dakota never checked who was on the other side before opening it. Dakota figured she'd just drop-kick a person if they were up to no good.

As soon as she saw the wicked smile and sexy dimple on the face of Ace Armstrong, she felt her heart thunder and her knees shake. He was standing on her doorstep with a bottle of wine and a dozen roses. She grinned at him as "Pour Some Sugar on Me" played loudly in the background.

"Nice choice in music," he said as he leaned in her doorway.

"It's my motivational music," she said, unable to help but grin back at him.

"I brought wine," he told her.

"I can see that," she said, her lips turning up even more. "I suppose you're hoping I'll invite you in?"

"That's the plan," he said. She had to respect the man for not trying to barge through her door before she gave him permission.

"I could just take the wine and close the door in your face," she pointed out.

"But I have flowers too," he pointed out.

"I'm more of a lily type of girl," she said, trying to sound unimpressed.

"I'll remember that," he assured her.

"I suppose you can come in for a few minutes," she said, swinging her door wide open. He didn't wait for her to change her mind. He stepped into her place with confidence, immediately making it seem much smaller than it was.

When Dakota cleaned, clutter took over. It always appeared as if a tornado had swept through the room before she got things organized. She was still in the things-strewn-all-over-the-place phase of her cleaning day. "I like it," he said as he looked around and laughed.

Dakota moved over to her music player and turned down the volume so they wouldn't have to keep shouting. Then she led Ace into her small kitchen and pulled down two wineglasses.

He uncorked the bottle and then waited as she poured them each a generous amount. Her first sip was heaven on her tongue. The crisp white wine was cold and refreshing. She most likely looked a mess, but he didn't make her feel self-conscious. Even though she was sure her hair was sticking out in every direction and there was probably sweat beaded on her forehead, he looked at her as if she was the most beautiful woman on the planet. He was certainly good for her ego.

"What are you doing in this neck of the woods?" she asked him.

"I haven't stopped thinking about you all day. I decided I'd rather see you in person than picture you in my head," he said, taking a step closer.

Dakota knew she could retreat, but there was nothing inside her that wanted to. Instead she closed the space between them, meeting him halfway. Ace's eyes flashed in delight as he took her wineglass away and set it on the counter, then slowly slipped his arms around her back.

"You aren't an easily forgotten woman," he said, almost sounding angry about it.

"It's always better to leave them with a . . . happy face," she said, and he laughed.

"Yes, a happy face works for me," he said before leaning down and kissing her on the corner of her mouth before his tongue traced her bottom lip.

"You know this is a bad idea, right?" she said, her voice already husky.

"Yep, I do," he assured her.

"Okay," she said, drawing out the word. "Since we have that out of the way, kiss me like you mean it."

Fire flared in Ace's eyes, and Dakota felt the burn all the way to her toes. He gripped her hips tightly as he pulled her up against him and his mouth crashed against hers. This was no exploratory meeting of the mouths. This was pure possession at the deepest levels. Dakota was immediately lost in his embrace.

Ace backed the two of them up against her counter, then easily lifted her up, pulling her to the edge and pushing himself against her. She felt his thickness pressing on her, and she wanted to reach forward and feel him. She was sure he wasn't going to disappoint her.

Ace groaned against her mouth before releasing her swollen lips and moving down her jawline to suck on her neck. She arched her back as his hands slid from her neck to her butt and back up again while he sucked on her skin.

She reached between their bodies and slid her fingers over the bulge in his pants, making him tense as he shook in her arms.

"You can't touch me like that—I'm afraid I might go pure predator," he warned through clenched teeth.

"Ooh," she said, heat flooding her. Instead of backing away, she squeezed him through the denim of his pants, and he bit into her shoulder, a warning nip that only served to turn her on that much more.

She reached for the buttons on his pants, finding it difficult to undo them. His thick erection had drawn the material tight. She was up for the challenge, though, and after a few fumbles, she managed to get his pants undone.

She slipped her hand into his boxers and then felt his velvety-smooth hardness. Her core pulsed with need. Her body knew exactly where she wanted this to end. Her nails traced over the head of his arousal, and his excitement dripped out, making her squirm on the counter.

Ace leaned back, and she whimpered. Their eyes met. She could swear she saw fire in his expression. That only made her wetter. She leaned forward and kissed along his solid jaw, reaching around and sucking on his ear.

He tugged on her shirt, and she felt the material give beneath his strong touch. Her T-shirt was shredded down the middle in seconds. Dakota wondered if she was going to orgasm from the excitement of his obvious hunger for her.

"Damn, Dakota," he said in awe as he leaned back, his gaze focused on her barely covered breasts, which were hardly contained in her bra. Her nipples hurt from rubbing against the lacy material.

He quickly solved that problem by undoing the bra and flinging it somewhere behind her. She didn't care where it landed. He leaned down to suck her peaked nipple into his warm mouth. She cried out as her fingers dug into his hair, holding him right where he was.

He moved from one breast to the other until she was a puddle on the counter, barely able to hold herself up. When he pulled back, she tried tugging him forward again, but he shook his head. He lifted her from the counter, and she wrapped her legs around him.

"Bedroom!" he said, his voice almost unrecognizable.

"Down the hall, on the right," she said, her own voice husky and weak.

Ace carried her the short distance down the hall into her room. Her bed was a mess, the blankets twisted, the pillows halfway off. Ace set her on the edge, then swept all of it to the floor before he gently pushed her back and then climbed on top of her.

His mouth connected with hers again, even hungrier than before, as he devoured her whole, his throbbing package cradled in the safety of her thighs.

"I need you now," he said.

"Then take me," she begged.

Ace leaned away only long enough to shed his clothes and grab a condom, quickly slipping it on. She was thankful, because she hadn't even taken a moment to think about protection. They didn't really know each other, and they were jumping into this fast. She didn't have time for regrets, though—didn't want them.

Ace pulled off her pants, and then he was on top of her again, his thickness poised at the entrance to her heat, his heart thundering against hers, his fingers gripping her face. He didn't move forward, didn't lean down and kiss her, didn't move so much as a toe as he gazed into her eyes. His look had such intensity, she felt too exposed under his gaze. She tried to turn away.

"Don't do that. Look at me," he demanded.

She wrenched her eyes back to his and felt the sting of tears prickle. This was too much for her to handle. It was just supposed to be sex—nothing more. But Ace wasn't allowing her that freedom.

"Ace," she said, her tone holding a warning.

His gaze never broke from hers as he surged forward, his thickness breaking through the barrier of her body and filling her completely. Pain shot through her for only a moment, and then the intimacy and fullness of him inside her was all she could think about.

But Ace stopped as his eyes widened, understanding dawning in his expression. He began to pull from her, and Dakota panicked. She'd been hoping he wouldn't notice she'd never gone this far with a man, that it could simply happen without any fanfare. She was too old to be a virgin, too confident. She was a cheerleader. Everyone just assumed she'd been sleeping with everyone for years. She didn't care what people thought.

"I'm sorry," Ace said, his voice strangled.

"Don't leave me like this, Ace," she warned, her hips tipping up as she moved against him, the friction causing her to burn in new ways. "I've done things before, but I've just never felt the need to complete the act," she told him, hesitating. "Until now."

He groaned as he held on to her hips tightly.

"We can't do this," he said, though she could see her movement was pushing him over the edge of sanity. Good.

"We already are," she told him, wrapping her legs around his back and wiggling against him.

It was obviously too much for him to take, because his eyes went wild again. He leaned down and captured her lips, thrusting in and out of her body. His powerful erection seemed endless as he rubbed against her sensitive walls while his tongue did the most delicious things inside her mouth.

Beautiful pressure built and built as he moved faster and faster within her. She felt sparks igniting, and she began shaking as her orgasm drew closer.

"Harder, please," she begged.

Ace lost control as he gripped her hips and slammed inside her body. And that was all it took. She shattered in his arms, squeezing him deep inside her. He cried out at the added pressure, and then she felt him pulsing within her as she clung tightly to him.

The pleasure lasted forever—and yet it ended entirely too soon. Ace collapsed against her, their bodies wet with sweat, their breathing loud in the small room. Dakota was in no way ready to let him go when he pulled against her hold.

He turned them so they were on their sides facing each other, and she felt almost bereft as he pulled out of her.

"You should have told me," he said, his voice much more controlled now. He looked angry.

"You wouldn't have done what I wanted if I had," she said.

At least he didn't try to lie to her. "You should have told me." He repeated that a few more times.

"You are killing my happy buzz," she said with a glare. He looked at her in surprise. "If you're going to keep grumbling, then you can leave."

"Are you kidding me?" he said, seeming to grow as irritated as she was now.

"Nope. Matter of fact, you leaving is a great idea. Then I can lie here and relive this moment of ecstasy, leaving out this after-sex talk, of course."

He glared at her. She gave him just as stern a look right back. They faced off for several moments before he let out an exasperated sound and jumped from her bed, snagged his clothes, and stalked off.

Dakota leaned down and grabbed her blankets, covering herself as she sat up, wondering if he was even going to bother telling her good-bye. For his sake, he'd damn well better do that.

When he appeared in her doorway, he was fully dressed. She tried not to show her disappointment. If he wasn't going to let her savor this moment, it was better for both of them if he left.

"I guess this means there won't be a round two?" she said with an innocent smile.

He looked at her again as if she was insane. She probably was. After all, look how long she'd waited to have sex for the first time. A sane woman wouldn't do that.

"No," he snapped. Then, he turned to leave and paused, facing her again. "At least not tonight."

He didn't say anything more after that, just turned and walked away. Dakota should have been furious, but she couldn't keep the grin from spreading across her face. That had been the single most incredible moment of her life. And she wanted to relive it again and again and—

There was a knock on her door, and she smiled. He'd been gone for less than an hour. Guess he wanted round two after all. She thought about going to the door naked, but though she was confident, there might be some neighbors passing by, and that was a lot more of her than she wanted to show the world.

Grabbing her silk robe, she threw it on, barely taking the time to loosely tie the sash. She should make him wait, but she was too excited. She thrust open the door with a big grin that quickly fell away.

Maybe she should have checked to make sure it was actually Ace standing on the other side of her door so late at night.

CHAPTER THIRTEEN

Ace had never been one to kick himself. He didn't believe in wrong decisions, or regrets. Everything happened for a reason. But what he couldn't figure out as he drove away from Dakota's place was how he couldn't have known how innocent she truly was.

He felt as if he'd taken advantage of her, and he really didn't like the feeling. He wasn't a man who slept with women who didn't know the score. Sex was as natural to the body as food and water. He didn't like going too long without it. But that's why he was always with women who believed that as much as he did.

He'd never have guessed Dakota hadn't been with a man before. And while he felt shame at having taken her so fast and hard, he also felt an immense sense of possession over her, which was making his brow furrow. She was now his—only his!

Ace wanted to push those feelings away, wanted to think of her as nothing more than a good time, but no matter how hard he tried to reset his mind, he couldn't do it. He cared about this woman. She'd just given him a gift unlike any he'd ever been given before. It wasn't something he could look at lightly. But there was still the problem of him having to leave again to get back to work. How could she be his, when he wouldn't be around to be hers? When in the hell had he developed a conscience?

When his phone rang, he ignored it. There weren't too many people who would be calling him, especially at night, and though it might be nice to get out of his own head for a while, he felt too powerless to do that.

He was consumed with thoughts of this woman who had appeared in his life, and whom he couldn't seem to push away. It didn't matter if he told himself all day long that he needed to walk away from her for his own sanity and her safety. That just didn't seem possible.

A second later his phone rang again, and he glared ahead at the dark roads before him. The phone stopped, and he thought maybe the person on the other end of the line would finally take a hint. Why he didn't just silence the damn thing, he didn't know.

Maybe it was his years of training and having to stay alert that made him incapable of cutting off all communication with the outside world. He didn't know. Ace would like nothing more than to get lost on some exotic island with no chance of talking to anyone, but he could never do that. What if something happened, like one of his brothers getting into another airline crash? He had to be able to access his family, even if he didn't like the information he was given.

When his phone went off again, he cursed before lifting it, not recognizing the number on his caller ID. He thought about tossing the device out his car window and smiled, but instead he accepted the call and grumbled a very irritated hello into the mouthpiece.

"Ace, we need to have a meeting."

The person didn't need to identify himself. It was his boss from the CIA, Bill Hammond.

"I'm on leave," Ace told the man, irritated. Ace hadn't taken a single day off in so many years he'd lost track of the count. He deserved this much-needed rest. He wanted that to be clear.

"Not anymore, you're not. Meet me at this address." Bill rattled off an address of a lavish hotel in downtown Seattle.

The phone went dead. Ace thought for a moment about calling Bill back and telling his boss to go to hell. He'd dealt with enough in the last eight years. He didn't owe any of them anything.

But Ace found himself exiting the side road he was on and turning around. The place his boss wanted to meet up wasn't far from his current location. Ace wouldn't be surprised if he was being tracked and the CIA knew exactly where he was at all times. It was their job to be informed.

Ace pulled up at the busy hotel and sat in his car for several moments. He was aware of people milling about, some just arriving, some stepping out in formal wear for a night on the town. No one looked suspicious. The situation was secure.

He handed over his keys to the valet attendant after checking him out, making the young man squirm. Ace knew he could be intense, but that kept people on their toes. He hoped he never lost that edge.

Once he stepped through the tall glass doors, Ace made his way through the lobby to the bar at the back of the hotel. It didn't take long for him to find Bill. He sat down without saying a word, but he had no doubt Bill was reading the look in his eyes very clearly.

"Glad you could get here so fast," Bill said. The man wore a long-practiced poker face that rivaled that of anyone Ace had ever known. There was no way to know what the man was thinking or feeling. Ace liked it, though. He'd tried perfecting the same look himself through the years.

"We both know I didn't really have any other option but to show," Ace told him. He wasn't even trying to hide the fact that he didn't want to be there.

Ace had thought he was out for a while. His last undercover job had taken him too long, and he needed a long break. He wasn't even sure if he ever wanted to come back. But that wasn't something he needed to share at the moment. If he chose to leave the CIA, it wouldn't be out of fear, and he wouldn't have regrets. He'd do it because it was the right move for him.

Bill gave his version of a smile, lifting of the right corner of his upper lip slightly. It was more of a scowl than anything else. Ace's expression didn't change.

"Why are you summoning me here?" Ace finally asked. He didn't feel like sitting around, shooting the breeze.

Bill pulled out an envelope and slid it across the table to Ace. Not sure why, Ace's blood ran cold as he looked down at the insignificant sealed yellow envelope. He didn't reach out for it, didn't think he wanted to know what was inside. What he knew for sure was the clock was ticking down. He knew he was going to be leaving, but that envelope in front of him ensured it would be sooner than he wanted. If he didn't open it, then he wouldn't have to go anywhere, he tried telling himself.

But after a long moment, he sighed. Ace had never been one to run away from things or hide his head in the sand. Still, the longer he was able to live in denial, the longer he could try to move forward with his life.

"What is this?" he asked Bill.

"We've been putting this together for months," was Bill's only reply.

Ace knew he couldn't turn and walk away like he wanted to do. He had to face whatever was going on. With dread, he opened the flap and pulled out the materials resting inside.

"When?" Ace asked. He'd wiped all expression from his face. This was the life he'd chosen. It was what he'd wanted, he thought with determination. He ignored the voice in his head telling him that that was no longer true.

"Two weeks, wheels go up," Bill said.

"Getting blown up doesn't give a person much time off," Ace grumbled.

Bill gave his best impression of a smile. "You weren't blown up," Bill told him. "Just blown onto the ground. And you've been through worse. We can't sit on this too long."

He'd barely been home. And now he had to leave again. Would his family forget all about him once more? Would Dakota? Why did he even care?

"And what if I don't want to do this one?" Ace asked. Bill looked surprised. It wasn't something Ace had ever said before. Bill schooled his expression and leaned back as he analyzed Ace.

"You're my best agent," Bill said. That wasn't an answer.

"I just . . ." Ace trailed off. What was he going to say? This was his profession. He couldn't tell Bill he wasn't ready to leave yet, that he wanted to be with his family . . . and with Dakota.

"In this line of business, not everything is black-and-white. You know that, Ace. It's why you stayed away from your family for so long. Maybe it's safer for you to get back to work sooner rather than later," Bill told him.

He knew Bill was right. He was only stating out loud what Ace had been thinking about for the past couple of weeks. But hearing the words spoken to him drove the guilt of putting those he loved in danger even deeper.

"I'll be there," Ace finally said, accepting what had to be. Bill nodded.

"I knew you would," Bill told him.

"I have to go now."

Ace stood up and moved swiftly through a group of high school cheerleaders checking into the hotel. A hand brushed down his arm, but he ignored it. His time with Dakota had begun ticking down, and the way he'd walked away from her earlier irritated him. He suddenly had to get to her—and fast. Yes, he was most likely the most dangerous person in her life, but he needed to say good-bye, even if she wouldn't know that was what he was doing.

Ace reached the stand and stood impatiently while his vehicle was retrieved. Why in the hell had he valet parked his car? He needed to go now. The kid running the booth obviously saw the urgency in his eyes, because he had gone scrambling away to collect his car. Ace needed to be with Dakota.

The kid pulled up with his car, and Ace jumped inside, throwing him a hefty tip in an attempt to make up for his brisk attitude. The need to get back to Dakota made a cold sweat break out on his neck. He should fight it, should force himself to drive in the opposite direction of Dakota's place. But he didn't.

The drive back to her house seemed to take an eternity. As he drew closer to her neighborhood, something seemed off, and his spidey senses were definitely on alert. He'd been too relaxed since coming home, hadn't been as aware of his surroundings as he should have been. That needed to change.

He pulled up near Dakota's home, and all seemed to be fine from the outside. But Ace was abnormally sensitive to things that were out of the ordinary. There was a black sedan parked half a block away. Ace knew something was wrong. He'd learned long ago not to ignore his instincts.

A couple of houses across the street from hers had their lights low. Ace could see the flicker of a television screen behind lace curtains, a couple relaxing on their couch as they watched some mindless sitcom.

Nothing seemed out of place, but Ace knew it was all wrong. Dakota was in trouble. And whoever had dared put her in danger was about to get the surprise of a lifetime. A murderous protectiveness filled his eyes as Ace went to his trunk and opened the secret compartment in the back, pulling out his sidearm.

He hadn't felt the weight of it for a few weeks, but it fit perfectly in the palm of his hand. It felt right. He was on high alert as he looked around the quiet neighborhood, screwing on his silencer.

Then he stepped forward, quickly getting lost in the shadows of Dakota's place. He slipped around the side of her house and checked any place someone could be hiding. There wasn't a soul in sight.

Though he didn't hear a thing, he knew someone, or multiple some-ones, were inside with Dakota. He also knew he might be too late. Pushing all emotion down, he moved to the back door. Anyone who attempted to hurt someone he cared about was going to pay the ultimate price.

CHAPTER FOURTEEN

Standing in her doorway, Dakota looked at the two stoic men in suits. A sliver of fear ran down her spine, and she didn't know why, but she did know it was better if she didn't ignore the feeling.

"Can I help you?" she asked, her voice slightly shaky, irritating her.

Everything inside her told her she was in danger, though the men didn't look particularly menacing. She forced a smile, knowing what she was feeling was utterly ridiculous. They looked more like Bible salesmen than muggers. Still, she didn't move from her doorway, somehow trying to block their entrance, even if they weren't attempting to push through.

Her body was pulsing with a need to protect herself, but she didn't understand why. She was in that in-between of not knowing if she should just slam her door shut and lock it or if she should find out why these strangers were at her home so late at night.

They said nothing, and that was only making her more nervous. Why were they just staring at her? But just as she was about to fully panic, one of the men took a slight step forward, not exactly blocking her door, but moving closer.

"Are you Dakota Forbes?"

The man's voice was calming, almost therapeutic as he spoke. It should have slowed the racing of her heart, but the guy beside him had a menacing demeanor that wasn't allowing her to escape her fight-or-flight mode.

"Yes, I'm Dakota," she told him, the words coming out almost like a question. Of course, she knew who she was, but what she didn't know was *how* they had her name and *what* they wanted.

"We believe you're in danger," the man said.

"Danger? Why would I be in danger?" she asked, her eyes narrowing in suspicion. They looked official, but that meant nothing. She'd been raised with brothers, and they'd taught her not to be gullible. Just because a person was wearing a nice suit didn't mean he was a good guy.

"There's been some vandalism in your neighborhood, and we believe you've been targeted," the man said. "Can we come in?" He took another step forward, and her heart thundered.

If he was speaking the truth, then she definitely wanted to find out what was going on, but if he was lying to her, then these men *were* the danger. She was torn on what to do. She was also wishing Ace hadn't left. Never had she needed a man to protect her before, but right now she wouldn't mind another person in her house, having her back.

"Where did you hear this?" she asked. Her grip on the door tightened as the need to close it intensified. She really needed to get away from these men. Whatever they were up to, it was no good. That was for sure.

"May we come in?" The second man repeated the first man's question, and his voice was as menacing as his appearance.

"No, I don't think that's a good idea. You can tell me what's going on from where you are," she told both men, making sure to look them in the eyes. She wasn't going to show them how afraid she actually was.

"No, it's safer for us to come inside," the first man said.

"I think you need to leave," she told him. This felt all wrong. She had no doubt about that now. She didn't trust these men, and she needed to listen to her screaming instincts.

"That's not going to happen," the second man snarled as he took a step forward.

Dakota decided she'd had enough. She pushed on her door, but it was too late. Both men stepped forward, easily pushing her out of the way as they barged their way inside. She took a step back, true fear filling her. She knew for sure she was in danger.

"I don't know what you think you're doing, but this is my place and I don't want you here," she said, her voice squeaking.

"Maybe you should think twice about opening your door to strangers then," the first man said, all the charm in his voice suddenly gone. He obviously didn't feel he needed to keep pretending he was a good guy.

She backed away, trying to decide where to go when they shut her front door behind them. Who were they? And what was going to happen to her?

"If you cooperate with us, this will go a whole lot smoother," the first thug said.

"I don't want any part of this," she told both men as she continued backing away from them, getting pushed into the far reaches of her house. She was making her way to the kitchen, where she could possibly slip out the back door and hide in the bushes or run to a neighbor's house.

"It's too late, Ms. Forbes," one of the men said.

They reached the kitchen. The men didn't try to grab her, but she had no doubt that if she tried to run, they would pounce. They were simply waiting for the right moment as they boxed her in. She didn't want to take her eyes away from them, but she was also thinking she might need a weapon. If they thought she was some meek woman who was simply going to roll over and let them do whatever they wanted to her, they certainly had the wrong gal.

Her skin was on fire as sweat dripped down her back. Dakota didn't know what she was going to do. When there was a loud crash behind her, she was too frozen with fear to turn and see what new threat was coming her way.

But she did see the two men in front of her shift their focus, their hands reaching for guns inside holsters attached to their chests. All color washed from her face.

"Dakota, get down!"

Both relief and disbelief washed through her at the sound of Ace's voice. She didn't hesitate as she dropped down. Ace flew over her, plowing into one of the men, a sickening thud echoing through her kitchen as the man's head hit the tile floor.

A shot rang out, and then a second one, her eardrums ringing as the sound echoed in her kitchen. Tile splinters broke apart, stabbing her in the arm and side of her neck. She couldn't focus on that as she tried to see what was happening.

Grunts could be heard as Ace turned, his fist slamming into the second man's jaw, making the huge guy stagger back on his feet. All of this happened in seconds, though time seemed to have stopped having any meaning whatsoever. The second guy fell, and then an unbearable silence swept through her kitchen.

Her eyes must have been the size of saucers when they focused on Ace, whom she barely recognized. He looked feral, clutching a gun in one hand while reaching for her with the other. She instinctively flinched away from him as she noticed blood dripping from his fingers. Her focus was on the red beads as they splattered to her floor, the sound seeming so loud, though she was sure she couldn't hear the splatters at all.

"Dakota?" Ace's voice was trying to break through the ringing in her ears. But she just shook her head as she gazed at this man she didn't really know at all.

"I . . . What . . . Who . . ." Dakota couldn't complete a sentence, much less ask any questions.

"It's okay, Dakota," Ace told her, reaching for her again. She took a step back. If he touched her at this moment, she might fall apart, and with two men groaning on her floor, now wasn't the time to let that happen.

"I'm just going to call the cops," he told her, his voice filled with authority. He lifted his phone and spoke for a few moments. The ringing was still buzzing in her ears. She shook where she stood as she tried to replay all that had just happened. He hung up and grabbed her fingers.

"Let me go," she said, hating how weak her voice was.

"I can't," he said. "You're in shock, and you've been cut. I need to look at the wounds."

"Cut?" she questioned. His hand moved upward, and he pulled a shard from her neck, showing her the piece of sharp tile that had her blood on it.

"One of the bullets hit your counter. It sent splinters through the air," he said.

She finally looked him in the eyes. That's when she noticed the pain on his face. She looked at his arm, which was hanging by his side. Blood was flowing heavily from his fingers.

"Were you shot?" she asked, more shock filtering through her.

"It doesn't matter." They heard sirens in the distance. Help was on the way.

"It matters," she countered. She shook off her fright and gripped his good hand firmly, pulling him to the stool not far from them. He didn't sit. "Take off your jacket," she told him.

"It can wait," he insisted.

"Damn it!" she shouted, and his eyes rounded in shock. "Take off the freaking jacket!"

Ace smiled at her, and she wanted to smack him. But then he took off the jacket. There were two ragged wounds on his arm, dripping blood. Her stomach turned over.

A loud knock pounded on her door just in time for her to turn and see it crash open. Two uniformed men slid into the room, weapons drawn. Both she and Ace held up their hands.

"We're in here," Ace called out. "My name is Ace Armstrong. I'm with the CIA. The culprits have been neutralized." He sounded so calm, so professional as he said all this to the officers, who moved forward, weapons still drawn.

They looked at the two men on the floor and then at Ace and Dakota.

"My weapon is here on the counter," Ace pointed out. "My badge next to it." Dakota was amazed he'd thought about having that out of his pocket for when the officers arrived.

Another siren cut off as one of the officers checked out Ace's badge before moving his gun away. Only then did they holster their weapons. One officer spoke into his mic, and then paramedics came through the door.

"You've been shot," the officer with the name tag R. Johnson said.

"I'll get it taken care of," Ace told him.

"We need to get you to the hospital," one of the paramedics stated.

"I said I'll get it taken care of," Ace repeated. The paramedic backed down immediately. There was so much authority in Ace's voice, Dakota could understand the man backing down.

"Can you tell us what happened?" Officer Johnson asked.

Dakota was the one to speak up now. "I was just in my house minding my own business when these two men showed up and pushed their way inside," she said in frustration.

The next twenty minutes saw her and Ace replaying the events as the officers took down information. They verified Ace was who he said he was, and the paramedic bandaged Ace's arm, though he was obviously frustrated Ace wouldn't go with him in the ambulance.

Throughout the entire event, Dakota watched Ace. He was so controlled. She was seeing a side of him she hadn't yet seen. The officers had the utmost respect for him.

Sure, he was the brother of her best friend's husband, but that didn't mean he was safe or even sane. She really didn't know much about any of the Armstrong men, though she'd thought, up to this point, at least, that they were a good family—a safe family.

The adrenaline from the last hour was wearing off. Dakota was standing there in nothing but her thin silk robe, tremors beginning to rack her frame. Ace tried to put his arm around her, but she scooted away and held herself. She didn't understand any of this.

"It looks like there has been a series of burglaries around your neighborhood," the officer stated. "Some people haven't been as lucky as you."

What resided in his eyes scared her even more. Those neighbors hadn't had GI Joe bursting in through the back door and jumping over counters to save them.

The officer talked a little longer, and then her house finally began to clear out—everyone except for Ace. She found herself standing there with him and a broken door. Ace didn't say anything as he went and looked at it. There was no way to lock it now.

"Do you have a hammer and some nails?" he asked.

It took a moment to process the question. "Yes, in the garage."

He left her standing there and then came back with a hammer, nails, and a two-by-four that had been out there since she'd tried to build planters before giving up on the project. It didn't take him long to seal the door shut, making it unusable. Air still drifted in through it, but at least someone couldn't push it open.

"I know you're a bit freaked out right now, but I think the best thing we can do is get out of here for a while and let you calm down," Ace told her.

Him telling her to calm down pissed her off all over again. She glared at him as she tried to calm her breathing so she wouldn't end up saying something she knew she might regret. He wasn't the bad guy here. She just wasn't exactly sure who he was.

"Telling me to calm down isn't going to make it happen," she finally said.

"I'm sorry," he replied quickly. "Let's get out of here, please," he added.

She looked around again at the mess that was now her kitchen. The bad guys had been caught, so she didn't understand why she was still so afraid. But she did feel as if someone could walk in her door at any minute. She felt like a target.

"Where?" she asked.

"We'll go to my brother's place," he told her.

"Okay." She said the words before really giving herself time to think about it.

The two of them moved to the hallway. She grabbed a coat, slipped on a pair of shoes, and followed him out the door. Neither of them said anything as he helped her into the passenger seat of his car before moving around to his side to drive.

As they moved swiftly through traffic, Dakota clutched her seat belt with shaking fingers. They took a corner entirely too fast, making her body slam into the locked door to her right. Ace had the heater on full blast, but she was still shaking uncontrollably.

"Ace, I . . . I don't understand how you came in my house like that," she said when the silence was stretching on long enough to make her feel as if she were beginning to lose her mind.

She heard his intake of breath, and though he didn't turn to look at her, she knew he was very aware of every move she made. This was a side of the man she hadn't yet witnessed. Yes, she'd known he was different, but this man beside her, this man she'd made love to only hours before, was a total stranger.

"It seems like danger is always following me around," he said, his voice calm. She couldn't see him well in the darkness, but she had a feeling that even if she could see his expression, it would give nothing away.

"Why would you say that? Those men had nothing to do with you," she said. "I don't even understand why they came after me."

Ace sighed as he ran his hand down his face before meeting her eyes briefly as he drove. Dakota didn't like the determination she saw in his expression. It didn't bode well for what was to come next. She had a feeling her ordinary life was about to take a drastic turn, and not for the better.

"I didn't come home for a long time because the cases I was working on for the CIA had me deeply undercover. A few months ago, we busted an operation wide open, and the head of the family was killed. I don't believe in coincidence. It scares me that you were targeted tonight," he told her.

"Do you think those men were after you? That makes no sense. The cop said there has been a string of robberies," she reminded him.

"Yeah, I'm hoping that's all it was. But in my line of work, I don't trust many people."

"What in the heck have I gotten myself into?" she asked.

He gave a mirthless laugh. "I bet you will be asking yourself that same question a lot over the next couple of weeks," he told her.

"Weeks? What are you talking about?"

"I don't think you should go home for a while, at least until we figure out what is going on."

"They got the bad guys. I'm going to be perfectly fine going home," she assured him.

He sighed, and she could see he didn't agree with her at all. She had no idea where that left her. One thing she did know, though, was that she was in for an adventure, even if she didn't want one.

CHAPTER FIFTEEN

Ace didn't know what was going on with him, but he knew for sure that he was in some serious trouble where this woman was concerned. He looked over at Dakota as she snoozed restlessly in the seat beside him. He also knew he was a sick bastard for noticing the sleek curve of her thigh as her robe bunched up around her.

He couldn't shake the feeling that he'd been the one to put her in danger. Yet he was still lusting after her. The best thing he could do for her would be to put her in a safe house and stay the hell away from her. But the thought of doing that had him feeling . . . panic. That was an emotion Ace didn't feel—didn't *allow* himself to feel.

What was this woman doing to him? He didn't know, but no matter how much he wanted to fight the emotion, he couldn't. He cared about this spitfire of a woman, and he didn't want her out of his sight. Not only because he knew he could protect her better than anyone else could, but also because he couldn't seem to let her go.

The more he was with Dakota, the more muddled his brain and body became. He hadn't been this infatuated with a woman since he was a teen trying to score with the band nerd who had a wild side.

Dakota was more than he'd ever imagined. She was beautiful, loyal, and fun to be around. She wasn't afraid of much in life, and he could see himself never growing bored with this woman by his side.

But settling down with a yard, and kids, and a couple of dogs wasn't in the cards for Ace. He'd chosen a solitary life, and he'd accepted it. But being back home around his very happily married siblings was messing with his head. Being around Dakota was making it that much worse.

Ace had been on red alert for so long, he'd forgotten what it was like not to be. Over these few short weeks, he'd let down his guard, at least partially. He hadn't been as aware of his surroundings, and all hell had broken loose because of it. The cops said it was robberies, but he couldn't fully accept that.

What would happen if he settled too casually into this make-believe world he was living in? If the general population had even an inkling about all the bad surrounding them, they wouldn't sleep so well at night in their comfy little homes. Ace was very aware of the danger, and even he'd grown somewhat complacent to it all.

His arm was throbbing, reminding him he'd been shot. The medics had wrapped it, but if he didn't get the bullets out soon, he was going to have some problems. His sister-in-law was a nurse. She'd take care of him. Right now, he had a call to make.

Turning down the volume on his car speaker, he dialed Bill and waited.

"Hello." The greeting was abrupt as always.

Dakota stirred in the seat next to him at the bold voice coming over the speakers, but then she settled back down, obviously exhausted from their ordeal.

"My friend Dakota was attacked tonight," Ace told him, coming straight to the point. "Could it have anything to do with me?" Ace tried desperately to keep the rage from simmering over. It wasn't working too well.

"I haven't heard anything," Bill said slowly, but there was a knot of suspicion in his voice. He didn't believe in coincidences, either. "Random attacks do happen," he added.

"I don't trust anyone," Ace told him. "Two men were in Dakota's house, both of them armed. I have no doubt they wanted to harm her. It was a good thing I showed up."

"I'm sorry, Ace. Maybe we should meet up and see if any of this has to do with you. But honestly, I don't think so," Bill told him.

"Not right now. Can you do some research without me? I have Dakota with me and I'm getting her to safety," Ace said.

"You know you don't have to do this alone," Bill told him. "I'm here for whatever you need."

"I'll take care of my own problems," Ace said with no room for argument.

"Ace—" Ace cut him off with the click of a button. He respected Bill, knew he wasn't a part of all of this, but he'd been wrong before. He wasn't going to allow anything to happen to Dakota. And that meant he was going to take her to his brother's home. Even after all these years, he knew where he could go for safety, and he knew he could count on his family above anyone else.

Ace continued toward Cooper's place. It had become the meeting ground through the years. He knew the rest of his family would drop everything and meet him there. He didn't know exactly why. He hadn't given any of his brothers reason to trust him in a very long time.

Ace dialed his phone again. Coop picked up on the second ring. "I have a situation," Ace said, forgoing the greeting.

"Are you on your way here?" Coop asked, calm and alert.

Ace didn't understand why, but his brother's words caused a surge of emotion to rush through him, and he wasn't able to respond immediately. Yes, he'd known he could count on his family, but maybe there was still a small part of him that had wondered when they would stop taking his bullshit.

"Yeah. Can you call the others?" Ace finally asked. "And maybe find sitters for the kids?"

"Are we in danger?" Cooper asked.

Ace paused. "I don't think so . . . but I still worry."

Now it was Cooper's time to pause for a moment. "If you think there's danger, of course, we will gather and make sure the kids are safe," he finally said.

Ace was still uneasy, but he needed his family. "Good," he said.

"What's your ETA?" Coop asked.

"One hour."

"I'll have the coffee brewing."

With that, Ace hung up the phone and picked up the speed of his car. He needed to get back home. Not only did he want the help of his family, but his arm was really throbbing. He needed these bullets out. And if the attack on Dakota hadn't been random, then he had to warn his family they could be next.

With that thought in mind, Ace felt the urgency to get back to his brother's place and be there for his siblings like they were doing for him. He'd feel much better having Dakota surrounded by people he knew would protect her. Not only would they do it because she was with Ace, but they already cared about her as Chloe's best friend.

CHAPTER SIXTEEN

Never in Dakota's life had she been so relieved to see a group of people as she was when they pulled up in front of Cooper's front door and she saw Ace's three brothers and their wives anxiously standing by waiting for them.

The vehicle didn't even have a chance to get put into park before they were swarmed by Ace's family, all of them wearing looks of concern as they yanked open both the driver's and passenger doors.

"You took longer to get here than you said. We were growing concerned," Cooper said as he leaned down and looked inside.

"Is that blood?" Maverick asked, instantly doing a visual of the yard, searching for danger before his eyes focused back on Ace.

"What in the hell is going on?" Nick piped in as he assisted Dakota from the car.

Cooper and Maverick tried to help Ace out, but he brushed away their hands, grumbled about being perfectly capable of getting out of the car on his own, and then wobbled on his feet as he stood.

Dakota rushed around the vehicle to his side, sliding her arm behind his back. When everything had begun at her house, she'd been afraid and needed someone to blame. Then she'd dozed in the car for a few minutes, and when she'd woken up, she'd instantly felt guilty about having yelled at Ace. He'd saved her from being attacked and possibly killed. She'd noticed the bloodstain on his arm growing larger as they drove and the color draining from his cheeks. She'd felt responsible. Now she felt protective. She hadn't been sure if she'd ever wanted to see this man again at the beginning of their traumatic night, but now she couldn't imagine leaving his side.

"Why aren't you at the hospital?" Mav's wife, Lindsey, asked as she nudged in on Ace's other side. Being an ER nurse, of course Lindsey was concerned about the obviously fresh wound.

"I just felt it would be best to get here," he told her. "Besides, I knew there was a nurse on site," Ace said with a grimace Dakota was sure was supposed to be a smile.

"I don't have all the things I need here, Ace," Lindsey scolded him.

"Yes, you do. I just need you to pull out the damn bullet and stitch me up," he told her. His face was ashen, and Dakota wondered how in the world he'd managed to continue driving them for so long after being shot. It had to be the adrenaline rushing through his system. It was the only explanation that made any sense.

"I don't have anything to numb you with," Lindsey insisted.

"I'm an Armstrong. A little bit of pain isn't going to kill me," Ace told her.

"We need to get him inside," Chloe said. She hadn't worked as a nurse for a while, but she would certainly be a good assistant for Lindsey. She'd been a nurse before deciding to go into physical therapy, which was how she'd met her husband, Nick. Dakota wasn't worried about the two of them getting Ace patched up.

"Yes, let's get them in the house. I don't know what in the hell is going on, but I don't like being out in the open like this," Maverick said. His years in the military had him more on edge than any of the others.

The group slowly made their way to the front porch. It took Ace a few tries to make it up the stairs. Dakota didn't miss how his brothers hovered around him in a half circle, trying not to be obvious about it but right there in case he did fall. Dakota's respect for this family was growing by the second.

"How are you doing?" Chloe asked Dakota once they were safely inside and moving toward the dining room.

"I'm fine. A lot has happened tonight, but I'm fine," Dakota said, her voice shaking the slightest bit.

"You are lying, but since it appears Ace needs the most critical attention, we'll cater to him first. But then you have some explaining to do as well—such as why you're standing here in nothing but a silk robe and jacket with cuts marring your normally perfect skin."

Dakota felt heat infuse her cheeks as her best friend pointed out her attire. She'd completely forgotten she was barely wearing a stitch of clothing. In all the rush from the time those men had shown up at her door, she hadn't had time to even begin to think about her appearance.

She had to be a mess, her hair in that just-had-sex disarray, and whatever makeup she'd started the day with had to be smeared and splashed across her face. Add to that the fact that her robe was hardly appropriate for a family gathering, and her jacket was too thin, and she was a sight. But none of them were paying attention to her—no one but her best friend. The rest of the group's attention was fully on Ace.

She looked at him as he sat down in the chair, his face white, his hand trembling, his lips pressed tightly together. The full impact of the intruders, and her flight with Ace through the city and beyond, was beginning to settle in on her, but she pushed it away. There wasn't time for her to fall apart—not yet. First, she had to make sure Ace was going to be okay. He had to be one of the strongest men she knew, and that was saying a lot, considering she had a heck of a lot of alpha-male brothers.

Lindsey and Chloe were examining Ace, and he smiled up at them before winking at his brothers, who grumbled.

"You two have done well in your choice of women," Ace said as Lindsey leaned over him and Chloe touched his arm.

"Yeah, yeah," Maverick grumbled. "Remember, you're in pain, and think a little less about flirting with my wife or trying to look down her shirt."

"I can't help myself when I have beautiful women with their hands all over me," Ace told his brother.

"You're such an ass," Nick said, but he was smiling.

"I can second that," Dakota said as she leaned against the wall. She was afraid she was going to rush over and run her own hands over him. No one needed to see that, or realize the strong connection she felt for this man.

"You got shot twice, Ace," Lindsey said with a frown. She then turned to her husband. "Get me some clean cloth and hot water. I'm going to grab my emergency kit from the car. He's dang lucky I have a much better one than the average person."

Everyone moved to get what was needed. Dakota pushed away from the wall and moved over to him. She leaned down, and Ace smiled at her. Damn, that look in his eyes took her to a place she had no business being.

"This is going to hurt. I think we should just go to the hospital," she told him.

"I've been through worse," Ace assured her.

"Not in front of me," she said.

"Are you worried about me, Dakota?" he asked, seeming to like that idea.

"You were shot. I think I can worry a little," she admitted.

"I like it," he told her. The seriousness of his words made her nervous. This thing—whatever it was—between the two of them was moving entirely too fast. She didn't trust or like it. But even knowing that, she couldn't seem to stop it. Maybe she and Ace were tangled up in a boulder shooting down a steep hill at top speed.

"Are you ready for this, Ace?" Lindsey asked.

She and Chloe were back, and their gazes shifted from Ace to Dakota in a knowing way. Dakota was going to need to set her best friend straight before Chloe's imagination ran away with her. Hell, Dakota didn't even know what she was feeling, so it would be hard to set anyone straight.

"I was born ready," Ace told her.

"The bullets are in farther than I'd like. I'm going to have to dig them out," Lindsey told him. "Be prepared to pass out."

"I'm tougher than your husband," Ace said before smirking at Maverick.

"I'm going to let you get away with that considering the state you're in," Maverick replied.

Dakota took a moment to look at Ace's three brothers. They might be cracking jokes and making comments to one another, but she could see the concern in their eyes, knew that they loved their brother, and didn't at all like the situation he was in. It made her feel a little homesick for her own family. They were just as protective of her, which at times was beyond frustrating and at other times made her feel loved and safe.

"Time to let me go," Ace said, and Dakota realized she was still clutching his hand.

She tried to pull away, but he tugged on her, bringing her forward. Right there, in front of his entire family, he kissed her. It was short and sweet, and she felt wobbly on her feet as she pulled away.

Yes, this was definitely so much more than she had expected. She refused to look at his family as she backed away. She couldn't imagine what they were thinking about the two of them—especially with the way she was dressed. Normally she really didn't care what anyone thought about her, but it was different with this family—with Ace. She knew who she was and didn't shrink away in sticky situations, but from the moment she'd set eyes on Ace Armstrong, her world had been spinning. The longer she was with the man, the more the wind whipped her around.

She didn't want to remain in the room as Lindsey and Chloe began cleaning Ace's wound. But she couldn't tear her gaze away from his face. He looked up and met her eyes, and she felt the sting of tears in her own.

He wasn't making a sound, but she could see how much pain he was in as his wound was being tended to. She wanted to stop it, but this had to be done. Ace gritted his teeth around a wooden kitchen spoon as Lindsey slipped a sterilized pair of tweezers into one of the small holes in his arm. Maverick was at his side, steadying his arm. Sweat began pouring from Ace's brow. He still didn't make a sound, but his teeth were biting hard on the spoon. He was even more pale than he'd been when they'd walked into the house.

Blood poured from the wound as Lindsey pulled back, a bullet easing from Ace's arm. She dropped it in a cup sitting on the table, the sound unusually loud.

"I know that sucked, Ace," Lindsey told him, apology in her voice. "But that was the easier of the two," she added. "The next one is going to be worse."

"Thanks for the pep talk, Doc," Ace said, his voice hushed as he tried to mask his pain.

"Can't we give him a break?" Dakota asked.

"We need to get it finished as quickly as possible," Chloe told her as she wiped his wound and put more antiseptic on the area. "The longer we draw this out, the worse it is for him."

"Just do it," Ace told her.

Dakota was shaking as Lindsey wiped the other wound before dipping the tweezers inside his tender flesh. This time, though she knew he was desperately trying not to, a groan escaped Ace's tightly clamped teeth.

Dakota moved forward, not wanting to be in the way but needing to comfort the man. Without thinking about it, her hand lifted and she wiped away some of the sweat from his brow. He wasn't even able to lift his face up and look at her. She just kept out of the way, comforting him as best she could.

"It's almost over," Lindsey promised. She began retracting the tweezers, and Dakota prayed she had the bullet, that this was truly almost over. She didn't think Ace was going to be able to take much more, no matter how strong a man he was.

Time dragged on endlessly, but then the tweezers popped back out of his skin holding the thing that had caused so much pain. Blood streamed from the wound now that the second bullet was out of his flesh. Tiredly, he turned and looked at the tiny piece of mangled lead before Lindsey dropped it in the cup holding the other one.

Chloe took over, cleaning up the area. Dakota was so impressed with both women. They had remained calm the entire time, offering words of comfort and steady hands. Dakota had always thought of her best friend as a hero, but she had an entirely new appreciation for her in these moments.

Chloe washed away all the blood, cleaned the wounds again, then began to wrap his arm to protect it. Ace didn't utter another sound, but Dakota knew the area was tender as hell. They'd given the man a healthy dose of painkillers. Still, they didn't compare to what he would have gotten at a hospital.

"We're all done, Ace. Before we talk, you need to rest," Lindsey told him.

"There's no time for rest right now," he said. His body was trembling, and Dakota didn't at all agree with his assessment.

"If you won't do it for yourself, then take a look at Dakota, who appears to be on the verge of falling over," Mav pointed out.

"I'm fine," Dakota argued.

"No, you're not. You need a shower and a change of clothes," Chloe told her.

"Okay, let's take an hour break," Ace agreed, his eyes meeting Dakota's. "I'll rest on the couch while you take some time," he told her.

"Good, it's a plan," Chloe said, not letting Dakota argue any more. Chloe grabbed Dakota's arm and began pulling her away while Ace's brothers helped him to his feet and led him into the living room.

Chloe didn't try talking to Dakota as she led her straight to the guest room's bathroom. She looked at her best friend with tears in her eyes. Dakota was too close to falling apart now that the danger seemed to be over.

"Take your time. There will be clothes on the bed when you come out," Chloe said. "Then we will talk."

Dakota nodded, and Chloe left her alone. She was in shock. She knew this, and still, she didn't know what to do next. People often said that when a couple was in a high-stress situation, they would misconstrue certain feelings that they believed were *real*. That might be the case for Dakota, because all she wanted to do was get back to Ace. She felt a connection with the man that she hadn't planned on ever feeling for him.

She was in serious trouble—and it wasn't because people were shooting at her.

CHAPTER SEVENTEEN

Standing in the bathroom, Dakota looked into the mirror, barely able to recognize herself. No wonder Chloe had seemed so worried about her. Dakota always smiled and was able to find joy in almost any situation. But she didn't recognize the image staring back at her as she turned her face to analyze her appearance.

She was washed out, with specks of blood on her hollowed-out cheeks. Her eyes were dull and her lips tight. She began shaking as she stood there, the shock of the night overwhelming her as she thought about the situation.

Never before had she even come close to experiencing what she'd just gone through. Fear and the need to escape had been with her from the moment those men had pushed their way into her house until Ace had charged in to save her.

She'd managed to catch a few minutes of rest in Ace's car, but he'd spoken on the phone, rousing her. She now knew just how dangerous Ace's job could be. She couldn't believe he was trying to blame himself, though. What had happened to her had *nothing* to do with him.

However, Ace had been shot. She'd never witnessed a person getting shot before. She'd seen it a thousand times in movies, had read about it in books, but the reality was so much worse than she ever could have imagined. It hadn't seemed real. She still felt as if she'd been placed in some script, or, for that matter, an alternate reality.

But all she had to do was look in the mirror to know it was all very real. She couldn't stand to stare at herself anymore. She found that her legs were growing weaker. She sank down onto the side of the tub and cradled her face in her hands as her first tears fell.

Dakota hated weakness, prided herself on her strength, but she decided she could forgive herself for having a small meltdown. She'd been through a lot this night, and it wasn't even over yet. She had to let out some of the anxiety before she would be able to put on a strong mask again and sit down with the Armstrong family to tell them of her crisis, which in reality wasn't that bad. Everyone had come out relatively okay. Well, everyone but Ace.

Tears silently streamed down her cheeks, and Dakota turned on the tub's faucet to drown out the sound just in case anyone happened to be outside the door. She didn't need them to see her falling apart. Chloe was worried enough as it was. If her own family had even an inkling of what had happened, they'd be rushing in through the private gate of Cooper's property, breaking it down if need be, to get to her. She didn't need that on top of everything else.

Dakota had known from the moment she'd met Ace that he was trouble with a capital *T*. She'd chosen to be with him anyway. Maybe she liked the appeal of danger. Being shot at hadn't been exactly what she'd had in mind, but sometimes her life was too predictable, too boring. After this night, that wasn't something she could ever say again.

Slipping out of her ruined robe, she sank down into the overly hot tub and felt prickles of pain shoot through her body. She wanted this reminder that she was very much alive and unharmed. She also needed to scrub away the blood and grime clinging to her.

As she adjusted to the temperature of the water, she hugged her knees tightly to her chest and rocked back and forth in the deep tub. She felt some of the terror of the night begin to fade. She would pick the pieces back up. That was who she'd been raised to be, and there was no use in falling apart now.

Uncurling, she found bruises here and there on her legs and arms. She wouldn't show those to Ace. He'd been so worried about her getting injured, he hadn't focused at all on his own much more traumatic injuries. She smiled as she thought about that. He wasn't as hard as he wanted the world to believe he was.

There was a protective spirit about Ace that made her want to stay plastered to his side. Was it possible to fall in love with a person after knowing him for such a short period of time? Dakota shook her head at the thought of that. She didn't think so.

To fall in love, a person needed to really know someone inside and out. Anyone could mistake lust for love. That was easy. Your body reacted to another's, and attraction was instant. But to fall in love with a man, you had to know him, know what he liked, understand who he was behind the many years' worth of barriers he'd built around himself.

She hadn't been with Ace long enough to feel anything more than attraction, but the thought of him being hurt any more than he already had been nearly broke her heart. She felt something much stronger than attraction for the man. She just didn't want to think about what that was.

When the bathwater began to cool, Dakota stood on legs that were much weaker than she liked. She left the tub carefully and grabbed a fluffy towel from the shelf. Stepping from the bathroom, she found a fresh set of clothes on the bed and her best friend sitting in the corner in a chair.

"They are new underwear, don't worry," Chloe said with a smile.

"I'm so glad we're the same size," Dakota told her as she began slipping the clothes on beneath the warm towel. She felt as if she were back in her dorm room getting ready for the day while speaking with her roommate.

"These are Stormy's, but she's about our size as well. This worked to our advantage tonight, since you showed up here in a skimpy robe. You know I want an explanation about that," Chloe told her.

"Ace is going to fill everyone in on what happened after he has a bit of rest," Dakota said as she turned and put on the bra before slipping a sweater over her head. She was feeling so chilled. She was sure that was from the adrenaline rush as well. Her body had used up all its fuel, and now she couldn't even stay warm.

"I know he is. I want to know the stuff he's not going to talk about," Chloe insisted.

Dakota could fight her best friend, but she knew she'd lose. When Chloe had been Nick's physical therapist, she had tried unsuccessfully to keep things from Dakota. That hadn't gone well for her. They had shared everything their entire lives. It's what best friends did.

"We went flying today, though that feels like a million years ago. We had an incredibly hot kissing session that I never wanted to end, then I left," Dakota said, wondering if she could get away with only half the story.

"And then?" Chloe prodded. She should have known that short explanation would never fly.

"And then he showed up at my house . . ." Dakota paused. "And we ended up in the bedroom."

"*Now* we're getting somewhere," Chloe said. Dakota looked at her best friend, who was grinning. It was so odd to see a smile after all she'd been through tonight, but it also was a relief.

"It was incredible," Dakota admitted as she sat down on the edge of the bed and looked at Chloe. "It made me wonder why in the heck I've waited so long."

"This is a *huge* deal," Chloe insisted. "You waited a long time to make love, and then when you do, a heck of a lot more than fireworks happened. You got shot at afterward!"

As she processed the words her friend had just spoken, it somehow hit Dakota's funny bone. She looked at Chloe's serious face, and suddenly, she couldn't keep in the laughter that was bubbling up in her throat.

"Seriously," she said between bits of laughter. "Who in the heck gives up the V card and then is chased by gun-toting killers?"

Chloe was looking at her as if Dakota was losing her mind. Then her lips twitched, and soon they were laughing together. It took several moments for both of them to become composed again.

Dakota stood and grabbed a comb, dragging it through her hair as she looked at Chloe. They were silent for several moments before Chloe spoke again.

"Was the sex great?"

Dakota couldn't help but smile. "Yeah, it was better than I ever imagined. Ace was worth waiting for."

"On one hand, it's very odd to think of my brother-in-law and you having sex, but on the other, I want to know every single detail," Chloe admitted.

"When he found out I was a virgin, I think I nearly gave the man a heart attack. He had the nerve to lecture me and ruin my happy buzz. So I kicked him out of the house."

Chloe's eyes widened. "You had sex with the man and then kicked him out of your bed?" Her lips twitched again. "That's so awesome."

"Yeah, well, it didn't last long. The doorbell rang, and I thought it was him coming back, maybe to do it again, but that's when all hell broke loose."

"You opened the door without verifying who was there again, didn't you?" Chloe reprimanded.

"I live in a safe neighborhood. I wasn't expecting thugs to be at my door," Dakota explained.

"I worry so much about you," Chloe said with a sigh.

"You need to worry about yourself. I'm perfectly capable of taking care of me," Dakota told her.

"I'm just glad that Ace came back," Chloe told her.

"Yeah, me too. But I'm also really pissed that those men ruined my happy buzz," Dakota grumbled.

"You have men break into your house, threaten you with weapons, shoot at you, and of course you're more concerned that your after-sex glow was interrupted," Chloe said with a roll of her eyes.

"It was my first time. The happy buzz should have lasted longer. If I ever get ahold of those men, I'm going to drop-kick them," Dakota assured her.

"Okay, I really need to know this entire story. Finish pampering yourself so we can get back downstairs. Ace rested for a few minutes, but he couldn't sleep. I don't think he liked you being out of his sight with all of this going on."

"Does he seem to be a little overprotective?" Dakota asked. Normally, that might infuriate her after growing up with brothers who smothered her. But with Ace, she kind of liked it.

"Yeah, I think he has it bad for you," Chloe told her.

"It's only because we had great sex, or at least it was great on my end," Dakota said with a wave of her hand.

"You aren't the humble kind of girl, Dakota. Don't try to make excuses. He likes you," Chloe said.

"Yeah, and I like him, but it's just temporary. We haven't exactly started in a place that allows us to pursue a relationship," Dakota told her.

"You'd be surprised. Men like sex and gunfire. He might just think he's in his own personal heaven," Chloe said, unable to mask her amusement.

"You are such a nerd. Have I told you that lately?" Dakota asked.

"You do it all the time."

They left the room together, and amazingly enough, Dakota was feeling stronger, ready to face whatever was coming. She was ready to do it right beside Ace.

CHAPTER EIGHTEEN

Before Dakota turned the corner into the sitting room, Ace felt her presence. She was drawing nearer to him. In his line of work, he had to be observant, but his senses were even more intensified when it came to this particular woman.

He hadn't been able to rest. Part of it was the fact that his adrenaline was still running on high, and part of it was concern for Dakota's safety. He had almost convinced himself that those men truly had been robbers, but still . . . just in case, he wanted her in his line of sight. Of course, that made him also worry about his family, but he knew his brothers could take care of themselves, and they would die before letting anything happen to their wives or children.

Dakota had him to look out for her. He realized he didn't know much about her, though. Did she have a big family? Would they want his head on a platter because he'd almost been too late to save her? Would she rather be with anyone other than him? Ace wasn't used to worrying about such things.

Still, he let out a relieved sigh when he saw her enter the room. She immediately sought him out, their eyes connecting. He felt that punch to his gut he was getting used to feeling when she gazed at him. That was a sign that told him he should surely head for the hills as quickly as possible. He was doing just that in two weeks. She might not forgive him for taking her virginity and then leaving her high and dry.

"You look better," Ace told her.

"Never something you should say to a woman," Chloe advised Ace.

"What?" He was confused.

"We *always* look great," Chloe said with a wink.

"Of course you do, darling," Nick piped in.

"Suck-up," Ace said to Nick.

"You'll understand sooner than I probably would have imagined," Nick responded.

Ace didn't want to go there, so he turned away from Nick and looked at Cooper instead. "I guess you're ready to find out what in the hell is going on."

"Yeah, definitely more than ready," Cooper told him.

They all sat down, and Ace was immensely pleased when Dakota curled up into a happy ball at his side. She kept a few inches of space between them, which was too much in his opinion, but he felt calmer just having her close.

"I think I overreacted. Now that my adrenaline isn't pumping, it looks like that's exactly what I did. As a result of being undercover in the CIA for the past several years, when I see danger, the first thought that comes to mind is someone is coming after those I care about in order to get to me," Ace told them.

"Explain," Mav said.

He told them about having a bad feeling when he returned to Dakota's place, about finding the armed men up to no good, the gunfight, and the police taking the intruders away. When he was done, he felt his blood pressure rising again at just the thought of what could have happened to Dakota.

"Damn," Cooper said with a long sigh. "I'm so sorry, Dakota," he added.

"I'm okay, thanks to your brother," she assured him.

"Do you really think it could have anything to do with you?" Mav asked.

Ace was quiet for a moment. "No," he said. "I just was scared for Dakota. And home is the first thought that came to mind. I spoke to my boss, Bill, and he assures me there's nothing on the wires about anyone being after me."

"It's better to be safe than sorry," Nick told him. "Coming here was the smart thing to do."

"Thank you," Ace said. It truly didn't matter to any of them how long he'd been gone. They were still family and he was still welcome, especially in a time of crisis.

"You can always trust us to be here for you," Cooper said.

"I know that. I should have done things differently over the years. I'm sorry," he said to his family. His apology was long overdue.

"All is forgiven. We're just glad you're home now, where we can be here for each other," Nick said. He patted Ace's unhurt shoulder. Ace looked over at Maverick, who shifted on his feet.

"I'm sorry, Mav," he said, knowing at least one of his brothers hadn't fully forgiven him.

"It's all good," Mav said.

"No, it's not, but I hope it will be someday," Ace told him. Mav looked down. But he didn't try to argue anymore. Maybe the two of them needed to talk it out alone.

"I really don't think anyone is chasing me, but maybe I should take Dakota on a vacation or something just in case," Ace said.

"That's not a good idea at all," Maverick said, his eyes snapping back up to give Ace an intense look. Ace could almost hear his brother's thoughts—that he believed all Ace knew how to do was run away. Ace wanted to change that image they had of him, but it wouldn't be long before he'd have to tell them he'd be leaving for his next mission. He also needed to assure them he wouldn't be gone so long this time.

"But what if . . ." Ace trailed off.

"You're back home now, and we stick together through the good and the bad," Cooper insisted.

"I don't want you guys in danger," Ace told them.

"And do you really think any of us are safer with you gone?" Nick asked. "If someone were truly after you, which they aren't, don't you think you would see the signs before we would?"

"Mav would. He has military experience. And if I'm the object of someone's vendetta, they would follow me," Ace said.

"And *we* don't back down from a fight," Maverick informed him.

"I'm not exactly asking that of you. I'm just saying this isn't your fight," Ace said, feeling frustrated.

"That's pretty damn shitty of you to say," Mav said, his voice rising. "For years, we didn't know if you had gone to the dark side or not. To push us out again is spitting in our faces."

There it was. Ace shouldn't be shocked at the anger in his brother's tone. He didn't know what to say to that. He had known he'd been hurting his family through the years, but he'd been doing it because it had been what needed to be done.

"You've been gone a long time, Ace, and maybe your instinct is to run at the first sign of danger, to do everything on your own, but you're back home now, and we're all here for you," Chloe said. "Besides that, Dakota is like my sister. There's nothing I wouldn't do for her. Just stay here."

Ace turned and looked at Dakota, who'd been silent this whole time. He was willing to drag her away where danger could possibly follow them, but not keep her in the safety of family. That made him an even bigger dick.

"What do you want to do?" he asked her.

She sighed before speaking. "I'm exhausted, and my brain is fried. But I will say this much," she told him. "I'm not letting those disgusting bastards run me out of my own town. I have commitments. Plus, they're locked up anyway."

Ace held so much respect for this woman beside him. Not only was she beautiful, kind, compassionate, and spirited, but she was brave and a force to be reckoned with. He was a lucky man to have met her.

"I just hate that you were nearly killed," he said, exhaling in frustration.

"*You* were the one shot," she pointed out.

"I've been shot before." He brushed off her words, which only seemed to annoy the woman more.

"That's not making the case for you," she told him.

"Everyone is tired, and we're just going in circles. Ace, you and Dakota are staying here tonight. You can use the guest cottage so you have privacy. You can sleep with ease," Cooper insisted.

"I just reacted and wanted to get away from Dakota's place. We don't need to stay here," Ace said.

"I have a house to get back to," Dakota agreed.

"This is no longer up for debate. We'll all get some rest here. Tomorrow, I'm sure this will all seem like nothing more than a nightmare," Coop said.

Ace didn't really want to argue with his brother about this. Besides, at the moment the danger had begun, he'd quickly decided to go to his brother's house, to have his family surround him. So why did he want to leave now? Because he was an idiot.

"I agree. It's late, and you need rest. Lindsey just pulled two bullets out of your arm," Mav said.

"We'll all stay here tonight. The kids are already sleeping," Nick added.

Ace looked around the room at the determined expressions on everyone's faces. He knew, at least for tonight, he was defeated. He'd been the one who'd wanted to come back home, anyway. Maybe underneath it all, this was exactly what he'd needed and wanted.

"For tonight, I guess that will work," Ace finally agreed.

"Good. Now that it's all settled, I'll take you down to the cabin," Stormy said.

"You stay with the kids. Mav and I will take them down," Cooper said.

Stormy smiled at her husband and then nodded.

"Good, let's get some rest," Nick said. "No more heroics, at least for tonight."

He turned to Chloe and wrapped his arm around her, then began pulling her from the room. She turned before they left and ran back to Dakota, throwing her arms around her friend.

"Don't ever scare me like this again," she said.

"I'll try not to," Dakota told her.

Nick and Dakota were the first to head up the stairs.

"Come on, brother. Let's get you settled down," Coop said.

Dakota didn't try to fight any of them anymore. She was just as tired as Ace was. She might not have been shot, but her life had been thrown into turmoil. She needed to feel safe so she could let down her guard and get some much-needed rest.

Ace had never slept all night in bed with a woman, but he knew he was going to tonight. He wouldn't be able to rest unless he was holding her, sure of her safety. Otherwise he feared she'd somehow slip from his grasp and the bad guys would get to her again. He didn't trust the jail system. Hell, he didn't trust much of anything right now.

It was a quiet walk down to Cooper's somewhat secluded guest cottage. Dakota stayed by his side, Maverick and Cooper as alert as Ace as they walked the path.

They reached the cottage, and Cooper unlocked the door before looking inside. No one was there, but with Dakota having been attacked in her own home, everyone seemed to be highly aware.

"Everything's clear," Cooper said as he stepped back out. Ace didn't want to admit how weak he was feeling right now, but a bed sounded like all kinds of heaven.

"Thanks," Ace said. "I think you're right. Some rest will refresh me."

"You should listen to your elders," Mav said with a grin. "And Coop is getting pretty old."

"Shove it," Coop said.

"On that note, we'll say good night," Mav told them as he chuckled. He grabbed Coop's arm, and they walked away. Maybe their little showdown had helped them. Maybe Mav could start forgiving him now.

"I guess it's just you and me," Ace said, unable to resist reaching out and touching Dakota's cheek, his thumb skimming over her bottom lip in a sweet caress.

"It might get dangerous," she told him, nipping his thumb and making him throb in an entirely different area.

"You take my breath away and make me forget about the danger of the night," he told her, utterly mesmerized.

Her body trembled beneath his touch, and though he knew both of them had been through far too much in the last few hours, he found that he wanted her. Their attraction to each other was more powerful than any other force he'd ever experienced.

"We should explore this place," she said.

With reluctance, Ace pulled back from her and Dakota took a step forward, not paying attention to where she was going. Before he was able to stop her, she tripped, tumbling sideways to the floor and landing with a groan on her perfect rump.

She groaned as she slid her hand over her hip and rubbed her ass. "Ouch," she said, looking up at him with a sheepish smile on her lips.

The yoga pants and fitted sweater she'd been loaned hugged her beautiful curves to perfection. That ache in his body grew as he wished it was *his* hands soothing her bruised backside. The pain in his arm was nearly forgotten as he gazed at her.

Standing up, she rubbed herself a bit more before moving inside the cottage. He couldn't tear his eyes away from her fantastic rear end.

What in the hell was wrong with him? That should be the last thing on his mind after the night they'd had.

Dakota disappeared down the hallway, and Ace felt a moment of panic. He knew it was just the stress of the situation. If this were any normal day, he wouldn't mind her being away from him. Normally, Ace enjoyed his solitude.

But like a puppet on a string, his feet carried him to her. For at least tonight, he wasn't going to berate himself about needing to be with her. He'd be back to normal soon enough. Not tonight—but soon.

CHAPTER NINETEEN

Stepping into the master bedroom, Ace found Dakota sitting in the corner, her legs crossed, her eyes intently watching him. There was confusion, desire, and so much more in her deep-green depths. He didn't know what to think.

"We shouldn't do this tonight," he said, surprised at his own words. "A lot has happened, and you're exhausted."

She smiled at him as she reached for the hem of her shirt and pulled it over her head, not leaving the chair. The pain in his arm was nearly forgotten as he gazed upon her beauty.

"And you've been shot," she said as she unclasped her bra, her eyes never leaving his. He was practically shaking as he watched her. She smiled as she finally looked down.

His eyes raked over her upper half, devouring her beautiful breasts. He kept his feet firmly planted on the ground, but it was taking all his strength to stay where he was. There was no way he could deny her or himself if this was what she truly wanted, but a part of his brain was resisting. He knew she needed to rest.

Dakota stood up. He found himself holding his breath as he waited to see what she was going to do next. She walked to him with confidence—just another thing he loved about this woman. Her arms wrapped around his neck, and she pressed against him, turning her face up to look him in the eyes.

"I need you," she told him huskily.

Escaping her was the last thing on his mind as her lips gently pressed against his. Unbearable heat surged through his body as he wrapped her in his arms and deepened the kiss. She opened fully to him, and their tongues tangled as his hands roamed her back, sliding into the waistband of her pants.

Moving them backward, he was ready to take her now, spending a lot of time memorizing every inch of her body, filling his entire essence with only her. He turned and they fell onto the bed, pain shooting through his arm as their combined weight landed on it.

Dakota pulled back and winced as she looked at his pain-filled expression. She was lying on top of him, her naked chest such a temptation. His pain was nothing in comparison to how she made him feel.

"Maybe we shouldn't," she said as she wiggled against him, trying to move. That made the ache in his pants even worse.

"I'm not even thinking about my arm, if that's what you're worried about," he said.

She looked at him uneasily, trying to assess the situation. He turned their bodies so no weight was resting against his bad arm. Then, he ran his fingers across her luscious chest.

"I need you, Ace. Please make love to me," she said, her desire greater than her worry.

When he closed his fingers over one beautiful breast and squeezed, she arched against him. The sight of her dark hair, creamy skin, and beaded nipples sent him over the edge of sanity.

Turning their bodies again, he lay on his back, pulling her over on top of him. She easily straddled his thighs, her hot heat scorching him through their clothing. The ache inside him grew by the second.

Dakota sat up and arched her back, rubbing against him as he used both hands to squeeze her chest. She groaned as she threw her head back and rode him. He wanted their clothes gone right now.

"Dakota," he said with a groan.

"*Mmm*, I love the way you say my name like that," she purred.

"We need these clothes gone," he insisted.

Dakota leaned down and kissed him, trapping his hands between their bodies. Her mouth was hot and hungry, and he was lost to her in a moment. When she pulled back, it was his turn to protest. She climbed from his body. He was getting ready to crawl after her when she hooked her thumbs in her pants and began pulling them down.

Ace was unable to utter words as she stripped away the rest of her clothing, leaving herself fully bare to him. Words weren't enough to describe how he felt. He had never seen such beauty.

Ace scooted from the bed, unable to take it a moment longer without having her in his arms. He threw off his shirt as he stepped up to her, then grabbed her from behind, pulling her perfect ass against his throbbing erection. He slid his hands around her, trailing them up her smooth stomach to the curves of her breasts.

She leaned against him as he squeezed her nipples. He should have taken the time to remove his pants. Now he was going to have to pull away from her again, something he definitely didn't want to do.

He leaned down and sucked the soft skin at the side of her neck, feeling her pulse pound out of control against his kiss. He sucked harder as he squeezed her nipples and pulled her more tightly against him. Then he stepped back and turned her around.

Her skin was flushed, her chest moving rapidly as she trembled before him.

"You are so unbelievably sexy," he said, his own voice almost unrecognizable. "Get on the bed." The second part came out a lot more commanding.

She turned to look at him, her eyes flaring. His erection pulsed even more painfully. When she stepped away from him and went to the bed, she lay down, giving him a perfect display of her luscious body. He wasn't sure if he'd make it through the night alive.

Ace quickly stripped away the last of his clothes and dripped his happiness when her eyes darted to the hardest part of him. She licked her lips. She was so sexy, so sensual. He had no idea how she'd waited so long to share herself with a man, but he was more than grateful she had. Because she was his—only his.

Their brief time apart was already too much. He joined her on the mattress, pulling her against him as he connected their mouths again. He kissed her hungrily, his tongue tracing her mouth, his teeth nipping at her lips, his gentleness long gone.

She reached between them and squeezed his throbbing member, her thumb rubbing against the head of him, coating his moisture down his pulsing length before slowly moving up again, squeezing it hard.

"You feel unbelievable," Dakota breathed.

"I feel like I'm going to explode," he replied.

"Stop talking and kiss me," she demanded.

He wasn't going to argue with her. Grabbing her tight, he pulled one leg over his and pressed his thickness against her wet heat while his mouth devoured her. He rubbed against her slickness while his tongue swept inside her mouth.

Dakota groaned before pushing him on his back and climbing on top of him. She gripped him in her hand and lifted her luscious body before sinking down on top him, her tight heat nearly making him explode with the first thrust.

Dakota quickly found a perfect rhythm as she moved up and down on him. Ace couldn't tear his gaze from her beautiful face. Sweat beaded on her brow. She bit her lower lip and groaned. She relished making love to a man who desired her more than life itself.

He lifted his hands and squeezed her chest, tweaking her nipples. He got lost in the passion the two of them were stoking higher and higher. Each time she pushed down on him, he drew closer to the edge. It was going too fast.

Pulling on her back, he tugged her into his arms and captured her mouth again, pushing his hips up to meet her thrusts. She cried against him, biting his lip and then sucking it while he felt the pressure continue to build.

Her body began squeezing his, and he knew she was building closer to an explosive orgasm. He would be right there with her. His hands grabbed her ass as he thrust upward, pushing harder each time their bodies met.

Tracing her back to the curve of her ass, he held on tightly as he moved his lips to her neck and sucked the skin. She cried out, her hips moving faster. And then her entire body tensed as she let out a scream that echoed through the room, her hot flesh squeezing him as she shook on top of him.

Ace didn't try to hold back any longer. He surged upward, his hot climax rushing from him, shooting deep within her tight walls. They shook together as the release washed through them, connecting Ace to Dakota even more than he already had been.

It was several moments before they were able to move, and still, when Dakota pulled off him, he felt an instant moment of aloneness he'd never felt before. He grabbed her before she could pull away too far, holding her against his chest as he reached for the covers and engulfed them in a safe cocoon.

Ace was exhausted, but as Dakota fell asleep in his arms, he lay awake for quite a while, his hand moving up and down her back, his eyes closed, his body relaxed. This was where he had always belonged.

What frightened him was that it was bound not to last. How could it? He was leaving in two weeks. Besides that, they didn't know the good, bad, and ugly of each other. They didn't know much at all. This had started out with a fiery passion and had literally evolved into a firestorm of bullets. For this moment, though, he wanted to forget all about that. He wanted nothing more than to have her wrapped in his arms, his heart beating against her cheek.

He wanted it all. With that thought, he closed his eyes and allowed sleep to claim him. A new day was coming and he could worry about it all then. For now, he was safe and content.

CHAPTER TWENTY

A smile rested on Dakota's lips as she slowly began waking up. Stretching her arms above her head, a slow ache burned through her body, and that only made her lips turn up more. She opened her eyes to the sunlight streaming through the windows. This was how she should have been able to wake up after her first time making love with Ace.

Whether her choice to sleep with him was a stupid or not, it was a choice she'd consciously made. She wouldn't allow herself or Ace to think of it as a mistake. Not when it was so damn wonderful between the two of them.

The bed beside her was cold, telling her Ace had been up for a while. She wasn't worried about it. The day before she hadn't wanted him out of her sight, but after the night the two of them had shared, she felt as if she were still in his safe embrace—at least for now.

The smells of coffee and bacon drifted into the room, and her stomach rumbled. Food had been the last thought on her mind the night before, but now that they seemed to be out of immediate danger, her body was demanding to be refueled.

Pushing the covers away, Dakota stood and walked into the bathroom, her leg muscles screaming at her. She had worked them pretty dang hard the night before. This must be her reminder. She thought about the night. It had been magical.

Turning the shower on hot, she stepped inside and sighed with relief. She ached in places she hadn't ached in a while. That was saying a lot, considering she was a cheerleader for the Seattle Seahawks and did all sorts of acrobatics during practices and on game day. *Heck, if I have enough sex with Ace, I won't need weight training anymore,* she thought with a laugh.

Too hungry and already needing to seek Ace out, Dakota got through her shower quickly before toweling off. She then went into the bedroom with a fluffy towel wrapped around her and looked at the room. She'd forgotten to get another change of clothes from Chloe the night before.

She found a thick robe hanging in the closet and slipped into that. She'd have to wear clothes she'd borrowed the night before, but she wanted food more than she cared to get dressed.

Dakota had always been a morning person. She hadn't been able to relate to those who weren't excited for a brand-new day, especially when the sun was shining and there were so many new possibilities in the air. What wasn't there to be excited about?

When she stepped from the bedroom, she heard the low beat of music playing, which automatically made her hips sway as she moved soundlessly through the surprisingly large cottage. She turned a corner and found Ace at the stove flipping a pancake. That wasn't what stopped her in her tracks, though.

A Garth Brooks song was playing in the kitchen, and Ace was singing along in a surprisingly beautiful baritone. She was completely mesmerized. Her heart raced, and she closed her eyes. She was falling a little bit in love with the man.

I'm shameless . . . shameless as a man can be . . .

His voice mixed perfectly with Garth's rich, emotion-filled voice. It was a song about love and how the man didn't care what the world thought. He was down on his knees, would do anything for the woman he loved.

. . . but I can't walk away from you . . .

Her heart thundered in her chest as she approached Ace, unable to stay away from him for even a second longer. She came up behind him and wrapped her arms around his torso, her hands sliding up his flat stomach and holding him where his heart beat.

"Good morning," she said, leaning against him and kissing his neck.

He stilled, his beautiful voice halting, which made her slightly sad. Maybe she should have stood back longer and enjoyed her one-man show. But to have his body pressed against hers was more tempting than any regret she might have.

"Morning," he murmured back, his deep voice sending sparks straight to her stomach and lower. They'd made love before the attack, before falling asleep, and then once more in the middle of the night. She would think her body was more than sated, but now that Ace had awoken a part of her that had been sleeping for a very long time, she didn't think she'd ever get enough.

"How's your arm?" she asked, nuzzling her cheek against his back.

"Hurts like hell today, but I'm dealing with it," he admitted.

He pulled the pancake from the pan, turned off the heat of the stove, and then turned around, quickly wrapping her in his arms. Her cheek was now pressed against his chest, and the steady thumping of his heart was the perfect comfort.

"I'm sorry," she told him, her hands sliding beneath his shirt and rubbing the hot skin of his back.

"I know what we can do to take my mind off it," he said as his hands slipped lower and he squeezed her sore butt cheeks.

"I think I need fuel," she said with a laugh. "And you have a beautiful singing voice."

"I didn't realize you were awake."

He sounded embarrassed, which shocked Dakota enough that she pulled back so she could see his face. Was that a blush on his cheeks? She would have never thought that possible.

"I didn't take you for a humble man," she said with a chuckle.

"Believe me, I'm not," he told her.

He bent down and took her lips with his. Hunger rushed through her, but also a strange sense of peace. He took his time, tracing her lips in a gentle caress that grew a bit more urgent the longer the kiss went on. When he pulled back, they were both breathing heavily, Dakota's heart beating wildly.

"Maybe food is overrated," she told him as she pressed more tightly against him.

His eyes dilated before he gave her one more hard kiss and then pushed her back from him. Disappointment filled her.

"My brothers are waiting for us, and you look as if you could be pushed over by a light wind, so I guess I'll put my unending desire on hold and give you that fuel you need," he said with a smile.

"You did cook for me, so it would be rude not to have some." Ace pulled down a couple of plates. Dakota looked at the food lined up on the stove. "There's enough here to feed your entire family," she said with another laugh.

"You haven't seen me eat home-cooked food yet," he told her.

They dished up, and Dakota eyed his plate with disbelief. "There's no way you can finish all that off."

"I take that as a challenge," he said as they sat down.

At the first bite of food, Dakota's hunger took over. Every other thought in her head and body faded as she gobbled a couple of pancakes far too quickly. Ace was eating as if he hadn't had a meal in a week, which made her feel a lot less gluttonous.

"I have to go back to my place today, Ace. I need clothes," she said when they were finished, her belly full and her other hungers awakening.

He'd managed to clear his own plate and had gone back for seconds. There wasn't an ounce of fat on the man. She wasn't sure where all the food was going. But then again, she'd seen some of the football players eat enough for ten people after a hard practice, so she knew how much fuel these men could burn.

"Clothes are already taken care of. Stormy dropped off a bag this morning when I began cooking."

"Your family has been very good to me," she said.

"I've been away for so long, I almost forgot what family was all about. I don't deserve their generosity after what I've put them through over the last eight years."

Dakota sipped her coffee as she gazed at him. He really believed what he was saying. She was learning there were so many more layers to Ace than she had originally thought possible. She reached across the table and took his hand.

"I put my family through hell for a lot of years. I grew up with four brothers, who all decided that because I was the baby, they needed to treat me like a toddler even when I was a teenager. I went through my rebellious stage, and many other stages along the way. No matter how much of a pain in the ass I was through the years, they always forgave me," she assured him.

"I was a monster," he admitted. "I was selfish and mad when my father died. I pretty much looked out only for myself." There was so much shame in his words. She felt her heart breaking a little bit for him.

"Something I learned along the journey of my life is that it's okay to love yourself enough to know you deserve to be treated with respect and dignity no matter what situation you are in. Even if you make mistakes, it doesn't define *who* you are. You can always pick the pieces back up. And you can always come back home," she told him.

"You are a one-of-a-kind woman, Dakota Forbes," he said with a smile.

"I had to define myself. When you grow up in a house full of alpha personalities, you learn a thing or two about being a unique individual. I was loved, and I always knew that, so it made feeling confident about myself that much easier."

"Not a lot of people have those same convictions. I've seen the worst of the worst in life and the horrible things people can do to those they say they love. It changes how you look at people and situations," he told her.

"I choose to see the gold at the end of the rainbow. It makes sleeping a whole lot easier when you don't have all that negativity clogging up your head."

"I might have to keep you around to remind me of all of this," he said with a smile. The seriousness in his eyes scared her the smallest bit. This was all moving at the speed of sound, and she didn't know what to think about it.

"When life gives you lemons, you make tea," she said.

He looked at her, confused for a moment, and then burst into laughter. She scowled at him. "Are you laughing at me?"

"Not at all," he said, still chuckling. "I just never know what's going to come from those pretty lips of yours."

"It's not the lips you should be worried about; it's the teeth," she assured him, snapping her jaw shut and showing her pearly whites to him. "They are sharp."

"*Hmm*, I might need to test that theory out," he said.

"Aw, there's that confidence that's so damn sexy," she told him.

"My family can wait," he said, his eyes dilating as they drifted to the opening of her robe.

Dakota chuckled as she stood up and took a step back. Ace was on his feet in less than a second. "You'll have to catch me first," she said before she took off running.

Ace was there before she'd made it a few steps. Then he was hauling her up with his good arm and marching back toward the bedroom. One hunger had been sated. It was time to cater to the other burning desire they felt.

They were very late to meet with his family—and Dakota didn't mind one little bit.

CHAPTER TWENTY-ONE

Dakota and Ace were having a standoff, and there was no way she was backing down. He paced the floor in front of her, stopping every once in a while to send a withering gaze in her direction. Dakota leaned back against the counter and shot him a look that was most certainly calling him several names.

"This isn't acceptable," Ace finally said, a dramatic sigh slipping from his compressed lips.

"I agree. You're being a controlling lout, and I won't have it. And if you think you're going to bed me into submission again, you have another think coming. I paid for flight lessons, and I'm going to have them. You either come with me or I am going there on my own. I'm sure Sherman will find me a new trainer."

Dakota didn't want a new trainer. She wanted to be in that tiny plane with Ace, and only Ace, but she wasn't going to sit by if he chose not to go with her. She'd let him keep her cooped up at his brother's place for two days. She was now done.

"But what if it isn't safe?" Ace said.

"We've been over this and over this," she huffed. "Robberies happen. It's certainly not something I ever want to happen to me again, but

I do live in one of the largest cities in the United States, and sometimes things happen. My brothers would prefer I live out on the family estate away from the drudges and city dwellers, as they say, but there I could be taking a walk and get attacked by a mountain lion. There's really no safe place, is there?" she pointed out.

"How often does a mountain lion attack happen?" he asked with a roll of his eyes.

"I'm not the Internet. How in the heck should I know?" she asked.

"Threats exist everywhere. It's important to be aware of that. I just want you safe," he told her.

There was such a pleading look in his eyes that it immediately mollified Dakota's anger. She pushed off the counter and slowly walked up to him. He was tense as she wrapped her arms around him.

"I know there's danger, Ace. I know it's impossible for you to look away from it, but you have to realize that by overprotecting me, you're actually restricting me. If you care about me at all, you won't do that," she reasoned with him.

She stood on her bare toes and kissed his solid jaw. It took a few moments, but finally he began to relax. His arms wrapped behind her and pulled her tightly to him, as if he would never let her go. On one hand, she wanted him to shield her from so much, but on the other, she couldn't give in on this matter or she feared it would define the rest of their time together. She would grow to hate him if she didn't stand up for herself.

"Logically, I know you're right," Ace finally admitted. "It's just that my gut says something isn't right."

"That might just be because of your job," Dakota told him. "You're always looking for the worst instead of the best."

"You might be right," he said, another sigh escaping him as his hands began moving up and down her back.

She felt a shiver travel her spine, and she knew how easy it would be to cave in to the demands of her body. But she was starting to look at this strange relationship with Ace as something that could possibly last for a while. And if that were the case, they certainly needed to have more going for them than just a great sex life. Though, now that she'd discovered the joys of having a man own her so completely, she knew she couldn't be in a relationship where the sex wasn't spectacular.

"Then you will take me for another flying lesson?" she said as she snuggled against his hard pecs.

"Yes," he said. "But I don't like it."

"You don't like flying?" she said, purposely misunderstanding him.

"I love flying. I get to be free when I do it," he admitted.

"Then it will be good for both of us. Well, if I don't send us spiraling toward the ground."

"I wouldn't let that happen," he assured her.

"Nope, you don't get to play the hero," she told him sternly. "I am going to be such a great pilot, the plane will have no choice but to obey my commands."

"Oh, really?" he said, a smile entering his voice.

"Really!" she insisted.

"I have no doubt you are great at whatever you put your mind to," he said.

"And I'm ready to go," she said. She pulled from his arms, the action making her feel slightly empty. The look on his face assured her he liked it even less. That helped.

"Be ready in ten minutes," she told him as she rushed to the back of the guest cottage and grabbed her tennis shoes. It was time to fly again. She was more than excited. The men who'd attacked her were forgotten. Okay, maybe not completely, but she wasn't going to allow them to stop her from living her life. That's how they won in their game of terror.

When she came back out, Ace smiled at her. His face was so beautiful, it took her breath away. This man was tugging on more of her heart each moment she was with him. She'd felt the need to soothe his battered soul from the moment she'd met him, but it seemed he was doing more for her than she was for him.

And she was more than okay with that.

CHAPTER TWENTY-TWO

Ace smiled as Dakota impatiently followed him around the plane while he took his time doing the preflight check. He made her look at everything after he did, and then check it off a list. He knew what she was feeling. She wanted to get into the air.

"I know this part isn't exciting, but doing it will save your life," Ace assured her.

"But we just did it a few days ago," she pointed out.

Ace laughed. "It has to be done every single time you fly," he assured her. "Otherwise disaster strikes."

"You think disaster is striking all the time," she told him.

Ace understood why she thought that, but she didn't have the same knowledge he did. She had never seen what he'd seen, and she just didn't understand true evil. He was glad she didn't. If she were truly aware, she wouldn't be the same woman. He'd seen too many instances of good people having their bubble popped, and then he'd had to watch the light go out of their eyes. He missed the light—he missed being that happy.

"If I promise to be more observant of my surroundings and to listen to you when it comes to all things about the plane, will you please let up just a little on your intensity?" she asked him.

Ace truly thought about her question for a moment before he forced some of the tenseness out of his shoulders. She was right. She was incredibly right. Maybe he felt this immense need to teach her because he knew that in less than two weeks he'd be gone. The thought of not being there if something else were to happen to her nearly sent him into a panic. That wouldn't do.

"Okay, I'll let up," he finally said.

"You can't just say it. You have to mean it," she told him, her stubborn face clearly pasted on.

Ace laughed. "Deal," he told her. "Are you ready to fly this beautiful girl?"

Dakota laughed. "Ah, we're back to calling the plane a girl," she said.

Ace smiled. "She sits here in the center of the room, and at the first sight of her, a hot flash of oxygen fills my lungs," he said. Her eyes widened. "Nothing but a sculpted, beautiful woman can inspire that kind of reaction. She's smooth, without blemishes. She's intoxicating. A plane can only be known as a she," he promised.

Ace saw desire flash in Dakota's eyes, and he felt himself grow hard—just that quickly. He'd been thinking about Dakota during his description, but the same was true of the smooth, sweet lines of the perfect plane.

"I know many people envious of a plane's beauty, of the confidence inspired while looking at her. She just sits there and begs you to climb inside and have a little dance."

"Are you now a romance novelist?" Dakota asked in a husky voice.

"You inspire me," he told her. He had to force himself not to step over to her and rip off her clothes. The thought of taking her against the beautiful machine in front of them had him aching in a way that should have sent him to the ER.

"I thought you were describing the plane, not me," she pointed out.

"I might have gotten that a little bit mixed up," he said with a shrug.

"We better get into the air, then . . . before we fly to new horizons without leaving the ground."

Damn, he loved being with this woman. She didn't shrink back from him, didn't try to pretend there wasn't massive attraction between them. She was real, and he wasn't sure what he was going to do when he had no choice but to walk away from her. That put a definite pail of cold water down his slacks.

"Let's do it," he said, a bit grumpily.

She looked at him as she tried to figure out his sudden shift in mood, but then she moved to the door of the plane and climbed up, giving him a delectable view of her butt before she disappeared inside.

He took his time walking around the plane. This was going to seem like a longer flight than last time, no matter how much time they were in the air. Her scent would still envelop him, but this time he'd know what it was like to be deep inside her tight body. Ace had been subjected to torture, but it didn't come close to what he was going to have to go through during the next hour or two.

Trying to convince himself he was stronger than average, he climbed in beside her and then sealed the door. He would get his mind out of the gutter and focus on her training. It truly was a life-or-death situation each time she went up in the air. The more he could teach her before he left, the better he would feel about her continuing without him. No one would train her as well as he could. Maybe he would skip this CIA mission—just let someone else have it.

As soon as he had that thought, he pushed it from his mind. He was CIA. It was his job to make the world a safer place. Nothing should stop him. Besides, he would never be happy simply giving private flying lessons. It was too mundane, too boring.

That decided, they got to work. They started the plane and began taxiing, Ace no longer in the mood to share witty banter with Dakota. That wasn't something he'd thought would ever happen.

She was doing amazingly well, getting her turns in, listening to everything he told her as they flew out farther from the airport, lifting higher into the air.

"I could do this all day long," she told him, her joyful laugh coming clearly through his headphones.

"Yeah, me too," he admitted.

"You don't find it boring after your millions of hours of flight time?" she questioned.

He laughed. "I don't have close to that many hours, but no, I honestly never get sick of flying," he admitted.

"I know I won't, either, even when I'm flying huge jumbo jets across the Atlantic," she said, bouncing in her seat a little bit, causing her leg to rub against his. He forced himself to ignore the shot of desire he felt.

"What makes you think you're going to be flying across the Atlantic?" he asked.

"This is my last year of cheering. It's time for me to grow up. I want to be a pilot, and flying small planes forever will never do. Sherman told me when I get the necessary hours and training in, I would be a shoo-in to work for Cooper's company."

Ace felt a tinge of jealousy at her words. He knew how the pilot community worked. A lot of those pilots had had too many affairs to count. They'd think they hit the jackpot the second Dakota stepped on board, those proud stars on her shoulders. She'd be hunted down from day one. He tried telling himself he wouldn't care. That was at least two to three years down the road. But with Dakota's determination, he'd bet she'd be flying every single day, racking up those needed hours.

She wasn't his—not really—so he didn't understand why he should even care. Maybe he wouldn't by the time that happened. He knew that wasn't the case, of course, but he refused to even think about it.

"Those long flights are pretty amazing," he said.

"Did you get to fly really cool places with the CIA?" she asked.

"Yeah, when the drug cartel on my last case thought I was working for them, we did a lot of international trips. Of course, they were up to no good, so that took some of the joy of flying away, but damn if she wasn't a beautiful jet," Ace admitted.

"You got them in the end, so that's the most important thing to remember," she told him.

"I try telling myself that," he mumbled. After a long pause, he said, "We should turn around and start heading back."

The pout on her face made him want to kiss her. She did a near-perfect turn despite her disappointment, and they began heading back toward the airport. Ace was about to speak again when a light began to flash on the control panel. Suddenly, the engine went silent.

Dakota looked at him with worry. *What the hell?* "Give me the controls," he demanded, his voice calm. It wasn't a big deal, but certainly not something a pilot in training could deal with on her second day out.

"This is bad, right?" she said. He noticed her voice remained calm, even if it was hesitant.

"This isn't what's supposed to happen, but we aren't in trouble yet," he told her.

She nodded as she watched every little thing he did. He was trying to get the engine to start again, but all he got was a sputter and then . . . nothing.

They were losing altitude, and Ace knew he only had seconds to decide what to do. He was sort of wishing he hadn't been trying to impress her by flying this plane, because it ran hotter and required a much faster landing speed, making it more difficult to set down in a short field. He began searching the ground, damn grateful they were outside the city limits. To their slight left were some fields. He didn't have a great visual to see if there were power lines, tractors, hay, any-thing that would make them flip once they hit the ground, but he had no other choice except to make an emergency landing.

"This is bad, right?" she repeated, her voice calm, but quiet.

"Yeah, this is bad," he told her before he keyed the mic to call in an emergency landing. He relayed his coordinates and said a little prayer as the ground drew closer, their speed too fast.

"Hold on," he told her, his voice tight. This would almost be a thrill for him if Dakota wasn't sitting right next to him.

Dakota's heavy breathing came over loud and clear through his headset, and all Ace could think about at this point was trying to control the plane. He didn't have time to wonder what was wrong or what was going to happen when they hit the ground. He had to play this by ear and pray he kept her alive.

"This is it," he said, not liking how fast they were going as the plane approached the field. Nothing was visibly in his way, but he didn't know about holes, low fences, ditches. He just focused his eyes and did his best to pull up the slightest bit so they didn't slam forward or tilt and hit the wings.

The plane hit the ground with a jarring impact, their bodies getting tugged painfully against their seat belts. Their harnesses were the only thing that saved them from slamming their heads into the ceiling.

He heard Dakota let out a sigh of relief.

"This isn't over," he told her. "Hold on tight."

The plane careened a bit to the left, and he did his best to straighten her out as they thundered down the grassy field. He tapped the brakes lightly, not wanting to hit them hard and send the plane tail over front.

Looking ahead, he saw a fence, and he knew it was going to be a close call. Tapping the brakes a little harder, he felt the plane resist as the tail began sliding sideways. Then they hit a mound of dirt, slamming the left wing into the ground, making them flip over.

Dakota's scream was the last thing he heard before his head slammed into the window, knocking him out cold.

CHAPTER TWENTY-THREE

Sirens were blaring when Ace regained consciousness. Dakota felt tears streaming down her face as she saw the beautiful sight of his eyes opening. She ripped off her headset and reached over and tore his off too.

"How long was I out?" he asked. He looked a bit dazed, but he was waking up fast.

"Only a few seconds, but you scared the hell out of me," she told him.

"We have to get out of here. She could catch on fire," he said. He ripped off his seat belt, then reached over and undid hers. Dakota's fingers were trembling.

The doors were jammed, so Ace leaned back and kicked with all his strength. It took a few tries, but he finally broke the window out. He pushed her through, and then he quickly followed her. He directed her away from the plane. They were damn lucky it hadn't gone up.

Dakota was trying desperately to be brave as fire engines and an ambulance drove quickly to find them. The whole ordeal had been terrifying.

"Still want to be a pilot?" Ace asked. He was trying to be calm, but she could see the fear in his eyes. She also knew it was because of her.

She had a feeling Ace was rarely scared for himself but was bothered deeply when someone he cared about was in danger. That meant she was on his list of those to protect. She sort of liked that feeling.

"That wasn't a fun part of training," she admitted with a wobbly smile. "But it won't stop me from going up again."

The admiration in his eyes as he brushed some hair from her cheek made her want to do a dance. The soreness in her body warned her it might be a few days before she was doing any type of cardio movement.

"You impress me, Dakota," he told her.

"Good. I like to be impressive," she said.

They were interrupted by the emergency vehicles pulling up and medics rushing to them. *Damn, this is beginning to become a thing,* Dakota realized. Maybe the two of them could finish out a single week without emergency personnel coming to their rescue.

It took a while for Ace to explain what had happened and for the paramedics to check them both out. She lost count of how many people told her how lucky she was to walk away from this with only some bruises and muscle aches.

In all honesty, she'd been scared to death. But Dakota wouldn't allow fear to rule her life. No way. She would get back into a plane. Not the one they'd just destroyed, but she would fly again, even if she was terrified the next few times. She'd give herself a week off, though. That wasn't wussing out; it was being smart.

"Ready to go?" Ace asked.

That's when another two vehicles pulled up and his brothers and their wives jumped out, the women with tears on their faces and his brothers with worry in their eyes.

"Oh my gosh, Dakota," Chloe cried as she rushed over to them. She grabbed Dakota and squeezed her so hard, Dakota whimpered a bit.

Chloe immediately pulled back and looked at her. "I'm sorry. I'm so sorry. I was just so scared," she said before apologizing a dozen more times.

"We're both fine. I promise. Just a little sore," Dakota assured her best friend.

"You were in a plane crash," she accused before glaring at Ace. "What in the hell is wrong with you boys that you keep on crashing?" she thundered.

Ace held up his hands as his eyes widened. "Trust me, it wasn't on my to-do list today," he assured her.

"I know. I'm sorry," Chloe said, moving over to him and throwing her arms around him. Whether he wanted a hug or not, he was getting one. Ace's eyes met Dakota's over Chloe's head, and Dakota smiled at him. When Nick had married Chloe, she'd taken on his siblings as her brothers. Ace would just have to deal with that and all the love that came along with it.

"We're okay," Ace said again, awkwardly patting Chloe's back.

"I know. I just had to touch you both to make sure," Chloe said.

Stormy and Lindsey both took turns hugging Dakota and Ace before the women stepped aside and let the brothers talk about the wreck. All four of them walked over to the plane.

"Do you know how it happened?" Stormy asked.

"No. One minute everything was fine, and then the next, the engine stalled and down we were going," Dakota told them.

"I can't even imagine," Lindsey said, her eyes widening as she took in the twisted metal of the plane.

"Ace did an amazing job keeping us safe," Dakota told them.

"That doesn't exactly look safe to me," Lindsey pointed out.

Letting out a sigh, Dakota ran through what she could say that would help ease everyone's fear, but she was at a loss. "He got us out alive," she finally said.

"That's all that matters," Chloe assured her.

"Well, I'm sure the plane isn't cheap," Dakota said with a wince. Her insurance was going to skyrocket.

"That isn't something you should even have crossing your mind right now," Stormy told her as she turned away from the plane. "I can't look at that anymore. It's going to give me nightmares for weeks."

"How did you guys find out?" Dakota asked. She and Ace hadn't had time to call his family, they'd been so busy with the emergency personnel.

"Sherman heard it and called," Lindsey said.

"Is there anything that man doesn't hear?" Dakota asked.

"No, not really," Stormy said.

"I'm surprised he wasn't the first one on the scene," Dakota told them.

"He wanted to be, but Maverick told him to stay by the radio so he could keep us updated. He promised we'd bring you to him right away," Chloe told her.

"More hugging is in my future," Dakota said with a laugh that hurt her bruised ribs.

"I think we should go to the hospital," Chloe said.

"I'm not being stubborn," Dakota insisted. "The medics poked and prodded. If there was anything alarming, they would have figured it out."

"What about internal damage?" Lindsey asked.

"You know more than anyone else that there would be signs."

"I think we need some X-rays, just in case," Chloe insisted.

With one nurse and one former nurse raising concerns, Dakota knew she was outvoted. She also knew any resistance from Ace would also be vehemently protested—and they were both going to lose. And they did.

CHAPTER TWENTY-FOUR

Sunlight streamed in through the guesthouse windows at Cooper's place. Dakota woke with a smile. She wouldn't admit aloud how frightened she'd been the day before when she and Ace had dropped from the sky. And though she hadn't wanted to go to the hospital, she was a little glad his family had insisted.

Though it had taken hours, they'd walked out knowing they were fine. She'd been aching when, with Ace's assistance, she'd gone to bed once again at the cottage, but the pain was endurable with Ace by her side. She was growing a little dependent on the man, and that worried her. Ace was unlike any other man she'd ever known, though, and she was enjoying her time with him even if she was scared of what that meant.

Though Dakota had always enjoyed her alone time—especially since she'd never had much of it growing up—these days, she felt this invisible string tying her to Ace. She rarely wanted to be away from him for too long. After the newness and exciting adventures they'd already been through wore off, she was sure that string was going to be severed.

But for now, she put on a borrowed pair of shoes and enjoyed the fresh morning air as she made the walk up to Cooper's main house. She heard voices coming from the dining room as soon as she stepped through the back door. The kids were laughing and the adults talking as Dakota rounded the corner. She stopped in the hallway and observed the family. They appeared not to have a care in the world.

She was mesmerized as she watched Ace laugh at something his brother said to him. The man was beautiful, but when he smiled and laughed he was breathtaking. She felt her heart skip a beat. Yeah, she really was in trouble.

"You're finally here. I thought you were going to sleep all day," Chloe said, making everyone in the room turn to look at her, which made Dakota's cheeks warm. "Must have been busy last night." The heat in her cheeks tried to confirm what they were all thinking, but in reality, Ace had just held her as she'd fallen asleep in his arms, safe.

"The last few days must have caught up with me, and I just needed the sleep," she told them.

The intense look Ace sent her reminded her how his hands had traveled all over her body two nights earlier, his mouth taking her to heaven before setting her on the ground again. He'd created a beast within her that it seemed only he could tame. She wasn't happy at all about it. One night of no lovemaking and she was ready to jump his bones in front of his entire family. What in the heck was wrong with her?

"Come get something to eat, and you will feel back to normal in no time," Stormy told her, taking her arm and leading her to the buffet, where a ton of food was sitting on warmers.

"We've waited for you to start," Lindsey told her as they began grabbing plates.

"You didn't have to do that. Now I feel bad," Dakota told the group.

"Don't worry. We would have come and gotten you very soon if you hadn't shown up," Chloe assured her.

"Good," Dakota said.

Ace moved through the crowd and came to stand directly next to her, leaning down and running his lips softly across the nape of her neck. A shiver slid down her spine. She realized her knees just might give out on her if she wasn't careful. She took a step away from him for her own sanity.

"It's only been a couple hours, and I was already missing you," he told her.

The glow his words caused inside her made her feel full enough not to need any food. All she seemed to need was him. This was a very dangerous road she was traveling.

"You should get some food," she told him, finally meeting his eyes. She could have sworn she saw disappointment flash there, but how was that possible? Was he feeling what she was feeling? Why couldn't she just admit to him that she had missed him too? Maybe because that made her feel too needy.

"Are we getting out of here today?" she asked as the two of them moved to the table with their plates full of food. She didn't want him to use the plane crash as an excuse to keep her sheltered again.

"Are you still feeling restless even after our harrowing adventure yesterday?" he asked. He began eating, and now she was sure she hadn't seen in his eyes what she'd thought she had. He was a confident man and didn't care what she said or how she felt toward him. Maybe she was putting more into this than was actually warranted.

"Yes, I'm used to being out all the time and very active. To be trapped in the house all day isn't something I can take for long," she told him, her voice definitely pleading now.

Chloe and Nick joined them.

"I can attest to that. Dakota has been the one to drag me out of the house time and time again when I wanted nothing more than to stay home. But I will admit, we've always had fun on our many adventures," Chloe said.

"We could go to town for lunch today," Nick said.

"Don't you think a day of rest would be better?" Ace argued.

"No. My body hurts, and it will be much better to get out and move it so the muscles don't lock up on me," Dakota insisted.

"I don't think that's what the doc would recommend," Ace told her.

"I know my body," Dakota insisted. The slow, measured look he sent her way told her he also knew her body—quite intimately. It was so easy to get lost in his damn eyes.

"I don't know . . ." He was still hedging. She wanted to smack him, but she needed a compromise.

"If you give me a day out today, then I'll lay off for a few days and rest," she told him with her most persuasive smile.

He sent her a stern look, but it didn't last once she reached over and ran her fingernails across his thigh.

"You're playing dirty," he warned.

"I play to win," she replied, which had the other couples at the table tittering.

"Just give it up, brother. You've lost," Maverick told him. Dakota sent Ace's brother a beaming smile. It helped to have other people on her side.

"Fine, we can go to town today, but then we are resting," Ace said.

Dakota threw her arms around his neck and gave him a hug. She enjoyed getting her way, and she was showing him he would be rewarded in turn.

They finished breakfast, and Dakota was shocked when the men performed the cleanup duty while the women went into the living room with the kids and visited while playing board games.

It didn't take long for the guys to join them, and then it was quite the domestic scene as Ace joined her on the couch, his arm thrown around her shoulders as he laughed with his niece and nephews and visited with his family.

If Dakota didn't know he'd been gone for the past eight years, she would have thought he'd never been away. They'd come back together perfectly, and they all seemed so happy to be around one another. It made her yearn to be a real part of this loving family.

"Are you sure you want to go anywhere? I'm content to sit right here," Ace told her.

"Don't tempt me," she said.

"I like tempting you," he told her, his hot breath brushing against her neck.

"Obviously," she said, her heart pounding.

"We could just go back down to the cottage for a while," he suggested.

She was more than ready to do exactly that. "I think you've spent enough time at the cottage. I've gotten a babysitter, and I was promised a trip to town," Stormy said.

Dakota smiled at her friend, not sure if she was happy for the rescue or disappointed.

"Okay, town it is," Dakota said.

Ace groaned when she pulled away from him and stood up. Then she reached out to take his hand. He slowly stood up and then pulled her into his arms and kissed her in front of his entire family. She was swooning by the time he pulled back.

"You sure you don't want to scrap this?" he asked with a wiggle of his brows.

"The wait will make tonight so much better," she promised, making his eyes flare.

"Now you're thinking," he said.

It took them a while to get out of the house, with them saying good-bye to the children and having to promise to bring them treats when they returned. They also had to take two vehicles when Nick insisted on driving his old truck, saying she was feeling neglected at having not been driven in a while. Chloe laughed at her husband but willingly joined him in the old thing.

In Seattle, they relaxed and ate a nice meal on the water. After eating, they went to the park to enjoy the sunny, windless day. Dakota realized she could very much get used to doing nothing other than lying in Ace's arms as she visited with her best friend and her family.

"We've had a fun day," Ace said as he looked around—he was always looking around. She kind of liked how safe she felt with him. "Now it's time to head back."

The girls all groaned, but they cleaned up their blankets and started walking toward the parking lot. That's when things went wrong. Ace stopped walking, his body on immediate alert.

"What is it?" Cooper asked. Nick and Maverick came to stand by them, all of them instinctively shielding the women.

"Something's wrong," Ace said.

"I don't see anything," Mav told him.

"I don't know. I just feel off," Ace told them.

"It's been a relaxing day. I think you're just so used to looking out for danger that you don't know how to relax," Nick countered.

"Not worth questioning it if the women are in danger," Ace insisted.

"Come on, brother," Cooper said with a laugh. "Relax."

"We need to get out of here. I've learned to trust my instincts," Ace said.

Coop looked at him for a measured moment, then sighed. "Okay, let's go," he agreed.

They stepped forward again, and the air seemed to grow denser. Nick was moving toward his truck at a relaxed stroll. They were less than a hundred feet away when an explosion nearby nearly knocked them off their feet. People screamed and ran away from the parking lot.

Nick stood there in shock, not moving as the heat from the blast engulfed them. They were far enough away they were out of danger, but too close for comfort.

Dakota watched as Nick's truck went up in flames. She turned to see his ashen face and didn't know what to say. They were all silent as they witnessed the devastation.

"Who would do that to my truck?" Nick asked, his voice revealing how numb he felt.

"What the hell?" Ace said. "I should have been paying more attention."

"How is this your fault?" Dakota asked.

"Because . . ." Ace trailed off. He didn't have an answer.

Cooper was the first to pull himself together. He lifted his phone, dialing the police. Someone else must have already, though, because they heard sirens as emergency vehicles were dispatched.

Another car suddenly blew up, and the people in the park who'd been heading for their cars wilted back. The sounds of screams and crying children could clearly be heard.

The fire department showed up and began to put out the flames that had ignited several other vehicles. The bomb squad screeched into the parking lot.

"What in the hell is going on?" Mav asked.

"I don't like this," Ace said. They all huddled together as Ace looked around the crowds, searching for faces that appeared out of place. He couldn't find any—just a hell of a lot of terrified folks.

The cops showed up, and Ace immediately approached them. Several members of the force began speaking to civilians.

"Did you see anything?" Officer Michelson asked.

"Yeah, I saw my truck get blown up," Nick replied with a growl.

"No, we didn't see who did it," Ace said.

"There have been other vehicles getting blown up. We think it's a group of radicals trying to prove a point," the officer told them.

"Are you sure about that?" Ace asked.

Dakota was listening to every word spoken. What else could it be? What wasn't the police officer telling them?

"No, we aren't sure, but there was another call an hour ago on the east side of the city."

They finished speaking with the officer and then had to wait as Cooper's vehicle was checked. It was fine, and they were free to go. It was tense when they got in the car. They all needed to go home and figure this out.

CHAPTER TWENTY-FIVE

Ace paced his brother's living room as he went through every curse word he could think of. He'd just gotten off the phone with Bill again, and his boss assured him no one was coming after him. He'd yelled, he'd threatened, he'd told the man to dig deeper. His brother's truck getting blown up couldn't be a coincidence.

His brothers were sitting there waiting for him to calm down, and it wasn't happening yet. He didn't even want to dull his senses with a glass of bourbon, though he was sure he could use it. *What if . . .* That was all he was thinking.

"You know, things do just happen," Cooper finally said.

Ace turned to him with an incredulous look. "Not to me they don't," he said through clenched teeth. He forced himself to calm down enough so his brothers would truly hear him. "I've lived in this evil portion of the world for a very long time. When you let down your defenses and relax, that's when people strike."

"I agree you've lived in a world that is full of distrust and evil, but you're back home now," Nick pointed out.

"And trouble has seemed to follow me," Ace told him.

"Or maybe shit just happens," Mav said.

"Yeah, like hoodlums blowing up my truck," Nick muttered. His shock was gone, and now he was filled with rage.

"Whoever did that will pay," Ace promised his brother. "And I'll get you a new truck."

Nick shook his head. "She can't be replaced," he said.

"I'm so sorry," Ace said. "I feel like it's my fault."

Nick was quiet for a minute, and then he smiled at Ace. It didn't seem to him like there was anything to smile about at this particular moment, but Nick had always been the one to see the rainbow at the end of the storm.

"I don't think this has anything to do with you, but even if it did, we're family. If one of us is in trouble, then we all are," Nick assured him.

"If the evidence comes in that someone is after you, we have your back," Cooper added.

"We're the four musketeers," Mav said with a grin.

"I don't know. I just don't know," Ace said. Maybe he was seeing danger where there wasn't any. But his gut had never steered him wrong before. He wasn't sure what to think.

"We should check on the ladies," Cooper told them.

"Lindsey and Stormy are putting the kids to bed, and Chloe and Dakota are talking. I think they'd rather be alone," Nick said.

"Yeah, it's been an intense few days," Mav admitted.

"I'm having a hard time backing off. If something happens to Dakota and it's my fault, I don't think I'll ever be able to forgive myself," Ace said.

"If something happens to her, I'm sure you'll be the one to save her," Nick pointed out.

"I'm no hero, and certainly not a knight in shining armor," Ace told them.

"She sure as hell looks at you like you are," Cooper said.

Ace had never wanted to be a hero, but the thought of Dakota seeing him as one did make him want to change his bad-boy reputation. She had far too much influence over him and over how he felt. He just wasn't sure how to process that information.

"Let's relax, maybe have a drink. If something is going on, I'm sure Bill will call you back."

"He damn well better," Ace said. He looked over at the liquor cabinet longingly, but he couldn't let his guard down right now—not yet. He didn't think the danger had passed, and he had a feeling it was going to get a lot worse before it got better. But seeing as he was the only person who believed that, maybe he did need to chill.

He didn't know. He felt as if he didn't know anything anymore.

CHAPTER
TWENTY-SIX

It seemed like any other normal day. Well, it would seem like any normal day for a regular family. But the day was odd for Ace. His family wanted him to go on like nothing was happening around him, but it was impossible for him to relax and enjoy himself with his gut tied in knots.

Dakota had insisted on everyone attending a charity event addressing violence against women. The other cheerleaders were all going. His sisters-in-law were thrilled to attend, leaving Ace the only one protesting. He'd been outnumbered. Ace hadn't been in the loop with his family in a very long time, and he couldn't say he'd attended any sort of event like this one before, but it would be much better if he wasn't so damn worried about something bad happening.

"Stop being paranoid," Dakota whispered in his ear.

"With strange things continually happening, I can't relax," he told her.

"Everything will be okay. I'm not allowing a few unfortunate events to alter my life. No way, no how," Dakota said. "Then all the villains of the world win."

"The guns they have make them victors," Ace told her.

"This event raises a lot of money for charity. You're simply going to have to suck it up and enjoy yourself. The event will have lots of security. No bad guys have been invited," she assured him.

"I know it's been a bad few days. And trust me, I'm unhappy about losing my truck, but we're all fine. In the end, that's what matters," Nick said as he eyed the crowd. He might be saying those words, but he was obviously growing a little suspicious himself.

"Your wife insisted we support Dakota in this, so you're just trying to stay on her good side," Ace grumbled.

"When you are married, you'll understand how important it is to make your wife happy," Nick assured him.

"I'm never getting married, so that's not something I will ever have to worry about," Ace responded.

He was glad Dakota had walked away to join her team. As a couple, she and Ace were nowhere near ready to talk about long-term commitment. Still, saying those words to his brother sent a pang through him. He didn't want Dakota to hear his feelings on marriage.

Maybe it was because she wasn't your typical woman. Normally he could sleep with a lady and forget about her by the time he woke up the next morning. That hadn't been the case with Dakota—not from the first moment she'd smiled at him in that perfectly sassy way she had. He didn't know how he was ever going to walk away from her. And he was scheduled to do that in just over a week.

The night could have been a fun adventure, but he couldn't relax. He ate a meal he didn't taste, his eyes constantly scanning the crowd for danger. Dakota moved through the room with ease, talking and laughing with big donors, making a lot of money for the charity.

There were too many people crowded into the glitzy hotel ballroom. He was constantly on the move as he made sure to keep Dakota in sight at all times. With her face flashed across television screens all across the United States, it wasn't as if he could easily hide her. He would be grateful when football season was over. That was a thought he'd never believed he'd have.

Cooper was speaking to Ace when Dakota walked through the crowd, her smile lighting her way as she approached him. Ace didn't hear a word Coop said to him. All his attention was focused on the beautiful woman coming straight at him.

"I'm going to be out of your sight for a few minutes. It's time for us to perform," she said. "I didn't want you to cause a riot when I go backstage."

"I will come with you," he told her.

"Not a chance. We have security back there. You sit down and have coffee while you enjoy the show."

Ace put his arm behind her back and pulled her to him, her eyes instantly dilating as she looked up at him and bit her bottom lip, something that drove him to insanity.

"You should learn to listen more," he told her, a low growl in his throat.

"And you should know that only good boys are rewarded," she said before giving him a quick kiss and then pulling from his arms.

He had no doubt she was adding a little extra sashay to her ass as she left him, knowing his eyes would be on her delicious rump. His brother's laughter pulled him from the dark place his thoughts had sent him.

"I think marriage is on the horizon for you much sooner than you think," Cooper told him.

"I can desire a woman without wanting to put a ring on her finger," Ace snapped.

"Yeah, there's desire, and then there's obsession. From the moment I met Stormy, I was a lost cause."

"That's you, brother, not me," Ace told him.

But he did feel lost as soon as Dakota was out of sight. He again tried to reassure himself it was only because of the current situation. If danger didn't seem to be lurking behind every dark corner, he wouldn't feel this unbelievable need to be with her twenty-four-seven.

The lights dimmed in the large room. Only the stage was illuminated now as a well-known host stepped out, a microphone in his hand. He announced a special treat for all the guests and asked them to sit.

Ace was much too restless to sit anywhere. He stayed where he was, with Cooper on one side of him and Maverick showing up on his other. All of them stared at the stage. Nick was sitting at a table with their wives, but even he was on alert. Nothing had been out of place the entire evening, but that still didn't make Ace feel better.

Music started, and the curtains pulled back. Ace let out a relieved breath when Dakota sashayed onto the stage with the rest of the cheerleaders. Ace felt the tension leave his shoulders as he enjoyed their choreographed routine. The way Dakota could twist and bend gave him a whole heck of a lot of ideas he'd love to implement when the two of them were alone.

As much as he enjoyed the show, he was more than grateful when it ended. The night had gone off without a hitch, but he still wanted nothing more than to leave this elaborate event. Dakota was too far away from him. He wanted to get back to his brother's place, where he felt a lot more secure.

Dakota stepped back out into the main crowd, and he wanted to break a few necks when people swarmed her, congratulating her on a beautiful performance and promising to write a nice, fat check to the charity.

She stroked egos and smiled, softly touched people on their arms, told each person they were special. Ace's gut tightened more when a businessman got a bit too handsy with her.

"Not the time," Mav said as Ace tried to rush in and stake his territory.

"That man is making a pass at her," Ace growled.

"Half the men in here have been doing that with all the girls. They handle it well, and they are making a lot of money for people who need it," Mav said.

"I don't think you'd be so calm if it was your wife flirting for money," Ace told him.

Mav tensed next to him for a brief moment. "Well, you have me there, but Dakota isn't your wife, is she?" Mav pointed out.

Ace sent his brother a cloudy look before pulling out of his grasp. He walked straight to Dakota and slipped his arm around her back, staring at the man she'd been talking with. He didn't punch him like he wanted to do, but he offered a forced smile instead.

"Ace Armstrong," he said, holding out his hand.

"Eric Winters," the man replied. "I haven't seen you at any of these events."

"You go to a lot of them?" Ace asked. He kept his tone civil, even though he was feeling feral.

"I believe in giving back, and I'm a huge Seahawks fan," Eric said.

"I've become a much bigger fan since meeting Dakota," Ace said, his hand possessively holding her perfect hip.

"Thanks again for coming, Eric. It's always a pleasure to have you here," Dakota said, giving the man her sweetest smile. It made Ace want to punch the guy in his perfect jaw.

Knowing he was dismissed, Eric told them both good-bye and walked away. "What in the hell was that about?" Dakota asked, no longer smiling.

"I missed you," Ace said.

"You knew I was going to be busy tonight. I warned you before we left the house," she said.

"I don't like watching you flirt with other men," Ace said. His own smile was long gone.

"That's part of the job, Ace," she said with a roll of her eyes.

"You aren't available to flirt with any other man but me," he told her. He knew that was exactly the wrong thing to say, but he was leaving soon. He couldn't call her his. He wouldn't be around to ensure she would be.

"What gives you the right to enforce such a rule?" she asked. He could see that fiery temper she'd told him she'd often used with her brothers. Maybe it should bother him more, but the fire in her eyes just made him admire her more.

"We're together," he said. For now, at least.

"Just because we are having a good time doesn't mean I belong to you," she told him.

Her words made him feel even more possessive. "You're mine," he said, his eyes narrowing. He didn't even try to analyze where these words were coming from.

"I belong to myself, Ace. Don't for one minute think you own me," she said, tugging against his hold.

"It's time to go." He needed to remind her what the two of them had together. He decided he was going to do it all night long.

"Maybe I don't want to leave yet," she said.

He just smiled at her as people passed by. This was going to be fun.

"We can walk out of here side by side, or I can throw you over my shoulder," he said pleasantly.

He could see that it took a few moments for her to process what he'd just said. Then her eyes lit on fire. She gave him a ferocious look that had his lower half throbbing with the need to take her.

"You're going to be very disappointed to learn I'm not some docile woman who will be at your call and beck," she snapped.

Ace smiled, deciding not to correct her. "I'll give you to the count of ten to decide what to do," he said.

"What?" This was growing more fun by the second.

"Ten . . . nine . . ."

"Are you seriously counting?" she gasped. She looked around as couples milled nearby. Ace would have no problem throwing her over his shoulder as he'd threatened, and she knew it. She was running out of numerals.

". . . four . . ."

"Let's go," she said. Obviously, she knew he wasn't bluffing.

Ace locked eyes with Cooper as he led Dakota from the room, and Cooper nodded at him. He'd let the rest of the group know it was time to leave. Ace was just grateful they'd all taken separate vehicles. He wanted Dakota all to himself. He didn't think he'd even last until they got home before he had to sate his hunger. It seemed lust took the edge off his paranoia.

They made it outside to the SUV he'd just bought. With everything that was going on, he'd decided his car was unsafe.

Suddenly, Dakota turned her wrath on him.

"Of all the foolish, macho-man, ridiculous behavior, this is so over-the-top, I don't even know where to begin," she snapped as she poked his chest.

Ace just grinned at her. "Damn, you're amazing," he said.

He pushed her against the side of the SUV, his body pressed tightly against hers.

"What are you doing?" she asked. But her voice had gone from irritated to hungry.

"What I probably shouldn't," he said. "But I need a taste right now."

Talking stopped as he took those lips the way he'd wanted to all night. He wanted to be sure everyone knew she was off the market. Truth be told, he was completely and utterly owned by this woman. With the snap of her fingers, she could have him on his knees, begging her to never let him go. He was too enthralled with her to let that thought scare him. She was his. But he was also hers.

When Ace finally came up for air, he realized he was out in the open with her with too many people around. That wasn't good. "We should get going," he told her, his voice strained.

"Is there a problem, Ace?" she asked in a husky voice. The little minx had a knowing look in her eyes. She knew what she was doing to him, and she enjoyed the power. That was the problem with a woman like Dakota. She held far too much power in the relationship.

"Yeah, I have a definite problem," he told her, taking her hand and pressing it to his pulsing arousal.

"That doesn't seem like a problem to me," she said as her fingers stroked over him, nearly making him come in his pants.

A scuffling in the parking lot made Ace stand at attention, his desire lessening as someone shouted. There were a lot of people leaving. He was sure it was nothing. The hair on the back of his neck had been standing on end since Dakota had been attacked. It was nothing new.

"He has a gun," someone yelled, and people in the parking lot scrambled to hide.

"Get down!" he yelled to Dakota half a second before several gunshots rang out, shattering the joyous voices of just a moment before.

Ace reached for his gun—he had refused to leave it at home. He glanced at Dakota, who was white-faced, her mouth open in shock. *There* was the sign of danger he'd been wanting to see in her eyes. Too bad it had taken another gunshot for her to take his unease seriously.

"Get in," he told her, thrusting open the door to the SUV. Ace crouched down, gun in hand. Another shot rang out, this one hitting the pavement where Dakota had just been standing. Two more shots rang out, and the only thing Ace cared about was getting Dakota the hell out of there.

There was no way *this* was a coincidence.

His heart thundered as he shoved himself into the SUV, pushing Dakota down as he revved the engine, his gun hanging out the window as he looked for the shooter. He was nowhere in sight.

Peeling out of the parking lot to the sound of police sirens in the distance and more shots, Ace's adrenaline continued pumping as he made a swift left. Another shot rang out, shattering his back window, hitting the passenger headrest. Ace had been in many sticky situations before, but never had he been so damn scared.

After he turned another corner, no more gunshots rang out, and he knew he was out of the shooter's range. Still, Ace didn't slow the car for even a second as he made his way down the road, taking side streets and altering his course to throw off anyone who might be tracking them.

Dakota spoke to him, but Ace held up a hand as he concentrated on where he was going. He was listening for more gunshots. She quickly took the hint. He felt bad as he glanced at her, huddled down in her seat, fear making her body tremble uncontrollably.

Though she'd been in danger at her place, the men hadn't drawn their weapons until he'd arrived and taken over. He punched in Cooper's number. His brother answered immediately.

"Are you all safe?" Ace asked.

"Yeah, why?" Cooper asked, seeming confused.

"A man opened fire at the stadium," Ace said. "Are you still inside?" What the hell. Ace was getting ready to turn back around.

"No, we all left while you were . . . um . . . having some time with Dakota against your vehicle," Coop said.

"Good. We're on our way," Ace said. He knew he should head in another direction. He now had no doubt that these acts were deliberate. Someone was after him, and going to his brother's place was putting his family in danger. But right now, he didn't have anywhere else to go. He had to protect Dakota as well as his family. And if whoever was doing this was openly attacking him now, Ace had no doubt they knew where Coop lived.

They drove for a good fifteen minutes before the tenseness in Ace's shoulders let up. He was still on alert, but at least he was speeding away from the danger.

"I'm sorry, Dakota," he finally said.

"Who is doing this?" she asked, still doubled over, her eyes facing the floor, her body shaking.

"I don't know," he admitted.

"I'm sorry," she said, on the verge of tears.

"It's not your fault, Dakota. None of this is," he said, forcing his voice to lower. She was scared enough as it was. She didn't need him making it worse for her. "It's mine. I should have figured this out sooner."

"Don't put all of this on your shoulders," she insisted.

"We just need to get to my brother's place, then we can get all of this figured out," Ace said.

Slowly Dakota sat up in the seat next to him. He glanced at her, impressed when he saw the determination on her face. Her lips were tightly clasped together. She stared at him.

"What?" he finally asked, wishing he could read her mind.

"You saved me again," she finally said, her eyes filled with awe. He didn't want her to feel that for him. He knew he would fail her if she did. He chose to stay quiet instead of responding.

She seemed to want something from him, so Ace reached across the space between them and gave her hand a reassuring squeeze as he looked into her brave eyes for a brief moment. They were going to be okay. He wouldn't rest until they were.

CHAPTER TWENTY-SEVEN

His phone rang, and he looked down to see Bill calling him back. He hit the green button on his wheel and waited to see what the man had to say. If he again told Ace he wasn't in danger, Ace wouldn't be responsible for his own actions.

"Ace?" Bill said after a moment, obviously irritated Ace wasn't speaking.

"I'm here," Ace said through clenched teeth. "You better have something for me, because I'm getting really tired of shit happening."

"You were right," Bill said, tightness in his tone. "Someone is after you."

Ace was silent for a beat as he tried to wrap his mind around his boss's tone. He knew someone was after him, but to have it confirmed nearly made his throat close. He was responsible for the threat against Dakota . . . and his family.

"Tell me," Ace said through his tight jaw.

"We know who it is," Bill said.

Ace's blood ran cold.

"Where did you get the information?" Ace asked.

"Isn't it more important to find out who it is?" Bill asked.

"Don't mess with me, Bill. Where did the information come from? I want to know that first before a name is thrown at me. I need to know if I even trust it," Ace said.

"This came from ops. It's legitimate," Bill told him.

His gut told him Bill was speaking the truth. "Who is it, Bill?"

There was a pause on the other end of the line that made Ace ground his back teeth together as he waited. The only thing that kept him from yelling at the man was the fact that Dakota was sitting next to him. He couldn't even look at her, didn't want to see the accusation in her eyes.

"It's Nestor Pavlov," Bill finally said.

"Pavlov?" Ace was now confused. "Explain."

Bill sighed. "We've found out that Anton has a brother. Obviously, he's seeking revenge."

"Why in the hell didn't we have this information before? We were on this case for years!" Ace thundered, forgetting about Dakota next to him. The fury in his voice echoed through the car and made her jump in her seat. Her eyes were huge as she stared at him, her fingers wrapping around the door handle. It was a good thing it was locked or he feared she might try to jump out.

"Sorry," he muttered at her, but he couldn't cover up the rage boiling within him.

She didn't say a word as her hand lifted to her chest. She rested it over her heart, which had to be thundering. This night wasn't going well for her—hell, the past couple of weeks hadn't gone too well. She'd not been safe since he'd stepped into her life. He was sure she was regretting the moment the two of them had met.

"He apparently is a half brother and was disowned by their father. Now that he's the last living relative, he's coming after you for revenge. I don't know why, though, as it doesn't appear there's any love in this damn family," Bill told him.

"I guess it doesn't matter at the end of the day," Ace said with a sigh. "Even when I gave my brothers every reason in the world to hate me, they never let me go."

Ace realized he was showing far too much vulnerability, in both his voice and his words. He instantly pushed his emotions back down to where they belonged and focused on the conversation at hand.

"We need a team on this, Ace," Bill told him.

"I have a team. I'll take care of it," he replied.

"You can't go rogue after this man," Bill warned.

"You told me my vacation is over. I'm officially back on duty," Ace informed his boss.

"You know what I mean," Bill said.

"I don't trust anyone, Bill. Don't ask me to fight you on this," Ace said.

Ace could practically see the steam spiraling off Bill's head the longer the conversation lasted. He also knew he'd won this round, which wasn't an easy feat on a normal day, not that this was a normal situation.

"Okay, then. Come to the office tomorrow and we'll strategize," Bill finally said.

"I will," Ace told him.

He hung up the phone and then slightly decreased his pressure on the gas pedal. He didn't need to get pulled over for speeding. The Pavlov family had ties in places that were unimaginable. He wondered if Nestor was as influential as his brother had been.

That's why his last mission had taken them so damn long. Ace had thought it was all over, had thought his life could return to some semblance of normalcy. He'd been wrong—so very wrong.

Now Ace didn't know how far Nestor's circle reached. He couldn't even trust the local police. His family was all he could turn to at this moment.

"Are we getting closer to the house?" Dakota asked.

"Yes," he said.

Dakota let out a sigh of relief. Maybe she wanted nothing more than to get away from him; he wasn't sure. She was in for a surprise, though, because he wasn't letting her out of his sight for a while, not without knowing exactly where Nestor was.

"Don't get too excited. It's gonna be you and me for a while," Ace said.

"I'm under witness protection," Dakota muttered.

"I'm not too bad a guy to have around," Ace told her.

She gave him a mocking look and then faced forward as he drove. That tingling on the back of his neck was there again, and he reached back and itched at the place. This night was only just beginning, and it had already been one hell of a day. At least he could never complain that life was boring—danger was a surety in his line of work.

They pulled up to the house, and Ace was tense. His brothers were waiting. Ace didn't waste any time telling them about the danger he'd brought to his family's doorstep.

"It's time for you guys to get out of here," Ace said. "They know where I am, and they know where you are."

"We're not leaving you, Ace," Cooper said. Nick and Mav nodded.

"This isn't up for negotiation," Ace thundered.

Cooper was silent for a few moments before he sighed and looked at his wife, who was white-faced as she stood next to Lindsey.

"We aren't hiding," Cooper finally agreed. Ace got ready to argue, but Cooper held up his hand. "However, we do need to get our wives and children out of here until we figure this out."

"Agreed," Nick said.

Stormy stood up. "We'll take the kids and get them settled," she said, "then we'll come back. We won't be able to stand by while this is happening. We'll go back and forth."

There was more arguing, but eventually Ace and his brothers agreed. Ace determined this would end, and it would end soon.

CHAPTER TWENTY-EIGHT

Ace was flanked by Cooper and Maverick, while Nick stood in front as they entered the secure building where they were meeting with Bill. Nick had been beyond ticked all morning. It was all fun and games until your truck got blown to smithereens. Now he knew the reason why.

Nestor had officially gone too far in his revenge scheme. No one else was going to get hurt. And there wouldn't be any further property damage, either, if Ace had his way. Ace was in his zone—he was one hundred percent the agent he'd been for nearly the past decade as he moved with ease, knowing exactly who he was.

Moving across the room, they came to the reception desk, where an alert woman sat. She remained emotionless as the four hulking men approached her, showing various scowls on their faces. "I'm here for a meeting with Bill Hammond," Ace said. The woman looked down at her screen before meeting his eyes again.

"Name?" she asked. Though Ace was sure she knew exactly who he was.

"Ace Armstrong."

"Yes, Bill is expecting you." She stood up, her sleek blue suit screaming all business and zero pleasure. That's how it was in the CIA, though. They weren't there for some frilly office party or just to earn a paycheck.

Being a part of the CIA was a calling. And though Ace was in full agent mode at the moment, he was beginning to wonder if his time was up. He didn't love it like he once had, and he didn't want to have to stay away from his family anymore, or from Dakota. When he had more than a few moments to breathe properly, maybe he would analyze that a bit more. Not today, though.

"Follow me," the woman told him. She looked at his brothers when they stepped forward with him. "The meeting was supposed to be one-on-one." She frowned disapprovingly at the other three men.

"It's been changed to four now. These are my brothers, and they're a part of it," Ace told her. His voice wouldn't tolerate any kind of argument from her.

The woman sat back down and lifted her phone to her ear. Ace internally rolled his eyes. He knew how this game worked, but they were wasting time, and he was annoyed. She hung up and stood again.

"Okay, this way."

They were led down a long hallway. When she reached an open door, she stepped aside and held her hand out for them to enter.

Ace was the first one in the door. He hadn't been to this particular building, but it seemed Bill had a decent setup here. A large desk sat at the back of the room, with papers scattered all over it. Two chairs faced the desk. There was a worn leather couch in the back of the room and an empty coffeepot on the table next to it.

Bill stood as Ace entered the room. He scanned Ace's brothers before his eyes returned to Ace. He must have deemed them trustworthy, because he didn't seem on high alert.

"Glad to see you here, Ace. I'm sorry it took us so long to figure this out," Bill said as he stepped out and shook Ace's hand.

"Do you have any useful information for me?" Ace asked, wanting to get directly to the point.

Though Bill was only in his early fifties, a life of chasing criminals had aged him. Dark circles were a permanent fixture on his face, and his lips rarely ever turned up into a smile. He'd been divorced twice and never got to see his children. That, almost more than anything else, had Ace thinking it was time to get out of the CIA. He didn't want to end up bitter and alone in some crappy apartment in a city filled with crime. Before coming back to where he'd grown up, he'd had no idea how important his home life was to him.

"I think we have valid information, but I'm having a difficult time knowing who I can trust at the moment. I only have six agents here in this building with me, and they are men I would risk my life for . . . so at least here, we're secure," Bill replied.

"I'm not sure I trust anyone but my family and you at this point," Ace told the man.

"Yeah, I can see why you feel that way, but not everyone is a bad guy in disguise, Ace," Bill said.

"That's not what I'm experiencing right now," Ace argued.

"You can't do this on your own, so you're not going to get much of a choice in getting assistance. I have a plan I want to go over with you, but you have to be willing to cooperate for it to work," Bill told him. "You were on a case that went very public. We knew there could be some consequences from it. Now, we're facing some of those. When we catch up to Nestor, we will get him behind bars, and this will be over."

"Until another long-lost sibling emerges," Ace muttered.

"Trust me, I've been through this case with a fine-tooth comb, and I don't see how anyone could have known this was coming. Nestor wasn't a part of this family. There were no documents until he stepped up and took ownership."

"I don't want to look back at what could have been done differently, I want to know what we're going to do from here on out," Ace said.

"We got the shooter from last night. He's been interrogated, and we got some information from him," Bill said.

That stopped Ace from speaking for a moment. He would really like to get his hands on even just one of the men who had put Dakota in danger. That had been an unforgivable offense.

"How do you know he isn't just feeding you a line of crap?" Ace asked.

"We don't know for sure, but he seems more than willing to cooperate to save his own ass," Bill said.

"Maybe *we* should talk to him," Mav piped in.

"That's not going to happen," Bill told Ace's overeager brother. Ace had been thinking the same, though. Great minds and all.

"The agent told us Nestor is pissed. You were an outsider invited into his family home while he wasn't. Then you killed off his brother. He feels he will never get to make the connection he so desperately wanted with Anton. Sounds like he has some issues of his own to resolve, and you have become the focus of his wrath. He wants you dead."

"I know he wants me dead. The bullets flying at my head tell me that much," Ace said with a huff.

"He's willing to kill anyone in his way—not only willing, but glad to do it," Bill said. "Apparently, torture and murder come easily to him. He likes to terrorize his victims before he does them in."

"Sounds like just another day at the office," Ace said with a humorless laugh.

"You might not like the plan I've come up with," Bill said.

Ace was ready for this to end, so he didn't care how it had to happen.

"Why don't you just spill it so we can prepare?" Cooper said, losing patience with this entire meeting. Ace could understand how his brother was feeling. He wanted it over with too.

There was a window in the back of the room. Ace moved over to it while Bill shuffled through the papers on his desk. There was a perfect view of Mount Rainier from where he was standing, and for some reason, it calmed him.

He'd hiked that mountain many times in his youth, had spent a lot of time there skiing with his brothers as well. He'd been away from home for a long time, and even with the bad guys still on his heels, he was where he belonged, and he had no doubt this would get fixed.

Ace didn't believe he was invincible, but he had been in sticky situation after sticky situation throughout most of his adult life. For that matter, he'd been just as reckless as a child and felt he had cheated death on more occasions than the average person.

What mattered most, he'd discovered, was not the adventure of cheating death, but the serenity of being back home. He'd lived out of the country for years and then back in the United States only when he hadn't thought he could take it any longer. Any time he'd come nearer to home, or had sneaked in to take peeks at his family, the heaviness in his chest had decreased.

This was no different. Yes, he was being hunted, but he was with his family. That made this whole ordeal easier. Finally, he turned away from the window and looked at his brothers, who were leaning over Bill's desk, looking at a paper he'd laid out.

"We can do this," he said. His tone was hushed, but it caught the attention of the four other men in the room. They looked up and waited.

"I'm not going to stand around and wait for this man to destroy what I want to build. Let's hear your plan, Bill," he said. He moved to stand beside his brothers.

"All righty, then," Bill said with his smirk smile. "We're going to use you for bait."

No one said a thing. A pin dropping on a vat full of cotton could have been heard. Maybe Ace should have been afraid, but he wasn't. His lips turned up as he looked at Bill and nodded.

"Let's do it."

Ace tuned out his brothers' protesting voices. They didn't believe this was the wisest plan. It was the only way they were going to draw Nestor out, though. The man was very good at hiding behind his goons, but the chance to personally get at Ace would be too much for him to resist. He'd have to show his face—and then this would end.

He was ready—he was more than ready, in fact. He actually felt damn good about what was going to happen.

CHAPTER TWENTY-NINE

Dakota stood in the cottage, not a muscle moving in her entire body as she listened to Ace try to explain how putting himself in danger wasn't the most idiotic plan she'd ever heard in her entire life. She schooled her expression, not wanting him to see how upset she was, afraid if she showed it he wouldn't finish telling her what his plans were.

There wouldn't be a way for her to stop him from acting the utter fool if she didn't know what was going on. She'd learned that much from growing up with brothers who were bred to be idiots. She'd identified *their* idiocy by the time she was three.

When she was sure Ace had finished his entire explanation, Dakota hugged herself, her body tense. It was either that or she feared she was going to come unglued and smack the guy in the head for being such an idiot.

"No." Just the one word slipped from her lips. Ace looked at her, clearly not understanding.

"What do you mean?" he asked. He was finally tuning in to her body language. For such an observant guy, he could sure be clueless sometimes.

"This is a foolish plan that only leads to you getting yourself killed," she told him. Now she wasn't even trying to hide her worry or fear. He'd told her his plans, and she'd told him they sucked.

Ace slowly moved toward her, afraid she might bolt. It was very dangerous for him to come toward her right now. She might just have to tie him down and not let him go anywhere.

Ace cupped her cheek as he looked into her eyes, utter confidence shining from his crystal-clear green depths. His confidence and independence were some of his best qualities, but at this moment, she would rather he not have quite so much arrogance.

"He won't kill me, Dakota. I'm not going to let it happen," Ace told her. "I know his family, know how they operate. This was a four-year mission for me, the most dangerous one by far. I might not have known Nestor was a part of the family, but I know what he was taught, because I learned everything about each and every one of the other family members. His overconfidence will be his undoing."

"Or your own might be yours," she told him.

"You have too little faith in me," he said.

Dakota didn't cry often, but she felt the sting of tears in her eyes as he spoke to her. She wrapped her arms around him and held on tight as she pushed back the urge to cry. That wasn't going to help the situation at all.

"It's not about having faith in you. It's about you trying to be a hero. I want you to be the man who is safe and sound, not the one stepping into gunfire," she told him.

"I can't be that man, Dakota, not for anyone. I couldn't live with myself," he said. His hand was weaving through her hair, and the gentle caress contrasted sharply with his words. His denial confused her.

"You are that man with me. You have done nothing but be a good man," she said.

"That's because you bring it out in me. You make me think of things I've never imagined before. But please don't ask me to be anything other than who I am," he said, his words almost sounding like a plea.

"I just want you to have a healthy fear of the man and the situation," she said.

"The man is a coward beneath it all," Ace assured her. "He hides behind his family name, behind the stolen weapons and drug money, and behind the goons he hires to do his dirty work. The only way to draw him out is to wound his pride. I don't fear cowards," Ace said, his voice tight. "I can't turn my back on this."

Dakota had been holding herself so tightly, she began to tremble in his arms. She would never respect a man who asked her to be anything other than who she was, so how could she ask him to change who he was? She couldn't. She just wished she'd maybe started to fall in love with an accountant. Life with an accountant would never stress her out this way. Boredom was looking pretty dang appealing at the moment.

"What if this all goes wrong?" she asked.

"We plan for it to go wrong," Ace told her. "That way we aren't taken by surprise. He will lose this battle, because his rage and pride will take him down as much as I will."

"You are hoping for that outcome," she told him. "He might be thinking the exact same thing, while working with a cool head."

"Criminals aren't rational, Dakota. He doesn't have someone like I have you, like I have my brothers. The people in his life are his employees. They are only loyal to him when times are good. They will turn on him quickly to save their own skins. He has no true allies. I have something to live for other than rage and pride. I have my family . . ." He paused, and she felt his steady heartbeat against her ear as she snuggled closer, wanting to hold on to him forever. "I have you," he finished in a whisper.

Her own heart thudded hard at his words. She wanted to ask him what he meant by that. But she was afraid to open that can of sweet peas at this moment. Some things just needed to stay tightly sealed where they were safe.

"I'm not planning on going anywhere. Just promise me you're not going to sneak off without telling me."

"It might be better if you don't know when this is going down," Ace said.

His hands were rubbing up and down her back. He was trying to get her mind off this conversation. She hated him a little for it, but he was beginning to succeed. His passionate words were making it hard for her to concentrate on the dangers of this mission.

"Don't do that to me, Ace. You owe me more than a note on the nightstand when you disappear," she said.

He sighed, his warm breath cascading over her head. "I won't sneak away," he promised.

"And you need to promise to come back to me. Don't let this man win," she insisted.

He stilled in her arms, and she wondered what she'd said to catch his attention. His hands resumed their languid movement on her back, slipping lower to feather over her butt and then drift back up to her hair.

"You want me to come back to you, huh?" he said, a smile in his voice.

"There's that pride," she told him, a smile in her own voice.

"When a woman as amazing as you is begging me to come back to her, I can feel a little bit of pride," he insisted.

"You're hopeless, Ace," she said, but she leaned back to look into his eyes.

"And you're unforgettable," he said.

"I take pride in that," she told him.

"Nothing is going to happen tonight, so why don't we try to forget about it for a while?" he suggested.

"I think those are the best words to come out of your mouth all night," she told him.

He winked at her before taking a step back and looking at her. The need to be in his arms was so great, she had to force herself not to take that step forward to get close to him again. She really did need him too damn much.

"I'm taking a bath," she said with a smile meant to entice him. She turned and began moving toward the bedroom, hearing him right behind her. Taking off her shirt as she walked, she enjoyed the intake of breath from him as he admired her back.

She had always taken pride in the person she was, deciding from a young age that if she didn't like something about herself, she was the only person who had the power to make the change she needed. She'd maintained that philosophy her entire life. If she wanted to have long hair, short hair, muscles, extra weight, or a lean build, it was all up to her. She respected herself, and she was happy because of it. She loved the look of awe in Ace's eyes as he gazed at her. She knew the same look was on her face as she looked upon him.

They entered the bathroom together. Dakota turned on the tub and added some lightly scented soap. Then she turned to find Ace bare of clothes. Damn, he took her breath away.

Looking into his eyes, she stripped the rest of her clothing away, feeling vulnerable and needy all at the same time. Ace pulled her to him, their hot flesh scorching each other. He finally kissed her, taking the rest of her worries away as pure need shot through her.

His hands stroked her flesh until the tub was full. She turned the faucet off as he stepped into the water and sank down. He held his hands out to her. She took them and slipped into the hot water, leaning her back into him.

Ace immediately pulled her tightly to him as he slipped his arms around her waist. She sighed as he kissed her neck, his thickness resting against her, making her squirm in front of him.

"I can't seem to get enough of you, Ace Armstrong," she said.

"I know exactly how you feel, Dakota Forbes," he replied.

With his arms wrapped around her middle, his fingers splayed on her stomach, and his thumbs pressing against the undersides of her breasts, Dakota was quickly losing the ability to speak. He moved up and rubbed the bottoms of her breasts, making them feel heavy and achy.

She pushed herself even more tightly against him, loving the feel of his erection pressed so tightly against the softness of her behind. Her only thought was how simple it would be to lift up and sit on him—and of how good that would feel for both of them.

She reached out and touched his legs on either side of hers. The bathwater was hot, but his flesh was downright scorching, making her breathing uneven and labored. Ace finally reached his hands up and cupped her breasts. He groaned against the back of her neck as he squeezed them, his palms pressed against her hard nipples.

When he opened his mouth and sucked her neck, she arched up, a moan escaping her lips. She ached so badly for this man that she couldn't think of anything other than him—as long as he was touching her, her worries floated away. She was filled with need, and he wasn't moving quickly enough for her.

"Please love me," she said. She arched into him and his hands squeezed her breasts in utter reverence before he moved a hand down the plane of her belly and slipped it over her slick flesh below. She moaned again as she opened her thighs to him, not easy to do with his legs pressed against the outsides of them. He dipped a finger inside her, her heat and wetness making his access easy.

Dakota turned her head. He took her lips while his hands played with her body. She was eager, ready, and she knew beyond a doubt that she was *his*. She wasn't at all frightened at how easily she surrendered to him. He tasted her lips before deepening the kiss, driving their excitement to unbearable levels.

Finally, she needed more. She twisted in his arms, wanting him inside her. He pulled her over him to straddle his lap, and he deepened their kiss. She teased him with her tongue, passing it into his mouth before retreating in slow, lazy sweeps until she was ready to explode.

Dakota pressed down on him, her slickness sliding along his erection, and he thrust upward, wanting them to be connected as much as she did, but she pulled back, teasing him as she bit down on his lower lip. He reached between them, finding her breasts again and squeezing her nipples hard in punishment.

She gasped into his mouth in pleasure and ground against him again. All traces of frustration were gone from both of them as they played with each other, stoking their desire to incredible heights.

"I need you so much, Ace," she told him before her lips trailed down his jaw. She sucked the flesh of his neck before biting it. She quickly soothed the sting by licking him.

"You have me," he assured her as he reached into her hair and tugged her back so they could see into each other's eyes. She felt a thrill of passion. She knew she brought that look of lust into his eyes, and only she could sate his need.

"Then take all of me," she demanded.

There was no more teasing, no more hesitation as Ace pulled his hips back and grabbed her behind with one hand, positioning her over him. He thrust upward and sank fully into her slick body. Not even the water could wash away their desire.

Dakota screamed as he filled her, and Ace grabbed her mouth and absorbed the sound before he gripped her hips and began moving her up and down over his thickness as he thrust into her.

Her breasts bobbed against his chest, her nipples rubbing his skin as he slid in and out of her. Their moans were swallowed up by the splashing water, and Dakota felt her head spinning as she climbed closer to the climax she so desperately needed.

"Yes, Ace, make me come," she cried before leaning down and biting his shoulder, where she stayed anchored as her body began clenching around him.

"Yeah, baby, let go with me," he demanded.

She cried out again as her orgasm ripped through her, clenching his arousal. Ace let go with her, their pleasure one as they pulsed together with the intensity of their release. She shook in his arms as he held her tight, until finally she collapsed against his chest, her breathing erratic.

She was exhausted. He held her tightly in his grasp, his arousal resting deep within her heat. She didn't want to ever move from this beautiful place. She relished the feel of his hands moving along her back.

"Remember your promise to me," she told him.

He was quiet for a moment. She wanted to know exactly what was going through his mind. If she could have any superpower, it would be to read thoughts.

"I will," he promised again.

They sat in the tub until the water cooled, then he took her to the bedroom and made slow, sweet love to her, sealing his promise with much more than a kiss.

CHAPTER THIRTY

Ace was busy over the next few days, having meetings with Bill and a special team along with his brothers. The more he met with this group, the more nervous Dakota became. He had made a promise to her that he wasn't going to put himself out there as bait without telling her. Yet she feared he was so confident in his plans, he might go through with the mission quietly and only tell her it was over when all the danger had passed.

This made her watch him all the more. Still, they fell into a comfortable routine as the two of them retreated to Coop's cottage each night. It seemed that the longer this danger went on, the more they clung to each other. Dakota knew it was only because it was a high-stress situation, but that didn't change her feelings about Ace.

She'd resisted falling in love for a very long time. She'd never found a man who stimulated her, made her feel like she was free-falling, and made her want to follow him wherever he chose to lead her. But this thing with Ace had been so intense from the beginning that she knew she was falling for him, knew that she most likely was already in love with him. The thought of anything bad happening to him made her entire body ache with a panic she couldn't quell no matter how badly she tried to push it back down. So each night as she snuggled into his arms, laughing, watching movies, talking for hours, or just silently being together, she fell a little bit deeper and deeper beneath his spell. And the longer this went on, the less she was frightened by it.

Dakota had a feeling she was getting to see a side of Ace not many people were fortunate enough to experience. He was in control and most certainly the king of his domain, but he was also tender and passionate. She loved all sides to his versatile personality.

The man insisted on holding doors open for her, making sure she was seated before he took his seat. He brought her morning coffee if she took too long to climb out of bed, and he made her meals that rivaled those of a gourmet cook. She wanted to know where he'd learned all these skills. She also noticed he didn't alter his behavior when his siblings were around. Attentiveness just seemed to come naturally to him.

Dakota had always been reliant on herself. Of course, she had a loving family she could depend on at any time, anywhere, and she had her best friend, who would drop everything to help her. But she'd never depended on a man before. Men had come and gone from her life. With Ace, it wasn't like that. She couldn't imagine a day without him. That frightened her, because she was losing some of her independence, which she had always clung so tightly to.

Who was she becoming? Would she like this new person if she were to analyze her too deeply? She wasn't sure. She'd been more than happy for Chloe when she'd fallen in love with Nick and had decided to marry him. Maybe she wasn't so frightened to be in a relationship anymore because she was with the right person.

With all the danger going on, she had agreed not to go to her cheer practices. It was her last year, and she might get cut from the team for not showing up. That hurt her pride a lot. But having been attacked a couple of times now, and with the FAA finding evidence that their plane had been tampered with, Dakota felt lucky to be alive. Still, the lack of freedom felt oppressive.

Ace stepped into the room she was sulking in. She turned to him with a forlorn look on her face.

"What's the matter?" he asked, carefully approaching her.

"I'm fine. I know Bill is waiting on you, so you should go," she told him.

"I have time for a kiss," he assured her.

Before she could even think about stopping him—which was actually the last thing on her mind—he grabbed her, knocked her off balance, and smoothly pulled her body against his. Even though they'd made love for hours the night before, one scorching touch of his chest against hers had her melting into him, her head thrown back to give him easy access to her lips.

Dakota didn't even try to hide the sound of approval that escaped her tight throat. She loved the spark of life in his beautiful light eyes. The attraction between the two of them was beyond hot, and she didn't see it ever fading.

"I hate walking away from you," he told her before kissing the corner of her mouth, making her squirm against him. She wanted so much more than a light peck from him. "And I hate it when you walk away from me," he added.

"But then you get to see me return," she pointed out, her hand slipping into his silky hair as she caressed his head.

"True," he said. Then he stopped trying to have a conversation and simply lowered his head, his mouth consuming hers in a kiss so hot, it was a wonder the floor didn't melt. She clung more tightly to him as she got lost in his touch, her body swaying. Ace's embrace was the only thing keeping her on her feet. She felt the evidence of his arousal against her stomach, making her squirm even more to draw closer to him.

Maybe she should just quit cheering, since she would most likely be fired anyway. Then she could have even more time with Ace.

As soon as she had that thought, she felt panic seep in. She'd promised herself her entire life she wouldn't be one of those women who gave up their dreams for anyone. If a man couldn't accept who she was, or didn't think her life was as important as his, then she had no business associating with him.

Though she didn't feel Ace treated her this way—at least not when there was no danger—she still pulled away from him. Maybe she needed to do some thinking. This thing between them continued to burn so fast and hot, she didn't know how to think about it.

"You have to go. They are waiting," she said when he leaned toward her again. He slowly opened his eyes, and though disappointment was obviously there, she knew they had to respect each other's obligations.

"Sorry. That was supposed to be a quick good-bye kiss," he said with a sheepish smile. "For some reason, the second I touch you, I lose all rational thought," he added with a laugh. "You might actually be a witch who has cast a spell on me."

"That might be the case. I have many talents I've yet to share with you," she told him with a wink.

He stepped closer to her, and she took a retreating step while she laughed.

"You shouldn't be allowed to get away with a statement like that," he told her.

"Oh, but I *am*," she said, taking another step back. "Because we will finish the conversation later . . . in the dark." She winked at him again, enjoying the glow filling her, even if it did scare her at the same time.

Dakota watched him walk away and felt an ache travel through her. What she needed now more than anything else was a small break to be by herself.

Changing clothes, she rushed from the cottage, glancing over her shoulder to make sure no one would stop her. She needed to take a walk and get her head clear before Ace came back. He was officially messing with her life if she couldn't think of anything other than him.

She made her way through the quiet streets of Cooper's neighborhood, knowing she couldn't go too far. She didn't want to get back late and then have to hear all about the dangers of being out on her own.

It just wasn't worth the lecture. But she figured she had a good hour or two to herself before she had to drag herself back and wait for Ace.

It wasn't that it was a hardship waiting for him, it was that she wanted him around her all the time. Knowing that was what she wanted made it clear just how stubborn and foolish she was being. She wasn't a weak woman, and she didn't need to lean on anyone. But with Ace's professional world leaking into his personal world, she was dealing with an element she'd only ever *heard* about. She'd never had any real-life experience with monsters before—not until they'd entered her house and threatened her because of her relationship with Ace.

She wasn't too far from the house when she heard someone behind her. Fear trickled down her neck and sent a shiver through her. It was light out, and she was sure it was some person who was also doing nothing more than taking a stroll. She had nothing to worry about.

She continued telling herself this until she was grabbed from behind. She let out one high-pitched scream before her mouth was covered and true fear invaded her all over again.

CHAPTER
THIRTY-ONE

Ace pulled back up to the house, cursing that he'd forgotten his phone. He needed to have it on him in case Dakota wanted to call. He avoided considering what it meant that he had to stay in constant contact with the woman.

He walked into the cottage and found her gone. He didn't like that one little bit. She had to be at the house. He moved quickly up to the main place and found she wasn't there, either. Where had she gone?

"I saw her sneak out through the front driveway," Stormy admitted when it appeared as if he was going to panic.

"And you didn't stop her?" Ace thundered.

"I figured she needed a minute by herself," Stormy said as she shifted on her feet.

Ace didn't say anything more. Instead he ran back to his car and peeled out of the driveway, his windows down as he frantically searched for her. He was sure there was nothing wrong, but he wouldn't feel better until he saw her.

He was pulling through an area where a trail started when he heard a scream. Without a second thought, he skidded to the side of the road, pulled out his gun, and began sprinting in the direction of the cry. He had no doubt that cry had come from her. What would have made her think taking a walk was a good idea?

Turning a corner, he found Dakota sprawled out on the ground. She whipped her head around, obvious relief filling her eyes at the sight of him. He didn't know whether to be relieved or throw her over his shoulder and smack her ass the entire way to his vehicle. Because they were in no way out of danger, he rushed to her and knelt down. He grabbed her arm to pull her to her feet, scanning the area around them the entire time.

"What happened? Why are you out here?" he fired off.

"Someone grabbed me," she told him, anger in her eyes. "I kicked him in the groin, surprising him, and he took off that way when he heard you," she said, pointing down the trail.

Ace was torn. He needed to get Dakota back to safety, but this might be his chance to catch the monster responsible for terrorizing her. But then again, it might just be another goon. He didn't know what to do.

"Go get him," she said, as if there was no other choice.

"I can't leave you alone," he told her, frustration mounting as the perpetrator ran farther away from them.

"I'll go right back to the house," she assured him.

"No, go back down the trail and get in my car. Drive back. I'll be right behind you," he told her. Then he ran off after her attacker. He hoped and prayed she listened to him for once in her life. The guy must have been watching the property for some time, just waiting for an opportunity—and that asshole had found it.

As Ace gained speed, he turned a corner and saw someone running at full speed up ahead, their head covered with a hat. Ace picked up his pace, his gun stable in his hand. He was going to get to this man, and he damn sure was going to make him talk.

A few seconds later, he heard the sound of traffic. He realized they were coming back out into the open. The man disappeared in front of him around another bend, and then Ace heard a vehicle peeling out. He moved even faster, his gun clutched in his fingers. He knew he was going to be too late, but that didn't stop him from trying to get to the guy.

When Ace broke out onto the street, traffic sped by, and he knew the guy was long gone. He had to get back to Dakota, and he had to do it now. Hopefully she'd listened and was at the house by now, but he went to where he'd parked his SUV instead. After all, she might not have left.

And what if this distraction had been their plan all along, and he'd played perfectly into their hands? The thought made his forehead break out in a cold sweat as he sped quickly back to the street where he'd slammed his car into park, praying he hadn't just handed her over to them. She'd be the ultimate bargaining chip. There was no way Ace was allowing the woman he loved to get hurt.

That thought sent his heart racing all over again, but he pushed it down. He didn't have time to panic. He had to get to Dakota and get her out of the open. Then he would be ready to take down Nestor. He'd die before he let that man hurt Dakota or anyone else in his family.

When he reached the street, he found Dakota standing by his vehicle. He felt his frustration growing. He was glad she was safe, but she should have done what he'd said—then she'd be safe with his family.

There were cars driving by and other people walking, so Ace quickly sheathed his weapon so he didn't scare the bystanders. But he didn't slow his pace. He wouldn't feel comfortable until he had Dakota in his vehicle and the two of them were back home.

Ace was still about four hundred yards away from Dakota when a vehicle with tinted windows raced down the road, doing a spin right in front of where she stood. Her head whipped up as she looked at Ace, a question in her eyes.

Ace was still running, but again, he was going to be too late. He had no doubt about it. He called out to her to get down, to roll beneath his

SUV. But she seemed to be in shock. It was all happening too fast. A few people were standing frozen on the sidewalk across the street, watching in confusion at the scene playing out before them.

The window on the car lowered, and though Ace reached for his weapon again, it was too late. A shot rang out, and he felt the burn of the bullet impact his side. It didn't slow him down. He moved forward, fighting against the pain.

He lifted his gun and fired, but his aim was off because of the wound in his side. He was winded from running full force toward Dakota. Another shot rang out. This one hit him in the same shoulder where he'd been hit before, sending him flying backward as additional pain ripped through him.

The pedestrians, who'd been watching in horror, screamed and dropped to the ground, quickly crawling into the nearby shrubs. Ace didn't even look at them as he jumped back to his feet.

This time when he took aim, the bullet went in through the vehicle's front window. A scream could be heard ringing across the nearly empty parking lot. The car squealed away, and Ace rushed forward to Dakota. He finally reached her and let out the smallest breath of relief.

He covered her body with his as he looked around, watching as the black car spun out of the lot. Maybe this would be the end of it. He somehow doubted it, though. They weren't going to give up this opportunity.

"Are you okay?" he asked her. "Have you been shot?" His hands were roaming over her body, his own wounds temporarily forgotten.

"I'm fine, Ace," she told him as she held up a hand to block the blood pouring from him. "But you aren't."

"They are just flesh wounds, trust me," he told her despite his breathing growing more ragged. "We need to get the hell out of here."

"I couldn't agree more," she told him.

He got to his feet, glancing around them before trying to push her into the vehicle.

"I'm driving," she insisted. "You were shot twice, and I want to get out of here before you pass out on me."

He thought about arguing, but he feared she might be right. He just nodded as he jumped across the seats into the passenger side of the vehicle, trying to stay as alert as possible even though tremendous pain was radiating through him.

"This time we're going to the hospital. Call your brothers. They can meet us there," she told him.

"That's really the reason you wanted to drive," he grumbled. "I'm fine. Go home and Lindsey can fix me."

"Not going to happen," she assured him. Ace was growing too weak to keep arguing, so he leaned back as she revved the engine and began moving down the street. She was sure the police were on their way, but they could talk to them once they were in the safety of the ER.

"Pick up the speed," he told her when she paused too long at a stop sign.

"Let me drive," she answered before she accelerated.

Ace could feel himself losing consciousness and fought against it. This wasn't the time to leave Dakota alone to defend herself. Just because they were in the vehicle moving along the roads didn't mean they were in any way safe. He didn't want to go to the hospital, but at least it would be staffed with armed security.

He picked up his phone with the last of his strength and called Cooper, explaining quickly where they were heading before he dropped the phone. All he could do now was try desperately to focus on the road while Dakota drove.

"Stay with me, Ace. Don't you dare pass out on me," Dakota scolded him.

He shot his eyes open and attempted to smile at her. He loved when she was fierce and commanding. It was just one more thing about the woman that he didn't think he could live without. Most women he knew would have been panicked in this situation, but not Dakota. She was taking charge, wouldn't allow herself to fall apart until she was sure someone else was there to take care of him. She wouldn't even worry about herself, which actually did frustrate him a little.

"I've been injured worse, Dakota. Stop focusing all your energy on worrying about me," he told her. But the weakness in his voice undermined his reassuring words.

Dakota was forced to slow down as she turned a corner, and Ace was fading, so he didn't see the car heading straight for them. But he felt the impact as the vehicle slammed into theirs, sending his body forward, his head slamming against the windshield.

Dakota's scream was the last thing he heard before he lost consciousness.

CHAPTER
THIRTY-TWO

Ace woke up, found himself strapped to a gurney, and felt a renewed sense of panic and fury. What in the hell had happened? He turned, trying to find Dakota.

"Dakota?" he called out, his voice barely a squeak.

"Sir, we're almost to the hospital. You've been shot and have a head injury," the paramedic hovering over him said.

Ace tried to move again, but he was held down tightly. There was a gunshot wound and a hit-and-run. They weren't taking any chances with him.

"I'm Ace Armstrong, I'm with the CIA," he said, but by the look in the man's eyes, the paramedic didn't believe him. They screeched to a halt in front of the ER, and the back doors flew open. It was only seconds before Ace's gurney was on the ground and he was being rushed inside the room.

"We have an adult male in a hit-and-run accident with an injury to the head and two bullet wounds, one to the side, one in the left shoulder," the paramedic shouted as a nurse began taking his vitals.

"I don't have time for this," Ace tried to yell, but his voice wasn't going to be scaring anyone any time soon.

He was rushed to a room and soon switched to a hospital bed, where he was strapped down again, his left arm free this time so they could assess the damage from the gunshot. He tried pushing them away, but he was too weak.

Even though Ace knew he couldn't do a damn thing at this moment, he still struggled against the people trying to help him. Time was of the essence, and if Dakota hadn't been with him in the vehicle, then it meant Nestor or his goons had gotten to her. These doctors just needed to stop his bleeding so he could get the hell out of there.

Ace was too angry to pass out again, so he continued cursing at the medical staff as he told them again and again he was CIA and he was on an important case. They either didn't believe him or they didn't care. It was infuriating. He demanded they call his supervisor, but he didn't have Bill's card on him. It wouldn't have mattered if he did—he wouldn't have been able to reach for it, since he was still strapped to the damn bed.

There was a commotion in the room. Ace had never been happier than when Cooper and Maverick ran into the room. The staff tried to slow them down, but one look at their fierce faces and they backed off. Only Nick wasn't there, since he was with their wives and children.

"You have to get me out of here. They have Dakota," Ace told Cooper.

The doctor numbed him and removed the bullets as Ace tried to remain conscious enough to get the entire story out to his brothers. They listened, and the medical staff became much more subdued, realizing he'd been telling the truth the entire time.

"She's got a tracking device on her," Ace said. "We have to trace it now before they figure it out."

"The bullets are out," the doctor said. "No internal organs were hit."

"I told you that," Ace snapped as the nurse took over for the doctor and began sewing up his wounds.

"You most likely do have a concussion, though, and will need to stay overnight," he said, glaring down at Ace.

"That's not going to happen," Ace told the man with just as strong a look.

"You aren't going to be able to do your job when you can't even walk straight," the doctor informed him.

"You don't know me," Ace assured the man.

"I know plenty of hotshots like you," the doctor grumbled before he turned toward Cooper, whom he seemed to deem the most responsible of the siblings. "He needs to take medication, and if he leaves, it's against medical advice."

"We have a couple of nurses at home. We'll keep an eye on him," Cooper promised, speaking far more rationally. The doctor sighed but nodded and told his staff to release Ace from his restraints.

When the straps were undone, he sat up too quickly and became ill, his head instantly spinning. The nurse looked at him with an I-told-you-so expression that irritated Ace all the more.

"Maybe you should let us and Bill handle this," Maverick said, obviously worried.

"Would you sit here if Lindsey was taken?" Ace fired back.

Maverick just shook his head. He didn't try to argue any further. He reached into his pocket and pulled up the app that would track Dakota, praying it was still active. It was the longest couple of minutes of his life while he tried to focus on it as it searched for her.

When the device stopped searching, it showed her in a steady location. They must have her wherever they planned on staying for the night. It was either that or else . . . No, he refused to even think about the fact that she might be gone from his life. They wouldn't kill her. She was too valuable to them alive. They had nothing to bargain with if she were dead.

"Let's go," he told his brothers as he slowly got to his feet. He could barely walk. It wasn't good.

"How in the hell are you going to save her like this?" Mav demanded.

Ace stood between his brothers as he left the ER department, waving off any effort at assisting him. "I'll have you with me," he assured them.

"Of course, we're more than willing to be there with you, but you have to call in help, Ace. For her safety, you have to let go of your pride," Cooper told him.

They reached Cooper's vehicle, and it took maximum effort for Ace to even slide into the back seat. He ignored the accusing look his brother sent him that told him he was a fool.

Without another word, he lifted his phone and dialed Bill, who picked up on the second ring.

"They got her, Bill," he said.

"Do you know where?" he asked.

"I have a location. I need men we can trust beyond a shadow of a doubt," Ace demanded.

"I know just who to send," Bill assured him.

"I won't hesitate to kill them if they try to betray us," Ace warned.

"I have my inner circle, Ace. No one else even knows about this," Bill told him.

Ace knew he could trust Bill, but that didn't make any of this easier. He wanted to be the one to save Dakota, because he couldn't trust anyone else to take her life as seriously as he did. But he knew he was too weak to ensure her safety. He'd be putting her at more risk by not accepting help.

He gave the address to Bill and agreed to a meeting place a block away. It was a full-on stealth mission. Before Ace hung up the phone, Bill had produced a map of the abandoned home on the outskirts of the city. The thugs probably figured they wouldn't be found in the location. Also, so far, they either hadn't found Dakota's tracking device or they had and this was a trap.

Ace didn't care. He would be going in for her, no matter what.

Though his brothers didn't like it one bit, they moved to the agreed-on location, and Bill's team of three guys was there within minutes, in full tactical gear with additional tactical gear for the Armstrong men.

"You really need to wait out here," Maverick told him.

Ace was having a difficult time breathing, his body hurt so badly, but he couldn't just stand by while they went in.

"You're a stronger man if you trust us to do this," Cooper said.

"You're too weak. You might give away our approach," Maverick added.

At his brother's words, Ace knew he was defeated. He couldn't be the reason something happened to her. Though it would kill him to stay behind, knowing she might be in mortal danger, or that he might be sending his brothers on a suicide mission, he had to be strong enough to trust all of them.

"We won't come back without her," Cooper assured him, placing his hand on Ace's unhurt arm.

"I want you both to come back to me too," Ace said. "I don't know if I can stand to wait idly by."

"You can, because it's what's best for her right now. Do I need to stay and babysit you?" Maverick asked.

"No. I need you in there," Ace told him.

"Then you need to keep your word and wait out here," Mav insisted.

"I will," Ace said, not looking at either of his brothers.

"Say it while looking in my eyes," Maverick demanded.

Ace glared at his brother, but finally he nodded. His vision was blurring again, and he knew he wouldn't be any good to them. He truly would be a hindrance. He was going to stay put and be there for Dakota the minute she was pulled out of the situation.

"We'll be back before you know we're gone," Cooper assured him.

"We won't let you down, sir," one of the agents said.

Ace nodded at him. Then he sat back in frustrated impatience as the three men and his two brothers disappeared down the street. Each second that passed felt like an hour. Ace sat in the vehicle, his eyes peeled for any movement as he listened for the sounds of gunshots or screaming.

It was silent. That silence nearly undid him. He'd made a mistake. He shouldn't have let them go without him. It was all going to go completely wrong. He had no doubt about it.

Struggling to his feet, he slid into a bulletproof vest while he gripped his gun in his uninjured hand. He needed to get in there and help them. Everything inside him screamed for him to do so. He hadn't been wrong about his instincts yet.

Taking a step forward, he pushed back the pain that was trying to pull him under, and he carefully made his way forward. When he had Dakota safely back in his arms, he wouldn't let her out of his sight again. No way, no how.

She was far too important to him. She was now a part of his life and his family, and he wasn't ever going to let her go.

CHAPTER
THIRTY-THREE

Dakota's head was pounding as consciousness slowly returned to her. She couldn't open her eyes, the throbbing was so great, and when she tried to lift her arm to massage her head, she was unable to raise it, which sent a jolt of panic through her.

Struggling, she finally wrenched her eyes open as she tried to figure out what was going on and where she was. The room was dark. She closed her eyes again and forced herself to calm down. She concentrated on what she remembered last.

Forcing her breathing to calm, she remembered rushing Ace to the hospital. Then they'd been hit by another vehicle. He'd flown forward. She would never forget the sound his head had made as it came into contact with the windshield of his SUV. She had to fight back tears as she lay tied to the bed.

She didn't know if Ace was alive or dead. One second she'd been panicking as she'd tried to help him; the next, someone had grabbed her, punched her in the head, and the world had gone black. Now she was in some cold, dark room.

Opening her eyes again, she strained to see around her. Not much was visible in this prison. Ace had been right all along. The people after him had gotten her, and she didn't know why she was still alive. Maybe they wanted to use her against him. That had to be the case. She knew he would feel responsible and he would stop at nothing to get to her.

She just wasn't sure if he would make it in time. Or if these sick fools would kill her right in front of him to teach him a lesson. She had hope, though, because if she was still alive, that meant they hadn't killed him yet.

Taking calming breaths, Dakota tried to listen for any noise of approaching people. Not a sound could be heard anywhere in the place. It was creepy. She would almost rather hear someone, even if he was making threats. At least then she would know where the danger was.

She had to escape. That was her sole purpose. If she could get away, then Ace wouldn't be in danger trying to find her, trying to rescue her. She should be more worried about herself, but her sense of panic decreased if she concentrated on Ace instead.

Focusing on the room she was in, her eyes began to adjust to the blackness. There was a window to her right, but it was sealed. She could see a bit of light coming in from low on the horizon, which meant the sun must be setting. But she had no idea where she was or how she was going to get out.

Dakota realized she was bound with rope. That was a good thing. She could eventually escape from knots. After all, she had grown up with brothers who'd enjoyed torturing her as they played their cops and robbers games. She'd always been the woman who'd had to be rescued. She'd eventually learned how to rescue herself.

She was finally beginning to make some progress when she heard voices outside her door, then the sound of the knob turning. She lay still as the door was thrust open and some men walked inside. It sounded like two of them.

"How hard did you punch her?" one of the men asked.

"She was screaming, and I was trying to shut her up," the other guy said. She could practically see him shrugging his shoulders as if he didn't really care.

"We need her alive, or she doesn't make very good bait," the first guy said. "Go and check her. Make sure she's still alive."

Footsteps moved toward her. She made herself take deep, even breaths as the man reached up and ran his hand down her chest, supposedly feeling for her heart, but taking his time groping her. She had to fight not to cringe.

"You're taking your time," the man standing back said, laughing as if this was nothing more than a big joke to him. It took all Dakota had not to lash out. Playing the victim wasn't an easy thing for her.

"She's alive and quite beautiful," the man touching her said. He seemed somewhat bored and somewhat excited. The excitement frightened her more than anything else. She was tied to some stinky cot and they had all the power in the world, while she had none.

"Okay, leave her be," man number two said, starting to sound irritated.

"Why? The boss isn't here. We could wake her up and play for a while," the guy running his hand down her stomach said. It took all she had not to shudder in revulsion.

"I don't think so. If something happens while we're playing, we're going to get shot," villain number two reminded his partner, who finally removed his filthy hands from Dakota.

"The guys are downstairs. They will keep a lookout," villain number one said, but he'd moved a few inches away.

"I guess you are right," the other one said. She could feel him step closer to her. She imagined him leering in the dark. She wanted to scream.

"Hey Tony, Pete, something is happening," a voice called. "Get down here."

The urgency in the voice gave Dakota hope. They were worried about something. Did that mean someone was coming for her? Was this nightmare going to end? She didn't want to hope for that, because she feared she would break into tears and give away the fact that she was very much awake.

The men left the room, their steps a lot more rushed than when they'd entered. The door slammed behind them, and she waited, holding her breath as she listened to their steps growing fainter. Only when she knew for sure they were gone did she allow a tear to fall down her cheek.

She began shaking, hoping and praying someone was there for her. She was a strong woman who didn't often give in to hysteria, but terror was currently tickling at her brain. She resumed trying to escape her binds.

She heard activity in the house, but she had no idea what was going on. When she finally began to feel a bit of give in the rope on her right wrist, she doubled her efforts to get it off. First one hand, and then the other.

She could do this. Yes, she wanted Ace to come for her, but she wasn't going to simply lie there and wait for rescue. She wasn't going to give up. She would get away if it was the last thing she did. And maybe she'd be the one to rescue Ace, she thought with a half smile.

Soon, she was able to slip a finger beneath a loose piece of the rope, and she tugged more. She heard voices coming closer to her room, heard shouts. But she didn't stop this time. If they were coming back, they might think they were safe—they might be coming back to continue what they'd started.

She wasn't going to allow that to happen. Her brothers had insisted she take self-defense classes when she'd gone off to college. She was more than grateful to them for that now. Finally, her wrist was free. She pulled up her raw arm and didn't take time to analyze the scraped skin.

She immediately began working on the other rope. Shouts continued being yelled in the house, and she could feel the anxiety of her captors growing. She wanted to be free by the time they burst into her room. She needed to be able to defend herself.

When her second wrist was free, she sat up in the filthy bed, ignoring the throbbing in her swollen wrists and the tingling in her fingers. She still had to undo her feet, and that was only the beginning in her escape. She then had to figure out how to get out of this house.

She didn't even know how many men were there watching her. She didn't know what weapons they had. She knew she was upstairs. Maybe she could get out the window somehow and be gone before they knew what had happened.

But even if she were able to do that, she didn't know if they were in the city or out in the country, if they had guard dogs. She knew nothing. But none of that stopped her as she finally got her feet free. She rubbed her swollen ankles and then tentatively placed her feet on the ground.

She could feel the tingling of the blood returning to her once-restricted limbs, so she waited a moment to stand. She didn't want to screw this up by standing up on numb legs and then crashing to the floor, alerting the men below that she was not only awake but free.

Every second that passed as she did nothing but sit on the bed rubbing her legs felt like an eternity. She was wasting too much time, and she knew it, but the other options were too terrifying to even begin to contemplate.

When she was finally able to get to her feet, she smiled. Her freedom was so close. She looked from the door to the window, not knowing which way she should try to go. Then she heard more shouting and the firing of a gun.

Her body froze for a moment before she sprang into action. Dakota wasn't a victim. She was going to prove that to them right now.

CHAPTER THIRTY-FOUR

Ace came around the corner, ignoring the pain throbbing through his body. He found Maverick, Cooper, and the other men who were there to save Dakota. He stood back as they spoke. He wasn't going to interrupt them if they could do the job, but he had to be close, had to help if he could.

"I can't tell how many men are in there," Maverick said. "I don't like going in against all these odds."

"We don't have a choice," Cooper responded.

"I know," Maverick agreed.

"I would be a lot happier, though, if we knew exactly where she was," one of the men said.

"We'll find her," Mav said, his voice sure. That made Ace feel a hell of a lot better.

Ace glanced around the neighborhood at abandoned businesses and crappy homes. These men were either arrogant or they had a lot more traps than what was obvious to the naked eye. Ace didn't believe in luck. He waited to make sure his family was being cautious.

"Okay, we're wasting time," Cooper said. "Mav and I will take the front of the house. You three take the back. We'll surprise them. Top priority is finding Dakota and getting her out. When Ace is better, he can come after these bastards."

Ace fully agreed with his brother as he stayed out of sight. Right now, all that mattered was getting to Dakota, getting her to safety. His revenge would come swift and hard—and soon. He didn't stay down for long. The bastards might have counted on incapacitating him with gunshots when they formulated their plans, but they obviously didn't know him as well as they thought they did.

"Let's do this," Mav said.

The five of them began moving swiftly. Ace was going to give them a few minutes' head start, and then he was going in. They didn't know he was there, so he wouldn't be a liability to them. But he was going in after her.

His heart thundering, Ace watched the three CIA agents disappear around the back of the house while Cooper and Maverick stealthily went to the front door. Mav lifted his gun and smashed the doorknob with the butt of his weapon. There were instant shouts and shots fired as Maverick and Cooper disappeared inside the place.

"Get down," he heard Cooper yell as more weapons were discharged.

All of Ace's pain disappeared as his adrenaline pumped, and he rushed forward. Smoke was coming out the front door. He feared a fire had started. He had to get to Dakota. Once he had her, he would radio the other men, tell them to get the hell out of there.

"Do not let them get to the girl," a voice yelled. Ace's fury rose. "Go upstairs now!"

Good. Ace now knew she was on the top floor. That narrowed down his search. He moved rapidly through the door, his lungs instantly filling with smoke. He ignored his labored breathing and quickly moved to the stairs.

A man was ascending them. Ace grabbed him, throwing him to the bottom of the staircase before the man knew what was happening. He landed with a thud, moaning as he gripped his broken leg.

Ace didn't give him another glance as he quickly ran up the remaining steps. He thrust open the first door at the top of the staircase. The room was empty. He quickly opened another door—the filthy bathroom was also empty.

Ace charged the remaining door, breaking it open. A scream came hurling out at him, and then a terrified animal launched herself at him, scratching his face with her claws.

The relief that flooded through Ace was incomparable. His arms wrapped around her as she kicked at him, his little minx unwilling to be anyone's victim.

"Damn, I love you," he said. He was too relieved and elated to realize his words or be worried about them.

Dakota stilled in his arms as she pulled back, instant gratitude in her eyes.

"Ace?" she gasped, her eyes brimming over with tears. "Is it really you?"

"Yeah, baby. And I do love this kinky side to you, but as you can hear, there's a hell of a lot of gunfire going on. I think this piece-of-shit house is about to burn down. We need to get out of here," he told her.

She leaned forward and kissed him hard before pulling back. "I'm so glad you're okay. I didn't know," she gasped.

"I promise we'll catch up when I get you to safety," he assured her.

He spoke into his mic. "Don't be pissed, but I have Dakota. We're leaving through the front door in exactly ten seconds, so give us some cover fire and then get the hell out of here," he snapped.

"Damn it, Ace," Maverick growled over the speaker, then it went silent.

Ace grabbed Dakota's hand and moved to the door, looking out into the hallway before pulling her from the room. All was clear on the upper floor. More shots were being fired down below.

"Get this bastard off me," someone yelled before another shot went off and the same voice screamed.

"Stay behind me," Ace told Dakota while he pressed her into the wall. They came down the staircase with great alacrity.

"You're hurt," Dakota told him. His wounds must have opened.

"Don't think about that right now. We have to get out of here," he said.

They reached the bottom of the staircase, and he looked at the distance from the stairs to the front door. The smoke was growing thicker, which was horrible for their lungs but gave them great cover.

"Get down," he told her.

She didn't argue as the two of them knelt down and crawl-walked to the front door. Ace's heart thundered as the firing of weapons became fewer and farther between.

"Are you out?" Cooper asked in his earpiece.

Ace pulled Dakota through the front door and launched the two of them down the front stairs. More gunfire erupted beside the house. Someone was firing from the back porch, someone else from the cover of the bushes. It was too dark for Ace to see who was who, so he couldn't assist.

"We're out of the house," Ace said quietly into the microphone. "Get out now. Flames are climbing the walls, and this place is going to collapse."

"All clear," repeated through his earpiece.

"Maverick?" Ace said, hiding behind an old truck with Dakota safely tucked beside him. He'd only heard four replies.

"Maverick, you need to answer us," Coop said, urgency in his tone.

"Where is he?" Ace asked. If something had happened to his brother, he would never get over it.

"I'm out," Maverick finally responded. "But the assholes got a shot into my leg. I'm on the west side of the house," he said before coughing.

"Got him," Cooper responded. "We will meet up at the car."

"Be there in thirty seconds," Ace said.

"We should wait for Maverick," Dakota told him.

She'd been silent during the exchange, but Ace finally looked at her, and though her face was pale and those bastards had hurt her, there was determination in her eyes. He would take her as his partner anytime.

"They are already out of danger. It's time to get you to safety," he told her, running his fingers along her dirty cheek. "I have never been as scared as I was not knowing where you were or who was after you."

"I'm okay, Ace. Let's go home," she told him.

"Yes, let's go home," he responded.

Everything inside him wanted to punish each man who had been responsible for hurting this woman. He could see the bruising on her wrists, and he had no doubt there were more injuries they would pay for. But he wouldn't leave her here on her own, so he had to get her away. He would come back for these guys. Maybe not today, but he would be back.

"We're not out of danger," he said. "So stay with me, and let's get the hell out of here."

"Let's go," she said, her lip trembling as she fought to remain cool under pressure.

"They never should have gotten their hands on you, Dakota. That's all on me. I'm sorry."

"Now is not the time for apologies," she said sternly. "And I will hurt you if you blame yourself for me being foolish enough to take a walk alone. I wanted to pretend the danger wasn't there, so I acted foolishly. Let's leave now, and then we can grovel to each other when we're safely away," she finished with a hint of a smile.

"But they hurt you," he said, his rage and anguish rushing to the surface.

"They are just surface wounds, and they will heal," she said. "I promise you nothing else happened."

The relief that rushed through him was indescribable. He had a feeling she wasn't telling him the entire story, but she would be much more traumatized if she'd been sexually violated. They'd rescued her in time, he assured himself.

Ace squeezed her hand, and then looked around. It appeared as if they were clear to leave. Still being cautious, he began to move from behind the truck. They were going to continue their conversation, but they'd do it when they weren't under attack.

"Ace, get down," one of the men shouted.

His worst nightmares came to life when one of the CIA men stood up and fired at a man who came around the back of the truck, his gun aimed directly at Dakota.

"You bitch," the man cried.

He fired the gun, and Dakota let out a moan as blood pooled on her chest.

It all happened so quickly. Ace didn't even have time to shoot before the other man took down his victim. Dakota fell into his arms, her eyes closed. Ace's heart stopped in his chest as he gazed at the woman he loved, not knowing how bad her injuries were.

"Let's go," the agent said, lifting Dakota into his arms as he began running.

Ace followed, his body numb. He was afraid to even look at Dakota. If he lost her, he didn't know what he would do. New determination filled him as he swore nothing would happen to her. He'd give his own life if he needed to.

CHAPTER THIRTY-FIVE

Ace didn't leave Dakota's side as she lay in a hospital bed, monitors hooked up to her, her heartbeat steady. The bullet had missed her heart, and they'd gotten it out without complication, but it had been way too close for comfort.

She was so pale and small lying there. She shouldn't be in a hospital room, shouldn't be in this situation at all. It was all on him. If he hadn't ever gotten involved with her, she'd be living her life, stress-free, happy. He truly was no good for her. But even knowing this, he couldn't walk away—not now.

A shudder racked his body as he thought about how close he'd come to losing her forever. If the bullet had penetrated even an inch to the left, she would be gone. One small inch and he never would have seen her smile again. It was something he couldn't even begin to imagine.

His brothers and sisters-in-law hadn't left his side in the waiting area those first twelve hours when she'd been in surgery. He'd practically torn off heads as he waited to see her, touch her, assure himself she was indeed alive.

Finally, she'd been taken to a private room, and he'd made his family go away so he could be alone with her. Her family had been called. Ace was sure there was a hailstorm of fire coming his way. They had been shocked by what had happened, so Dakota obviously hadn't told them a thing.

They would need a target for their grief and anger, and Ace was more than willing to be that person for them. After all, he hadn't protected her like he should have. He'd allowed her to be kidnapped, and then he'd been standing next to her when she'd been shot.

The doctor walked into the room, looking at her charts before nodding.

"How is she doing?" Ace asked anxiously.

"Are you family?" the doctor asked.

Ace froze up. No. Technically he wasn't anything, but he swore if this man didn't share with him what was going on, he'd put the doctor in a bed next to her.

"I need to know," he said.

"We need her next of kin," the doctor told him. Ace stood up to his full height, having no problem at all intimidating the good doctor.

"I'm her father," a man said as he stepped into the room, flanked by a small woman and four large men Ace was assuming were Dakota's brothers. None of them appeared happy at all as they glared at Ace. "I want to know what in the hell is going on."

The doctor turned toward the man and nodded. "Mr. Forbes?" he said.

"Yes, I'm Lucian Forbes, and this is my wife, Juliana, and our sons, Kian, Owen, Arden, and Declan. Please tell us what is happening with my daughter."

Lucian moved across the room and came to stand beside the bed, his hand instantly taking Dakota's. Ace wasn't surprised to see the man's fingers tremble. Hell, Ace was having a difficult time keeping it together. This wasn't exactly how he'd pictured meeting her family.

"Your daughter received a gunshot wound to the chest. We successfully removed the bullet, and she is expected to make a full recovery from her injury," the doctor said. Ace let out a breath of relief.

"Is there a but in there?" Lucian asked.

"No, sir," the doctor replied before sending a glance Ace's way. "However, we ran several tests so we would know what medications to give her," he continued before he paused again.

"Can you just spit it out?" Lucian demanded. Ace was beginning to respect the man, though he kept quiet.

"Your daughter is pregnant," the doctor said. He again glanced at Ace before turning away to look at Lucian again. "The baby appears to be fine."

The room went deathly silent as Ace stared down at Dakota. They'd been so cautious, had taken precautions. How in the world could this have happened? Well, he knew *how* it could happen, but he didn't understand when it had happened.

Ace could feel the burning gazes of Dakota's family focused on him now. As he was the only unrelated man in the room, they were easily putting two and two together.

"You are sure both my daughter and the baby are fine?" Lucian asked.

"Yes, we are sure. She should be waking any time," the doctor told them.

Much to Ace's surprise, her father looked up and smiled at Ace. That wasn't the reaction he'd been expecting at all. He looked from her father to her brothers. They didn't hold the same expression in their eyes at all. He had a feeling they'd like to draw and quarter him if they got the chance.

"Our first grandchild," Juliana said as she placed her hand on her husband's arm and looked down at their daughter. "This certainly isn't the way I would have liked to have heard the news, but how can I not be happy about that?" She spoke so quietly, with a slight accent Ace couldn't quite place.

Ace's head was spinning. A baby certainly hadn't been in the cards for him. Actually, it was the farthest thing from his mind. But as the doctor's words settled in his brain, something inside his chest expanded, making him ache with overwhelming emotion.

A child. His child. He couldn't even comprehend it. There was fear inside him, but it was drowned out by the overwhelming love taking its place. He was going to be a father. Just last night he'd almost lost the woman he loved, and now all of a sudden, he was being told he was going to be a father. And his baby's mother was going to be just fine.

It was almost too much for him to take in. His blissful moment was soon interrupted, though, when Dakota's oldest brother stepped forward.

"You have some serious explaining to do," Kian said. There was definitely murder in his eyes.

"I think you need to wait for Dakota to wake up. It's not my place to explain," Ace told the man. He could certainly understand her brother's wrath, but Ace feared her, not her family. And if he told them about their affair, she was going to kill him.

"I can certainly beat the information out of you," Kian said. Her other brothers nodded, indicating they liked that idea.

"Want to go outside?" Ace asked, smirking at the man. He saw fire explode in his eyes before his lips turned up in a menacing smile.

"Let's go," Kian said, holding out his hand.

"You both need to calm down," Juliana said, glaring at all of her sons before turning her disapproving look to Ace. "I'm assuming the child is yours."

Ace didn't want to look away from Dakota's brothers, but he couldn't disrespect her mother and ignore what she was saying to him. He slowly glanced at her, suddenly feeling shame as she gazed at him with a knowing look.

"Yes, ma'am," he replied, with a lot more respect than he had given the brothers.

"And do you love my daughter?" she asked, her intense, nearly purple eyes not allowing him to look away, though he did shift on his feet.

"Yes, ma'am," he said quietly. He'd realized it the night before, and the feeling had grown while he'd prayed at her bedside. He could try to lie to these people, but they needed to know he would die for Dakota. Maybe it would ease some of their tension.

"And I'm also assuming you have something to do with this mess," Juliana continued.

"Yes," he said, not elaborating.

"Since my daughter makes wise choices, I'm going to give you the benefit of the doubt and let you tell us what is going on," Juliana said as she accepted the chair her husband offered her. She sat next to her daughter, never taking her eyes off Ace.

"Mom, this douchebag touched Dakota," Kian said, obviously still wanting a fight.

"Your sister is an adult and can choose who she wants to be with," Juliana told her son.

"But . . ." Juliana held up her hand, and Kian instantly stopped. He obviously respected his mother, which made Ace think a lot more highly of the man.

"Are you in trouble?" Juliana asked Ace.

Ace sighed as he sat back down in the chair he'd been in all night—that was, when he wasn't pacing. He didn't want to tower over her.

"I'm CIA," he told her honestly. "I finished a case, and one of the members of the family is seeking revenge. Dakota got caught up in the crossfire."

He felt so much shame as he told her family that it was indeed his fault she was lying in a hospital bed and had been fighting for her life all night. They should kick him out of her life and take her far, far away. The thought of that had his heart burning in pain.

"My daughter never has been one to run from a fight," Juliana said, surprising him when she chuckled. "It seems like you might just be strong enough for her."

Ace didn't know what in the world to think about Juliana's words. It appeared to him as if the woman was giving him her blessing. That didn't make sense at all. Not when they were having this conversation across a hospital bed.

"You will marry her," Kian growled.

Ace's glance flew up to Dakota's brother. He hadn't even thought about marriage. But she was carrying his child. Of course, he had to marry her. The thought of marriage had filled him with dread for so many years, he was shocked that it didn't scare him now.

"Of course I will," Ace said.

He hadn't expected those words to escape his parched throat, but now that it was out there in the open, he knew that's just what he was going to do. He couldn't leave this woman carrying his child. Even if she hadn't been pregnant, he knew he wouldn't be able to walk away from her. She meant too much to him. He couldn't imagine his life without her.

"Good," Lucian said. He'd been quiet during the entire exchange.

"I'm sorry we're meeting like this," Ace told them.

"She's alive. That's all that matters right now," Lucian told him.

"Maybe we should just bring the preacher in here and get the ceremony done now so this fool doesn't change his mind and try to run away," Kian said. Her other brothers were oddly quiet, and that worried Ace a little bit. He couldn't judge what they were thinking if he couldn't hear their voices.

"I might have a problem with that."

Everyone went silent as Dakota spoke while slowly opening her eyes. Her brothers moved forward, surrounding her, probably making her a little claustrophobic.

"I'm glad you're all here," she said, her voice weak. "But you aren't trying to give me a shotgun wedding, are you?"

She smiled a little. Ace didn't understand how she could be making a joke, even a small one, after what she'd been through.

"Did you hear what the doctor said?" Ace asked, forgetting about her family being in the room.

"No. I began coming to a couple minutes ago. I heard you bickering with my family. I felt right at home," she told him. He'd never seen anything as beautiful as her open eyes.

"We're pregnant," he said softly, his hand caressing her cool head. Her eyes widened as she gazed at him. He couldn't tell what she was thinking. Then she gave him another soft smile.

"So my family is demanding a wedding?" she said.

"Of course we'll marry," he told her.

"I might not be old-fashioned, Ace Armstrong, but I do have a romantic side," she told him. "And no one tells me what to do."

"I know that," he said. It was only one of the many things he loved about her.

"So we have a baby together; that doesn't mean we get married. If I accept a proposal, it will be because I am so in love I can't imagine my life going on without the guy."

"I do love you," he told her.

"And we've also been on one long roller-coaster ride. Let's see how you feel when it stops," she said.

"But . . ." He was at a loss for words.

"Don't argue with me. I'm weak and pathetic right now," she told him.

"I'm sorry," he said.

She smiled, her face stunningly beautiful even while pale and sunken. It didn't matter. She was his, and he would prove to her she couldn't live without him, even if she would be much better off without him in her life.

She turned away from him and looked at her brothers. "You be nice to Ace. He's saved me more than once," she scolded them.

Her big brothers nervously shifted on their feet, making Ace feel like smirking at them. He managed to keep it in, though. He liked it much better when her controlling nature was turned on someone other than him.

The doctor came back into the room, and Ace slipped away. He'd been put through a lot of emotions in the past twenty-four hours, and he needed a few minutes to process it all.

His phone rang, and he lifted it to his ear without thinking about it. Maybe he should have just let it go to voice mail. He wasn't sure.

"Hello," he said.

"It's time you and I meet."

The deadly voice was on the other end of the line. Ace smiled. It was Nestor, and he'd picked the ideal time to call.

"Yes, it is," he replied.

CHAPTER THIRTY-SIX

Ace felt confident as he went to the location Nestor had agreed to meet him. Of course, it was a trap. Ace wasn't a fool. But Nestor's ego was going to be what took him down. Yes, the man would have his goons there, but he wasn't prepared for Ace's backup, either. He wouldn't be so foolish as to assume Ace would come alone, but he knew Ace had injuries, and he was counting on that to make him weak.

The man didn't know who he was. Rage was all he needed to wipe this man out. There was no way Ace was going to leave any more stones unturned. Not only had this idiot been foolish enough to come after Ace, but he'd attacked Dakota. Ace wasn't going to allow that to happen again—not ever. This ended today—one way or another.

His body was weak, and Ace didn't try to hide that fact. The worse off Nestor thought he was, the more victorious the creep would feel. His overconfidence would be his undoing.

All along Ace had planned on being the bait. He had done it before, and this was no different. What amused Ace was the saliva practically dripping from Bill's mouth at the thought of getting this guy. If anything went wrong, Ace would have to punch his boss. The man was almost as eager as Ace to get Nestor behind bars. However, Ace didn't care at this point if they caught him dead or alive. He just wanted him out of the picture.

"We can see you clearly. There's no sign of activity," Maverick said into Ace's earpiece.

His foolish brother had insisted on being there, even though he was sporting his own injury from the night before. The bullet that had ripped into Mav's leg would require him to use a cane for the next few weeks, but Maverick had insisted on being a lookout. He was too good a shot not to include on the mission, so Ace had reluctantly agreed.

Ace didn't say anything back but nodded his head the slightest bit. If Nestor was watching, he didn't want the man to get spooked.

"I would feel a hell of a lot better being down there on the ground with you," Maverick said.

The slightest of smiles tilted Ace's lips. He knew sitting by wasn't any of his brothers' styles. Ace hadn't let Cooper or Nick come along, as he was too worried Nestor wouldn't show and would use the opportunity to get to their wives. They were all at the hospital with full security and communication so they knew exactly what was happening.

"When this is over, you're going to have one hell of a pissed-off woman on your hands," Cooper said. "She won't let me leave the hospital room. Her brother also said if you get killed, that counts as running."

Ace lowered his head as he fought the smile trying to pop up on his lips. He could just imagine the hell Dakota was giving everyone, especially since he'd slipped away without a word. The time had come, and he'd had to move fast. He hadn't been left with a whole hell of a lot of choices.

"It's showtime, Ace," Bill spoke up. Ace tensed. "Reports show Nestor entering the premises."

Ace's eyes glowed with a renewed rage and concentration. All joking was pushed aside as the intercoms went silent. They knew he needed to listen, needed to be fully in the moment.

Ace adjusted the bandage wrapping his shoulder, letting the fire in his arm remind him of how alive he was. He sat still at the outside table in the remote café as he waited for his showdown with Nestor.

Nestor's choice of a meeting place had made Ace happy. The man thought he would be safe in a public place, but the patrons had been swapped out with undercover agents, and the scene was most definitely secure. Ace knew Nestor would have his own men around, and that's where it got a bit more dangerous, but the good guys were definitely going to win this one. Ace had a reason to survive.

Nestor was working off pure hate and revenge. And while Ace wanted his own revenge for what had been done to Dakota, he also wanted this ended for the safety of his family. That trumped anything Nestor could carry with him.

A sleek sports car pulled around a corner, and Ace's body tensed. He had no doubt this was Nestor arriving in all his glory. The car stopped, and Nestor stepped out, a huge goon with him.

Looking up, Nestor's eyes met Ace's, pure evilness in the other man's expression. He smoothed his jacket with the palm of his hand and then walked toward Ace with confidence.

Ace wanted nothing more than to order the kill shot and have this over with. But he waited, his body on alert, his attention focused on the man he wanted to strangle with his bare hands.

"Just in case you have anything planned," Nestor said, with a smile that sent a chill down Ace's spine, "you should know that bombs are strategically placed through the area and my men are watching. If anyone so much as sneezes on me, no one gets out alive."

Ace's skin crawled at the man's words. He wasn't sure if he was bluffing or not. But he didn't allow his worry to show in his expression.

"If you planned on this being nothing more than a bloodbath, then why even ask for a meeting?" Ace asked smoothly.

"We're scanning for bombs to see if he's speaking the truth," Bill spoke into his headpiece. Ace didn't tear his gaze away from Nestor.

"Because I've had my fun with you. Now I'm bored with it," Nestor replied.

"I'm pretty sick of it myself," Ace told him. He picked up his cup of coffee and took a sip, loving the flare of anger in Nestor's eyes. The man wanted Ace afraid and cowering. That wasn't going to happen.

"How is your little woman doing?" Nestor asked, a smirk on his lips.

Ace's legs twitched with the need to jump on the man and pound his face. But that was what Nestor was trying to get him to do. He was too professional to sink to this man's level.

"She's made a full recovery," Ace said then forced a smile onto his lips. "How's your brother doing?" He said it with such a deadpan expression, it took a moment for the words to process with his enemy.

He got exactly the reaction he'd expected. Nestor took a menacing step forward, only halting when his goon held out a hand and said something in a foreign language.

"You are a very stupid fool," Nestor said through clenched teeth. "To speak of my brother, whom you so ruthlessly killed."

"He got what he deserved," Ace told him.

"We can't confirm any bombs, Ace. Give it a few more moments," Bill said, knowing Ace would want an update on that situation.

"He trusted you instead of his own flesh and blood. He paid for that, but I am a better brother, and I have gotten his revenge for him," Nestor bragged.

"Really?" Ace taunted. "What exactly have you done?" He smirked at Nestor again, fueling the rage that the criminal was barely managing to control.

"I got to your family," Nestor said. "And I made you run like the coward you are."

Ace hated that he was right. "We do a lot of things we might not normally do to protect the ones we love," Ace said. "But this ends today."

"Yes, it certainly does," Nestor said. He stood behind his goon and pulled out a weapon.

Ace had been prepared for this moment, but he was still shocked when the first bullet flew. Nestor's goon's eyes widened before he dropped to his knees and then fell to the ground. His agents had shot at Nestor and missed.

That gave Nestor time to fire his own shot. Ace dived out of the way, but not quickly enough. A bullet buried itself in Ace's leg, making him unable to stay on his feet. He quickly moved behind a wall, realizing his mistake immediately.

"You're out of my sight," Maverick thundered into his ear.

Before Ace could turn, Nestor was on top of him, the tip of his gun pressed against Ace's temple. How in the hell had things gone wrong this quickly?

"I know you have men here, Ace, but so do I," Nestor said with a laugh.

That's when Ace heard yelling over his coms and Bill's furious voice telling the men to get back. Ace smiled at Nestor, not allowing him to see that anything was wrong.

"You can't win this, Nestor, whether I live or die," Ace told him.

"That's where you're wrong. Your death will be a statement to the world not to ever mess with my family again. After you die, I will finish the job of killing off your woman and your brothers. An eye for an eye," Nestor said gleefully as his gun pushed deeper against Ace's temple.

"You're not getting out of here alive," Ace said.

He reached for his blade tucked in at his side. He couldn't get to his gun, but he could stab this bastard with no problem. He just had to keep the man and his ego talking.

"I win this, you worthless grunt," Nestor said.

The click of his gun cocking sent a shot straight to Ace's heart. He knew he had only the briefest of moments to get this guy off him. And he didn't think anyone was going to be able to step in and assist.

Turbulent Intrigue

Getting his elbow loose, he jammed it up into Nestor's throat, making the man drop his gun as he sputtered, trying to catch his breath. Ace threw the man off him and reached for Nestor's dropped gun.

The older man was obviously used to torture, though, because he recovered remarkably well, rage boiling over in his eyes as he kicked the gun away from both of them and pulled out a deadly looking knife.

He slashed out, and Ace managed to block him, but he still couldn't get to his feet. The bullet in his leg had numbed the limb, and he was losing more blood by the second. He had to get control of this situation fast, or he was going to pass out and Nestor would get his victory.

Nestor circled, his blade in his hand. "I am going to enjoy this," he said, not underestimating Ace this time. "I wish I had more time to make this nice and slow, but you are going to die."

"Come on, Nestor. What are you waiting for?" Ace taunted him. "Are you really afraid of a man on the ground?"

His words did the trick. Nestor lunged at him again, and Ace pulled out his knife at the last second, thrusting it upward. Nestor's eyes bulged out in pain and shock as Ace's weapon made contact with his stomach.

But Nestor got the last laugh, though, as his knife sank into Ace's already ravaged body. Darkness overtook Ace. The injuries were just too great. He heard voices in the distance, but it was all fading fast.

"Ace!" someone shouted. It sounded like Mav. Maybe he was speaking to him through his earpiece. At the moment, he didn't know what reality was. "Hold on, brother. The ambulance is on the way."

"Nestor?" he managed to squeak out.

"The bastard is alive, and he will pay. We have him," Bill said. They were both there. Nestor had been captured.

Ace attempted to nod, but he couldn't even manage that. He allowed the blackness to finally take him under. This was over. It was all over. His family was safe—Dakota was safe. That was all that mattered.

CHAPTER
THIRTY-SEVEN

Ace was having déjà vu when he awoke to the sound of hospital monitors and the smell of antiseptic. This time, though, he wasn't worried about his safety. This time he knew his family would be there, and Dakota couldn't be far away.

He didn't hesitate to open his eyes. His head was pounding, but he blinked away the blurriness of his vision as he tried to focus on who was in the room with him. He was pleased when he saw his uncle Sherman, his mother, and his brothers. He wasn't happy when he didn't find who he truly wanted to be there.

"Where's Dakota?" he asked.

"We're happy to see you too," Sherman said with a half smile.

"Where is she?" he repeated.

"She's in the room next to you, just as grumpy as you are," Cooper told him.

"Take me to her," he demanded.

"You have been shot multiple times, stabbed, and you have lost a lot of blood. You shouldn't be going anywhere," Nick said.

"You can either help me or I'm ripping out lines again," he threatened.

Cooper sighed as he stood up and pressed the call button. A woman came in, thankfully not the nurse he'd threatened a month earlier. Ace almost felt bad about how he'd behaved then.

"We need a wheelchair," Cooper told the nurse.

"He can't go anywhere," she said.

"I'm going," Ace told her. She looked at Ace and rolled her eyes.

"I've heard about you," she said. "I'll be right back."

"At least your reputation is preceding you," Maverick told him with a laugh.

The nurse returned several moments later with a wheelchair, and then Nick and Cooper helped Ace move from the bed to the contraption while the nurse moved his IV bags to the hanger on the chair. She grumbled about stupid, stubborn patients, but at least she was doing what he wanted.

"You're all set," she told him. Then she turned and walked from the room. Ace's body was at least numb from whatever they'd been giving him. But the move from bed to chair had exhausted him. He was having a hard time even holding his head up.

"Take me to her," he told his brother.

Cooper didn't say a word as he began wheeling Ace from his room, then moved a door down and pushed Ace inside. Dakota looked over from where she sat up in her bed, her eyes bloodshot.

"You're okay?" she asked, a tear falling. "I should kick your ass for making me worry about you so much."

"I'm sorry," Ace said, thinking he might be saying that to her quite often. He didn't know how he'd gotten lucky enough to have her, but now that he did, he vowed he wasn't going to ever let her go again.

"It looks like the bad guys did all the ass kicking already," she said, another tear falling.

Cooper pushed him to her bed, and Ace reached for her, not feeling better until her beautiful fingers rested in the palm of his hand.

"You can do it again when I'm back to full health," he assured her.

She smiled at him, and it was more vibrant than the rays of the sun. He didn't need painkillers; he just needed her.

"He's gone, Dakota. There's no more danger," he assured her.

"And you were a fool to go after him in your condition," she told him.

"I know," he agreed. "I promise not to do anything like that again."

"You can't promise that in your line of work," she told him. "And I would never ask you to change."

"You don't have to. I'm telling Bill I quit as soon as I see him," Ace promised.

"Don't do that for me," she insisted.

"I'm doing it for me, for you, *and* for our child," he told her as he reached down and rubbed her flat stomach. "I want to be with my family."

She didn't try to stop her tears from falling as she looked at him with what appeared to be hope.

"I wouldn't want anyone to ask me to change who I am, so I certainly wouldn't ask it of anyone else, especially someone I love," she said quietly.

The warmth in Ace's heart was overflowing as she admitted her feelings to him. He might have been shot at, stabbed, and kicked around, but none of that mattered anymore. Because it had all ended well, and now he was home—right where he belonged.

"I think I'm going to become a full-time flight instructor," he said with a chuckle.

"Oh, really?" she said, a grin on her lips. "Your only student better be me. I know what you do in those planes."

Ace wanted so badly to kiss her, but he couldn't lean forward.

"Come down here, closer," he told her.

Dakota instantly lowered the bed, and he laid his head next to hers and carefully took her lips with his.

"I adore you, Dakota Forbes, and you will be my one and only the rest of my life. You don't have to worry about that," he said.

"I might hold you to that, Ace Armstrong," she said.

"Good. You can do so every single day that you're my wife."

She smiled at him again before grabbing his face and kissing him with a bit more steam this time. They didn't stop until Cooper cleared his throat.

Ace turned and looked at his brother. "Help me up into this bed and then get out," he said.

Cooper rolled his eyes. "I think that should be the last thing on your mind," Cooper said.

"I just want to hold my future wife," Ace said.

Cooper laughed, but he finally did help his brother. The second Ace was in bed beside Dakota, holding her curled up in his arms, everything was right in the world. Cooper walked from the room, and Ace realized he was no longer in a hurry to get anywhere—he was exactly where he belonged.

EPILOGUE

Looking into the mirror, Dakota couldn't quit grinning, though her cheeks now hurt from doing it all day long. Today was the day. Today she had married the man she couldn't live without. He was not only her hero and protector; he had saved her as much as she had saved him.

He'd wanted to marry her that day at the hospital, but not only had she insisted on having her fairy-tale wedding, but her mother would have beaten Ace alive if he'd deprived her of an extravagant wedding celebration. Dakota was her only daughter, and Juliana had dreamed of this day for her daughter's entire life.

And so far, it was more perfect than Dakota could have ever imagined. Her brothers had put Ace through hell for risking her life, but with time, they'd seen how much Ace loved her and how much she loved him, so they'd loosened up—a little.

The wedding had been planned in three months. Ace had been a mess the entire time. She didn't know why. They hadn't spent a single night apart until last night, when his brothers and her new sisters-in-law had insisted on giving them parties. They'd both been assured it was bad luck for the bride and groom to be together the night before the wedding. Both she and Ace had pouted mightily at that, but they'd had good times in spite of it. Still, when she'd met him at the end of the aisle, she felt as if she hadn't seen him in years instead of a measly eighteen hours.

The wedding had been a blur. She'd been lost in Ace's eyes the entire time, except when she'd shed some tears when her father had walked her down the aisle, his eyes growing misty. She'd never once in her life seen her larger-than-life father shed a tear. She knew how much he loved her, but it filled her with so much joy to see him so happy for her, and yet so sad to be letting her go. She'd held him extra tight before he'd released her to Ace. Before stepping away from the couple, Lucian had warned Ace never to hurt Dakota. Ace had promised he never would.

They'd cut their cake and laughed as the speeches were made. She'd never wanted it to end. Well, that wasn't entirely true. She did have her wedding night to look forward to. She'd insisted on waiting a day to leave for their honeymoon. That was, until Ace had assured her they were traveling in a private jet—with a bedroom.

Now Dakota was changed into her traveling outfit, and she'd been away from Ace for too long. She rose from the bench in the bathroom and walked back out, spotting him right away where he spoke with his brother Mav.

She was more than grateful the two of them had cleared the air. Mav had been suspicious of Ace for a while after his return, and only Dakota knew how much that had broken Ace's heart, though he felt he deserved it. But things were back to normal with them.

And though Ace had insisted on still training her in her flying lessons, she was absolutely his only student. He'd opened his own detective agency, and he was already swamped with work. He said she could be the pilot of the family now, though he did still have to go up and let off some steam in his private plane at least twice a week when the weather permitted. Washington had too many rainy days, he often complained. She'd offered to move anywhere he wanted, but he'd said he had been away from home for too long. She was more than grateful to stay where she had her family and her best friend nearby, and where Ace had his brothers. They would never be alone.

Ace spotted her and broke away from his brother midsentence, which made Mav laugh, his merriment carrying over to Dakota through the crowds of people there to celebrate their day.

"I missed you," he told her as he pulled her tight and led her to the dance floor. One look at the band was all it took for them to begin a slow song.

Dakota rested comfortably in her husband's arms. He swayed with her, and her heart was so full, she felt as if it would explode. That's when she noticed that Sherman and Joseph had made themselves very comfortable with her father over at a corner table, their heads bent together.

Dakota laughed with joy, and Ace pulled back to look at her, a questioning gleam in his eyes.

"What is going through that brilliant mind of yours?" he asked her.

"Look over in the corner," she said, turning his head. It took him a minute to focus on her father and his uncle and Joseph.

"What?" he asked without a clue.

"Oh, I think my brothers are in for some trouble," she said with another merry laugh.

Ace's eyes widened before he sought out her brothers. There was sympathy in his expression.

"Are you thinking married life isn't for everyone?" she asked with another laugh.

"Not at all. I don't know why I was so afraid of it," he said. "But I've heard rumors about my uncle Sherman and his best friend, Joseph Anderson. I have to say, I'm feeling a bit of pity for your brothers."

"They are stubborn fools, and it's about time they get knocked down a few pegs," she countered.

"Are you planning on helping?" Ace asked her.

"Most definitely," she said with glee.

Then Ace kissed her like she'd been waiting for him to do the entire night. All thoughts of her unfortunate brothers evaporated as she melted into the arms of the man she refused to live another day without.

ACKNOWLEDGMENTS

This is always the hardest part for me to write, because there are hundreds of people who help me, influence me, and make it possible for me to succeed. I can't do this alone, and I never would want to. Being an author is a privilege that I will never take for granted. There are still days I don't want to blink for fear that it will all have been nothing more than a dream. Then I wake up, come to my computer, and realize it's real, that I'm living this dream of a life.

First off, thank you so much to my fans. Thank you for believing in me and my stories, for sharing my love of writing, for sharing your experiences with me, and for always being there. I love to talk with you, meet you, and share our lives together. I am nothing without you, and that is something I will never forget.

Thank you to my amazing editors. Again, this process can't be done alone. I don't want to write the same story over and over again. I don't want to repeat myself, or get lazy in my writing. I love to be challenged, and I love having people I trust help me through the process. I lucked out with getting Lauren, who doesn't allow me to be lazy, but is one of the most positive people I've met and always makes me feel good about my writing before pushing me to do it the best way possible. I also lucked out with Maria, who is a positive force of energy whom I enjoy talking with, and who makes me feel like I can always be better.

Thank you to my entire Montlake team. Not one person has been less than positive, encouraging, and engaging. I look forward to conferences where we get to laugh, talk business, and also have a lot of fun. They have also learned I much prefer a fun country bar to a five-star restaurant any day of the week—time to slip on the yoga pants and go dance instead of worrying about what fork to use with each new plate.

Thank you to my author friends. Our talks are cherished, and I love building a brand together. I am awed by your continued support. Your laughter, craziness, and midnight talking sessions help me get through writer's block, and your make-believe worlds take me to happy places. I read far more than I write. J. S. Scott and Ruth Cardello are certainly my partners in crime, and I cherish our time together. There are many more authors I love, but I could write a book on that alone, and I'm sure you want to get to the story instead.

Finally, but certainly not least, thank you to my family and friends. The kiddos constantly put a smile on my face and remind me that I can choose to be young forever. The adults give me much-needed breaks. I love to laugh and stretch my boundaries. I love to do things I never thought I could do before. I love to be scared, happy, sad, exhausted, and energized. I want to feel all emotions. I don't think I can be a good writer without that. Thank you for giving that, and so much more, to me, for loving me, and for taking me away from my fantasy worlds when I forget to leave my house for weeks on end. Thank you for sharing this journey with me.

ABOUT THE AUTHOR

Photo © 2014 Edward Hart

Melody Anne is a *New York Times* and *USA Today* bestselling author who has written a number of popular series, including Billionaire Bachelors, Surrender, and Baby for the Billionaire. Along with romance and young adult novels, Melody has also recently collaborated with fellow authors J.S. Scott and Ruth Cardello for *Taken by a Trillionaire*. *Turbulent Intrigue* is the fourth book in Melody's Billionaire Aviators series.

A country girl at heart, Melody loves the small town and strong community she lives in. When she's not writing, she enjoys spending time with her family, friends, and beloved pets. Most of all, she loves being able to do what makes her happiest . . . living in a fantasy world (for at least 95 percent of the time).

Made in the USA
Middletown, DE
26 March 2024

51805386R00154